Debut authors Marion and Barbara are siblings. Inspired by their love for literature and arts, *Kabaslot,* is a collaboration born from respect of each other's unique literary talents.

Marion lives with her husband, Walter, in Maryland. Her children, Osi and Olayinka, are her pride and joy. She grew up in Sierra Leone and moved to the U.S. in 1996.

Barbara lives in Toronto, Canada, to be near her two children, Kenye Ezra and Yema. She hopes to move further north in the future to live off the land and make more time to write.

J.W. Morgan is the pseudonym they chose for this joint venture.

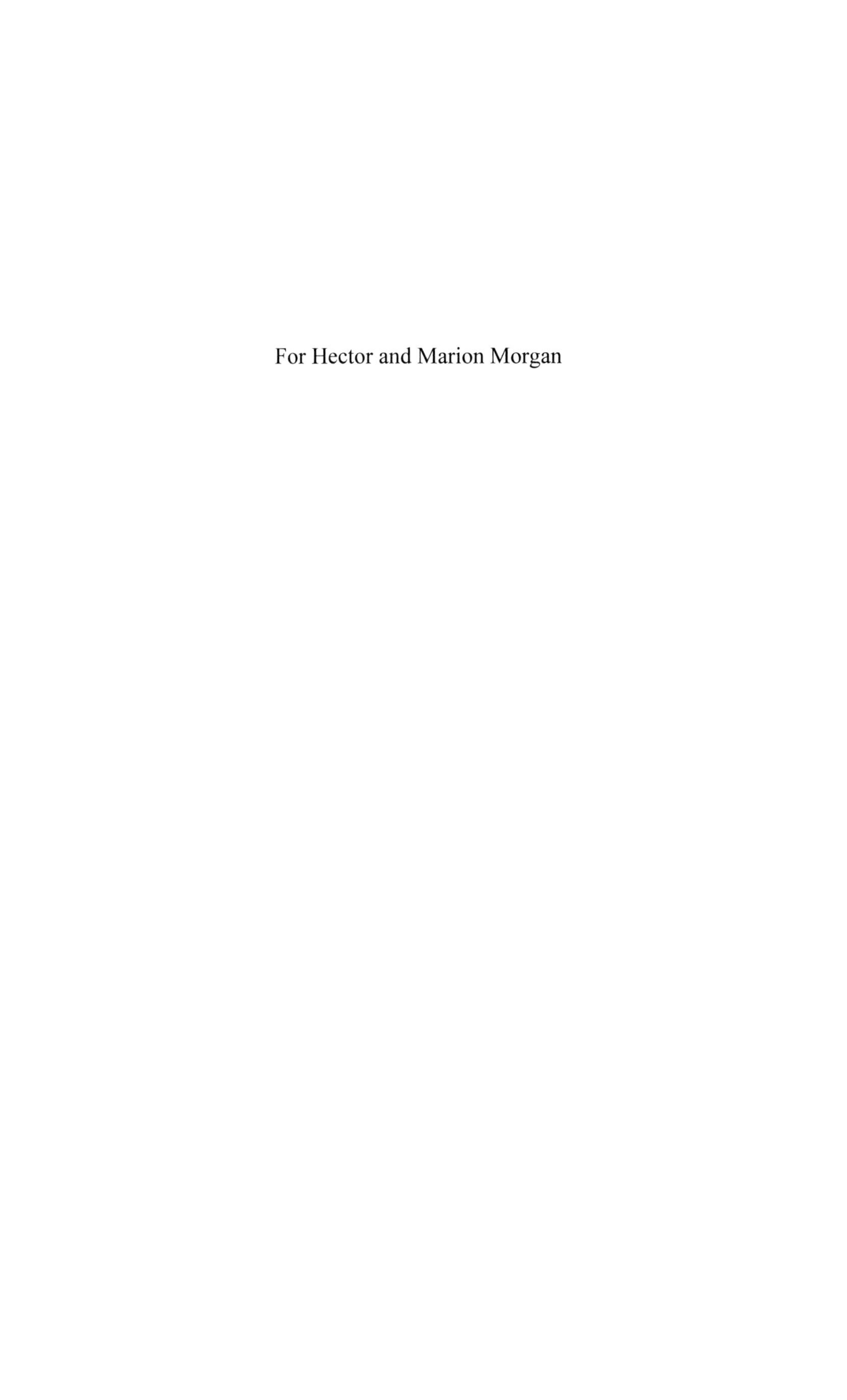

For Hector and Marion Morgan

J.W. Morgan

KABASLOT

AUSTIN MACAULEY PUBLISHERS™

LONDON • CAMBRIDGE • NEW YORK • SHARJAH

Ordering Information
Quantity sales: Special discounts are available on quantity purchases by corporations, associations, and others. For details, contact the publisher at the address below.

Publisher's Cataloging-in-Publication data
Morgan, J.W.
Kabaslot

ISBN 9781685627485 (Paperback)
ISBN 9781685627492 (Hardback)
ISBN 9781685627508 (ePub e-book)

Library of Congress Control Number: 2023912525

www.austinmacauley.com/us

First Published 2024
Austin Macauley Publishers LLC
40 Wall Street, 33rd Floor, Suite 3302
New York, NY 10005
USA

mail-usa@austinmacauley.com
+1 (646) 5125767

Yema and Kenye Ezra, your love and positivity are ineffable. I could not have gone through this process without your kindness and support throughout. Thank you. Utmost gratitude to our remarkable parents, Professor Hector Goddard Morgan and Mrs. Marion Elizabeth Joyce Onanu Morgan, who from the beginning created a space where our imagination could flourish. Our amazing big sisters, Ing Trudy Morgan and Mayor Yvonne Aki-Sawyerr OBE, for setting the pace, believing in us, and supporting us all the way, and to their beautiful families. Linda Williams, and Yabome Gilpin-Jackson for invaluable hours sharing their personal experience as writers. To my co-author and sister, for inviting me into your story, and committing to the process. Thank you.

1 Peter 5:10 'But [a]may the God of all grace, who called [b]us to His eternal glory by Christ Jesus, after you have suffered a while, [c]perfect, establish, strengthen, and settle you.' Throughout my journey in writing this novel, those words have stuck with me. I am grateful to God for allowing me to see this project through. I echo BJ's sentiments about our parents and our siblings. We have truly been blessed. Without Walter, Osi and Olayinka who I call my jewels, I don't think this manuscript would have been anything more than a wishful dream. To my co-author and sister, BJ, here's to many more shared successes.

The model is wearing the typical embroidered dress worn by Krio women.
The Kabaslɔt has long sleeves, a belt and a lace petticoat underneath.
The headscarf, straw hat, drawstring bag (kotoku) and a shawl (jojo lappa)
are used to accessorize the outfit. The footwear comprises Victorian pumps
made of a special embroidering described as "marking carpet"; hence the
term carpet slippers.
Wardrobe created by SheBar Concepts
Photo credit – Edwin Johnson of Jay's photography
Make up by Chantell Abie

Kabaslɔt ɛn kotoku, carpet slippers, straw hats too!
Old men doze while grannies shout "oo u oo!"
Brought by sea. No longer chained but free
From north, south, east, and west
Assembled under the Great Tree.

Kabaslɔt ɛn kotoku, jollof rɛs ɛn beef stew
A mix of memories, old and new
Bonga fish, cow bɛlɛ, foo foo
Time for tea in the afternoon?
Kabɔ settler, ow yu du?

Kabaslɔt ɛn kotoku, not mini-skirts or fancy hair-dos
Nyolɛ, pull na do, forty day-kabudul
Put stop for me, dɛn put stop for you?
Church every Sunday, to stay in the faith
Faith of our ancestors, holy faith.

Kabaslɔt ɛn kotoku, our children inherit all we do
Betrayal is no match for wey we tɔk true
At dawn of independence denied our due
Our roots and heritage for years to come
Will live on and on in our daughters and sons.

Our great-great-grandparents told stories, preserving our heritage through song and dance as their kin had, an ocean away in chains. Told and retold, embellished or understated. Their stories of love, loss, pain and death are a testament. They are reborn. They survive.

Through time on unfamiliar shores, they returned to make their mark under the Great Tree of the Freedom Colony. Maroons and Loyalists and many more, joined hands in the face of white scorn; the folly of division was as clear as the blue waters of the wharf before them. As their numbers swelled the people unique in their diversity, united by long-sought freedom, birthed the Krios.

For their independence, Krios earned a place at the bargaining table, shoulder to shoulder with their long-lost brothers. African tradition mixed with western influence. Bits of this and hints of that. The bod hos unlike any other in the region, tasty dishes prepared from memory, the Krio way of living, loving, of being.

My great-great-grandparents were among those who told these stories of love, joy, loss, pain and death. Today those stories are my testament. We are reborn. We survive. My name is Allison Regina Frederica Johnson. I am a Krio and this is my story.

Chapter 1
June

Freetown

Comfort knocks softly on the door that opens out to the verandah of the big house. In the fading light of dusk, the skyline of the sprawling city in the distance looks smudged, but Comfort does not notice. In her haste to seek out her missis, she forgot to turn on any lights when she came through the house, so the long shadows that spilled down the walls an hour earlier filled the corridor behind her.

"Yes, Mammy Comfort na wetin?"

Mrs. June Johnson asks in a hushed voice to avoid waking up her slumbering husband.

Instead of speaking, Comfort beckons June to join her, clasping and unclasping her hands nervously as she waits.

Comfort had come to work for Eric and June Johnson a year after their wedding. The two led busy lives and Eric's Saturday morning cricket at the open field in Kingtom was a welcome routine. When he returned home, usually in the late afternoon, June had his bathwater drawn and dollops of the soothing balm she kept in steady supply for his aching muscles. Feeling refreshed he wolfed down his lunch of foofoo and plasas chased with a cold beer, then would promptly doze off in the winged rattan chair out on the verandah, lulled by the hillside breeze.

June glances at her snoring husband as she sets aside the crochet needles and bundle of yarn on the whiskey stool beside her. She is terrible at the craft but determined to master it so she can make blankets and hats for her children when they eventually arrive. She follows the older woman through the house to the kitchen.

Out in the yard, they cross the short path that separates the workers' quarters from the main house. When they arrive, Comfort holds open the thin curtain hanging over the door and shows June into the dimly lit room.

June is surprised to see Comfort's daughter Stella propped up on the wooden cot in a corner. Comfort kneels beside the girl.

"Missis, a beg do ya nɔ, vex," she says, avoiding June's gaze. She is doubled over, and her head is bowed.

Confused and hardly able to hear the other woman's words, June moves closer, taking in the sight of a blood-soaked lappa that lay crumpled on the floor. Stella is seventeen but her doe eyes lend her a child-like appearance. She looks exhausted, skin slick with sweat. Her eyes widen in terror as June approaches. The smell of blood and feces lingers in the small space and June turns to Comfort, confused. Comfort offers no explanation and instead continues to beg forgiveness.

June's eyes are adjusting to the dim light when she notices tiny fingers and a nose peeking out of the cloth Stella clutches in her lap. Her sharp gasp caused the infant to startle and then settle back against his mother. Her mind swirls in panic. *Surely, this is impossible,* she thinks. *Had she not seen Stella only yesterday? There had been no hint of anything out of the ordinary. How could she have missed this?*

June looks again at the girl sitting on the bed with the baby in her arms. Her heart is beating wildly now. She understands why Comfort seems fearful. Stella had hidden the pregnancy well. June does not know if she should be afraid, worried, or angry. Mammy Comfort was her elder, so out of respect June never commented on how the woman raised her child. It was only a matter of chance that June herself was not in the unfortunate position of being a single mother forced to do menial work or rely on the kindness of a benefactor in order to afford a decent life.

She had assumed Comfort kept Stella under lock and key like most Krio mothers did with their daughters. Other than to attend school and church, or visit with relatives, young women mostly stayed at home. They were not allowed to gallivant about town, and certainly, no male suitor was permitted to call except to declare permanent intentions. This was an odd imposition since the Krio men, especially older, wealthier gentlemen, were not discouraged from having as many lady friends as they liked. So long as they were discrete, society was happy to turn a blind eye.

The little girl with the happy smile was not the same young woman June saw before her now. Perhaps Comfort had been too strict, and Stella had rebelled. June smiles weakly at the child who is avoiding her eyes. She turns hastily and stumbles from the room, hungry for fresh air.

Mammy Comfort joins June in the narrow space between the quarters and the wall that borders the Johnson property. The housekeeper who occupies the other room is away visiting her family for the weekend and June welcomes the privacy this affords them.

"Was she—?"

"No ma'!" Comfort's retort is swift.

June exhales sharply. There will be no cause to involve the police. This at least is good.

She waits for Comfort to continue, "Sissy, ow we go do now—?" Comfort asks.

"What will we do!" June retorts.

She had not meant to snap. She suddenly feels exhausted. She has been burning the candle on both ends. Their home was abuzz with visitors most weekends, and she poured what remained of her time into managing the new civics wing at the British Council library where she worked.

Eric's legal practice was extremely busy, the demand for sound legal opinion in the country was perpetual. He was also working hard to push forward with Independence preparations. June distractedly thinks that when the time comes to raise her own daughters, she will be firm enough that they keep to good Krio values, but flexible enough that they can still have fun and not hide things from her in their teenage years.

Her husband is a traditional man, and she fears that with this discovery he will send mother and daughter packing. It is a well-known fact that some older Krio gentlemen often sows wild oats, so rumors would surely fly about Eric's role in all of this. Speculation on the identity of the baby's father would be on the wagging tongues of the Krio mammies. She could imagine them now now, sitting on the stoops of their bod hos homes, signaling to each other, 'oo u oo! Making sure an extra set of ears was around to receive the juicy morsel of gossip.

Some might view her husband as a victim, entrapped by a fast girl's calculations. Others might not be so sympathetic, especially as Stella is so young. Either outcome would no doubt threaten Eric's burgeoning career. And Stella, what will become of her?

June forces her thoughts back to the present. No use worrying about how Eric might be scrutinized or the two of them chided for allowing such a scandal under their roof. She must consult with Eric.

Mammy Comfort was from a humble background. She met June's mother Ethel Walcott-Taylor at school and the two became fast friends. Comfort, a good student, and hard worker earned herself a scholarship to the prestigious Fourah Bay College. When she and Ethel graduated in the nineteen forties, they were two of a small number of women in the entire country who could claim such an achievement.

Soon afterward, Comfort fell head over heels in love with Segun, an apparently wealthy diplomat from Nigeria. He promised her a life of fancy parties, nice clothes, trips to Las Palmas, and a flat in Edgeware. But Segun was a good talker and a good liar. He spun stories faster than Anansi. Comfort was swept off her feet, landing squarely on her backside in a strange country, living with Segun's brother and several sisters in a small house outside Lagos.

When Comfort returned home with no husband and a little girl she dragged by the arm, she had turned to her old friend Ethel, who did not press her for an explanation but instead welcomed her in. Comfort started working as house help for the family, and when Ethel fell terribly ill, Comfort had been at her side tending to her day and night. Ethel gave up her fight one Christmas morning, leaving young June and her brother Robert distraught.

The children were urged to be stoic in the face of their loss.

"Mi pikin dɛm una gɛt for tie unu at," they were told.

The Walcott-Taylor family took charge of the orphans. Aunts and uncles sent well wishes, but it was Mammy Comfort who cared for them until they were sent abroad for further studies. In June's world, the life of an unmarried mother is not an easy one; she is left with fewer choices for her future. Bearing this in mind along with a sense of duty when June and Eric returned to the country, they took in Mammy Comfort. June had admired the love Comfort lavished on Stella, which made this new development even more heartbreaking.

"What do you mean June?" Eric exclaims looking like he'd been slapped. "How can she have a baby? This is impossible!"

June knows Eric can be intimidating when he is angry. His bulky frame seems to double in size as he fusses and puffs up his shoulders.

"I will show him to you when you calm down," she says.

Eric eases back into his chair, taking his wife's cue as she does her best to elaborate on what she knows of the matter. Anticipating Eric's next question, June quickly adds that she has no idea of the identity of the father. Although she is disappointed, Mammy Comfort hadn't come to them before the baby arrived, this can no longer be helped. Now, there are decisions to be made.

Eric bows his head, staring at his feet as he often does when deep in thought. June watches him out of the corner of her eye. She is already forming an attachment to the newborn and feels protective of him, but a delicate balance must be struck. She can be more persuasive, if need be, but she does not want to be at odds with her husband. When Eric eventually speaks, she allows the breath trapped in her throat to escape her lips.

"We will raise him in our home!" Eric's declaration is definitive, and June feels relieved.

"Now show him to me!" he demands.

They both make their way outside, their strides quick with excitement.

"Mammy Comfort!" June calls out as they near the bungalow.

"Ma?" the response comes promptly, and they can hear shuffling sounds from within. Comfort emerges through the curtain. She looks worried and her hands tremble slightly.

June speaks first. "I have told Mr. Eric about the baby, and he is happy for you. We do not want to send you or Stella away because of what has happened."

"But—" June continues, "you of all people know that Krios have a standard to live up to and a child out of wedlock in any household is bad."

Comfort nods her understanding, lowering her eyes. She knows the norms and customs well, especially the ones that go unspoken. She is painfully well aware that June will bear the brunt of the gossip that is sure to make the rounds in her social circles. Despite Comfort's long history with the family, June is the mistress of the house and must demonstrate that she has the situation in hand.

"All eyes are on us now, so it would be even worse if we put you out," June continues. Her voice chokes, her eyes glisten with emotion.

"Sissy," Eric starts to speak, glancing at his wife as she struggles to compose herself. He clears his throat and tries again. He uses the more formal title to address the older woman.

"Sissy Comfort, we are not angry with you or Stella. Just taken aback."

Eric considers how best to approach the delicate question on his and June's minds. There were recent cases of prominent young Krio men siring children with their house girls, and some of the stories even made the newspaper headlines. If his chances of rising to the high court were to remain viable, he needed to ensure any seeds of doubt in his integrity were not allowed to take root among the rumor mongers eager to clip his feathers.

"We know you hid this from us because you were scared," Eric says, "and so we only thank God that Stella is safe."

Comfort clasps her hands together; she looks hopeful for the first time since they began to talk.

"If you accept," Eric was saying, "we will keep you all here, provide for the child and send him to school."

"Thank you. Tɛnki, tɛnki!" Comfort responds. Dusk has faded into night, and in the pale-yellow lamplight, the relief that sweeps across Comfort's face is visible. She reaches out and touches both their arms.

Still apologetic, she says, "I am also very sorry. I did not see or suspect that she was pregnant until she was far along. May God bless you." Her words tumble out quickly.

"We promise to do everything we can to make this right. She is a big girl now. She will need to find a job because my salary will not be enough for all of us now—"

She is interrupted by movement at the doorway as Stella emerges. Stella looks clean and has changed into fresh clothes but still appears to be weak. She stands next to her mother, cradling her son close to her chest.

"Mr. Eric and Ms. June," she says, "I am sorry for what I did. I was very scared and did not want you to send my mother away." Then she burst into tears.

June and Comfort rush to reassure Stella while Eric stands apart with an awkward expression, shifting his weight from one leg to the other. The women are soon cooing and giggling at the gurgles and soft whimpers coming from inside the wrapper. June catches Eric's eye and they share a warm smile. Eric was an intelligent, progressive, hard-working, and handsome man who had a great future ahead of him. In that moment, she felt incredibly lucky to be his wife.

She'd invited Comfort and Stella to bring the baby inside the house, so they could see him better.

"I will call Dr. Cole right away. I hope he can come quickly to examine you and the baby," she says, already dialing the number.

While they wait for the doctor to arrive, June asks Stella what the child will be named. Both she and Eric cannot hide their surprise at the girl's firm response. Abdul Othame Kamara was not the sort of name they would have expected. Nothing about the entire situation was what they would have expected. June bites her tongue. She will not query further.

♋

An air of celebration flowed through the compound in the days following while, June kicked her planning into full gear. Comfort did not object when she wasn't consulted on details of all the arrangements. She'd known June long enough to deduce it would be a waste of breath, even for her own grandson.

According to their shared Krio culture, the naming ceremony should be held soon. June fixed the date. Next, she called the priest of the most noted Anglican Cathedral in the city to arrange for the baby's christening. The old ways—the naming ceremony, the cook, nyole, and all of their rituals coexisted alongside orthodox Christian rites, in harmonious counter-intuition.

June flits busily around the house, driving into town on several expeditions. She needs to shop for a new pair of shoes and set up an appointment with her hairdresser. The new addition to her household has her giddy with excitement at the prospect that soon she and Eric will have children of their own, and King's Lodge would be filled with the pitter-patter of little feet.

Like many young Africans from affluent families, June and Eric met, courted, and married while studying abroad, their families marking the union back at home with a performance of the traditional rites by proxy.

When the newlyweds returned from Britain, they were not keen to live in a typical wooden house. The traditional Krio bod hos is built on a sturdy stone foundation with an outhouse in the backyard and neat hedges of hibiscus and Dipladenia commonly called the yellow bell, in front. High ceilings kept the open concept living areas airy, and lattice shutters over box windows were a favorite spot where grannies set their highbacked cushioned chairs and spent hours crocheting, dozing, or just watching the goings on in the neighborhood.

Eric was adamant that not having running water or indoor toilet facilities were inappropriate for their station in life and June agreed with him. To climb the social ladder as quickly as he hoped would require a residence fit to host dignitaries, the educated elite, and whoever else he dreamed of rubbing shoulders with. As much as the bod os has a certain old-world charm he preferred to build a multistory modern structure on four town lots of land and called it King's Lodge.

June took pride in her home. The main house was an imposing concrete building, with a white-washed stucco façade. Ornate tiles and African rosewood panels adorn the parlor, dining room, and Eric's expansive library.

The workers' quarters were divided into a bachelor unit and one single-family unit consisting of two small rooms and a living area. There was a shared washhouse at the back and a separate kitchen for the staff to prepare their meals, although June always made sure there was enough food from the big house to keep everyone in the compound well fed.

In many ways, the Johnsons considered their domestic staff to be family, paying them above the going rates and treating them with consideration. Eric provided pro bono legal services to their relatives on more than a few occasions, and June was most charitable when called upon in a time of need generously giving money and using her extensive social connections to help many find gainful employment.

Mr. Johnny the groundskeeper and gateman did not live in the compound but rented rooms nearby. He arrived each day before the crack of dawn and left after the house was locked up for the night.

Rosetta the housekeeper was a spinster from Goderich village, referred with glowing praise by a fellow congregant at the church the Johnson's attended. A tough wiry stern woman, Rosetta carried out her duties, cleaning, and washing with quiet efficiency. Mama Comfort's main role was to manage the kitchen and stores. June had a well-developed palate and welcomed her experience preparing traditional and western fare. Comfort was great at driving a good bargain at the butchers which June appreciated.

In the early days before June worked full time, her days were filled only with the concerns of domesticity and entertaining. She often joined Comfort outside by the smokehouse to chat. The smokehouse was a low hut-like structure made of red clay, with an open roof. It was installed at the end of the south wall of the Johnson property, obscured from the main house by a cluster of banana plants that provided much-needed shade during the hottest days.

On those occasions the women chatted and gossiped while Comfort repaired any holes in the woven grass shopping baskets or braided Stella's hair. They mostly shared stories about mundane things. But when they happened to be alone, the conversation became quite intimate and personal June usually talked and Comfort listened, only offering words of advice when asked. One day the older woman surprised June by opening up about her past.

She had been perched on a bench, casually examining her newly manicured fingernails while Comfort prepared kanya. The dried roasted peanuts and gari jumped up and down the narrow walls of the wooden mortar as Comfort pounded away at them with a heavy pestle.

"Mi wan shilling rope," she proclaimed wistfully of her only child. Comfort swore never to have more children and after hearing her story, June could understand why.

The *thump thump* of the pestle against the mortar bowl was like a background rhythm to Comfort's low tones while she talked about her days abroad. As she described how Segun rejected their daughter June sensed the pain Comfort must have felt. Barely able to understand the trauma of being trapped in a place where your worth was judged by whether you conceived a son, June moved to console the older woman, but she was politely waved away.

Feigning as though her tears were sweat from pounding the mortar so hard Comfort used the corner of her lappa to deftly wipe her face dry and carried on with the task at hand. She added white sugar to the contents of the mortar, pounding the ingredients into a smooth blend as she talked.

"After three miscarriages, Stella's birth was my miracle Ma!" Comfort beamed through damp eyes. June nodded with empathy. Trying to conceive and failing so many times sounded devastating.

If only Segun and his family could have been more sympathetic. In their eyes, the many miscarriages were of no consequence. Bearing a girl after all the losses was not a consolation either. A girl could not carry forward the family name. Then there was the issue of the dowry. Segun was not pleased, and he blamed this misfortune on Comfort. June learned from reading books that this charge was nonsensical. If there was any fault to be had, it was not with her, but she knew her old beliefs were too ingrained and immutable even in the face of facts to change her husband's mind.

Comfort was lucky to find a job teaching English at a nearby village school. There she enjoyed a little respite from the acrimony at home. She was treated kindly by the people there, and her baby was cared for while she worked. However, with each passing month things grew worse. Segun took to drinking more than usual. He got involved in the local politics as just another means to swindle people, and when he came home, he harassed and beat Comfort for her money.

Comfort had heard of a Krio woman by the name of Mrs. Freeman who had lived in Freetown many years prior who might be able to help her. She learned that Mrs. Freeman had a house in Rivers State near Port Harcourt about an eight-hour bus ride away, but Comfort had no idea how she might find her.

One day, an entourage arrived from Segun's village bringing with them a young woman who was pronounced as his new wife. She would be a real woman and give Segun the son he deserved. That same night, Comfort packed her few belongings and when the house was all quiet, she left with her baby strapped to her back and nothing in her hand but an expired passport and a little money.

Curious and fascinated to hear more about the story June asked Comfort if she ever did make it to Mrs. Freeman and was itching to know what had happened next. All she knew was a vague recollection from family gossip about a treacherous trip that Comfort had made across country borders, on bus and sometimes on foot, till she eventually returned home.

June's nudging seemed to irritate Comfort and the corners of the older woman's mouth turned down distastefully. She clicked her tongue in a manner that meant 'tɔk af-lɛf af'; some things were best left unspoken. She pounded the kanya silently, hooded eyes flooding with more tears.

ᴖᴦᴖ

The morning Rosetta found Comfort splayed on the ground under the drying lines, a basket of laundry toppled by her feet was chaotic. Stella had been inside the quarters studying for her secretarial exams when she heard Rosetta's crying out, 'Una kam oh! Una kam!' She screeched at the top of her lungs.

Stella rushed outside, stopping only to pick up Abdul from where he had been frolicking on a playmat. By the time she was outside, Eric, Sullay the driver and Mr. Johnny were struggling to place Mammy Comfort in the back seat of the car. Rosetta squeezed in beside Comfort and the car sped away. June instructed Eric in a terse tone to be sure to call with updates the minute they arrived at the hospital. Eric waited till he came back home. Shattered and deflated he shared the awful news with June that Comfort was pronounced dead by the time the porters carried her on the gurney into the Accident and Emergency Department. The doctors said her heart had given out.

Comfort's sudden passing left everyone in shock. The day of the burial was one of the hottest that year. Rosetta glanced across to where Stella stood. Rosetta thought the girl looked frail; her shoulders hunched as she stared at the hole in the earth in front of her. Rosetta worried Stella might faint.

The mourners parted as two cemetery workers dressed in khaki approached and started to remove the wreaths from the top of the casket, preparing the rails and ropes they would use to lower the shiny grey metal with their beloved Comfort in it into the ground. Rosetta saw how Stella's face contorted as the reverend recited final burial rites. Stella wept softly and called out to her mother.

"My Mama, nɔ lef me so—ay mi mammy!" she moaned.

Abdul squirmed in Stella's arms and Rosetta reached out to take him. Stella refused to let go at first, clinging instead to Rosetta's neck. Abdul started to wail, and Stella finally surrendered him.

"The Lord giveth, and the Lord hath taken away," the reverend finished with a solemn chant.

The mourners responded, "Blessed be the name of the Lord."

Stella's moans grew into sobs, and Rosetta stepped aside to allow her mistress room to approach the girl. June had pulled out a white handkerchief from her purse and dabbed gently at the tears streaming down Stella's face.

"Ɔsh ya mi pikin, take heart," June said kindly. "We all loved Mammy Comfort, but Jesus loves her more, so He has taken her home. Be strong ya. Tai yu at." Her soothing tone and touch calmed Stella down.

As the sun set, the weight of the day and the unease from the oppressive heat began to lift. The final hymn was sung and a group of six or seven women who had been standing to the side approached the graveside. They were members of Comfort's church. Contrasting the mourners who wore black or navy blue, the women are dressed all in white with the matching blue pins of the Regent Village Mother's Union.

They linked arms, supporting the weaker members while one woman, a distant cousin of Comfort's, needed to be restrained from throwing herself onto the open grave Her wails caused Rosetta to pinch up her nose in annoyance, especially since she was aware of the rumors spread by the mourner and others who disapproved of the way she left Segun and her life in Nigeria under what they considered disgraceful circumstances. Comfort being an upstanding Christian woman had forgiven those who spoke against her. She served the church faithfully and spent much of her time in the village community where she had grown up, earning the respect and affection of those who knew her real character.

Despite herself, Rosetta felt hot tears pricking the backs of her eyes. The woman's wailing subsided and the single bugle player from the Boy's Brigade sounded the familiar tones of Taps. When it was all over, the congregation filed out, weaving through dusty path beside gravestones and headstones until they reached the cars parked under the mango trees that lined the Racecourse Cemetery Road.

The repast was held at the home of Comfort's maternal grandmother Ama Caulker, in Kissy. June and Eric spared no expense, ensuring that Comfort was buried in a plot beside her relatives and providing the family with enough money to cover the costs not only of the repast but also of the coming awujoh and nyole ceremonies, to be held forty days after burial.

Stella felt extremely shy around the Caulker clan. Her mother had not brought her around the tightly knit Sherbro family because she herself was raised by her father's family up in the mountain village of Regent. Being fiercely proud, the Caulkers, only reluctantly accepted the money contributed by the Johnsons.

The crowd from the church and cemetery now filled the Kissy Road compound. Stella felt overwhelmed with all the introductions.

Most of the mourners were seated on benches in the yard. The clergy, respected visitors, and elders were led up to the second-floor dining room of Mammy Caulker's stately three-story bod hos where the double doors to the living room had been opened up to create a spacious reception hall.

Rosetta busied herself in the outside kitchen, joining the women of the family to set out food and drinks on trays that the young nieces and nephews served the guests. The foo-foo and white sorel sauce was reserved for the household meal the next day, but there was jollof rice and beef stew for the everyone, with plenty of finger food-meat pies, akara, buns, and ham sandwich squares. There was also pound cake and rice bread, with ice cold ginger beer to wash it down.

Stella stuck to Rosetta's side the entire time, carrying Abdul awkwardly on her hip as she wondered what she could do to make herself useful. She looked on in awe as the women orchestrated feeding the crowd expertly and in an orderly fashion. A woman who looked familiar to Stella was sitting on a stool in front of a huge cast iron pot that had just been lifted off a smoldering three-stone fire. It had taken the strength of four people to set it down.

Working rhythmically, the woman scooped steaming rice from the pot onto plates being handed to her one after the other. Each plate was whisked away to the next station and received a dollop of stew. The plates made their way down the assembly line of goodies and every now and then when someone popped a morsel into their mouth instead of a plate, loud protests would erupt.

This was followed by a jovial concession allowing all the workers to sample a snack. With a pang, Stella realized she was witnessing a routine her mother must have also shared with those women on days when she would leave the house dressed in her starched white dressed and polished black shoes, returning home late at night looking spent but happy.

Stella protested when someone whisked Abdul away, but soon forgot her anxiety when she saw how content and happy, he was from all the attention he was getting. After that Stella only saw him when he grew hungry. She fed him but he was clearly exhausted from being passed around from one aunty to another. As his eyes drooped and his head nodded, she wished she had a lappa to strap him to her back and free her arms. Abdul was growing well and was quite heavy. Seeing her discomfort her aunt beckoned Stella into one of the bedrooms on the main level and indicated towards a bed she could lay him down on. She left the door ajar in case he woke up though the noise was much less as the evening wore on.

Rosetta found herself an empty chair leaned up against the corrugated iron fence. She checked that the creaky metal bench was sturdy enough to hold her weight before she sat down to rest with a cup of ginger beer in her hand. The yard was illuminated by a string of pale-yellow light bulbs which lent the place an oddly festive feel. It was part of the culture. Death was a sad affair, but a funeral was an opportunity to gather together, as much a source of succor for the living, as it was a memorial for the departed.

She had been on her feet since they arrived, and it would soon be time to return with the Johnsons to Signal Hill. She welcomed the moment to rest and listen to the quiet chatter around her.

Rosetta's mind runs to Stella who has gone into the house to look after Abdul. Having no children of her own, Rosetta is already feeling maternally protective toward the girl. She used to praise Stella for her graceful features, and her midnight black skin that glowed with vitality. The girl was blossoming into an intelligent and beautiful young woman. Rosetta is glad the Johnsons did the right thing and did not abandon Stella when she needed their support the most.

Rosetta's mind was on Stella and did not notice the young boy approaching her until he was only a few feet away. Startled, she waits for him to speak, expecting he is a street urchin who has ventured in to beg for scraps of food.

"Good evening, ma," he says politely. "A dey luk fɔ Ms. Stella."

"Yes, na mi nem Stella," Stella has just returned from the room where she put Abdul down and answered "Na wetin?"

The boy explains that a man outside is asking for her. Before Rosetta can question the boy, he scurries away.

Stella cranes her neck toward the gate.

"Son tɛm na mistek?" Rosetta muses.

"Mek a go luk," Stella replies uncertainly, half asking Rosetta's permission to go and see who it is.

Rosetta stands up and gestures for Stella to go. She follows close behind. When they reach the corrugated iron gate, Stella hesitates. Rosetta goes ahead of her, stepping through the main door. She is briefly blinded by the light from oncoming traffic.

The young man standing on the sidewalk looks well groomed, with his blue shirt neatly tucked into his trousers and his hair combed. Rosetta's curiosity is piqued.

"Capri!" Stella cries out in surprise.

"Stella," the young man gushes. Remembering his manners, he stops and turns to Rosetta, "Ma. Good evening, ma," he greets her.

Rosetta guesses the identity of the young man and insists they go back inside. The street is no place to discuss family matters.

Stella leads Capri into the yard. As the young lovers reunite under Rosetta's watchful eye, Rosetta learns that Capri Kamara had been an eighteen-year-old with aspirations to be a seaman when he and Stella met down at the government wharf. She was sixteen and quite impressionable. She'd been strolling through the fish market distractedly taking in the sights and sounds while Comfort shopped. The two were separated briefly while Comfort haggled over the cost of a freshly caught barracuda, and when she bumped into a lanky young man with a winning smile Capri and Stella had got to talking the attraction had been instant. When Stella hurried away to rejoin Comfort, her heartbeat wildly in her chest. Not many days later Capri found where she lived, and in the months that followed the two continued to meet secretly as their love bloomed. Then one day, without any notice, Capri vanished leaving Stella heartbroken and confused.

As they sat and talked, with Rosetta listening in uninvited, Capri explained that he had been posted to a cargo vessel leaving port on short notice. He had waited all year for a chance to join the crew as an engine room apprentice and when the time came, he hadn't been able to find Stella to say goodbye. Capri had been devastated and prayed that Stella would understand and wait for him. He wrote letters but did not want to risk getting her in trouble so he could not send them to King's Lodge. He knew calling the telephone at the King's Lodge was risky.

He explained that his boat was only in the Freetown port for a short while on its way to Malta. He had headed straight for Signal Hill to look for Stella when a neighbor had given him the news about Comfort and directed him to the repast.

Rosetta pretends not to listen as Stella explained to Capri how afraid she was when she learned she was pregnant. Rosetta could see that that Capri was genuinely shocked to learn about Abdul, clearly not aware that he was a father.

Rosetta feels more inclined to trust the young man now that she knows he did not deliberately abandon Stella. Rosetta goes inside to fetch Abdul and allow the pair some privacy. She is not too concerned that onlookers will notice the tearful interaction between the young lovers since they are gathered in mourning after all. She herself feels torn by the bittersweet moment. Capri's boat departs in the morning and there was no telling if and when they would see each other again. When Rosetta returns, Capri holds his son for a long time weeping and kissing the infant's placid face. His determined expression speaks volumes. Without question, Rosetta agrees that Capri can send money through her to pass on to Stella until Stella is able to set up a mailbox of her own at the central post office. Capri thanks Rosetta for her kindness, embraces Stella chastely and kisses Abdul one more time before he disappears into the night.

♋

Stella's search for a secretarial job has yet to yield results. She took the correspondence course offered by Crown secretarial college and was very pleased the day she received the telegram with her results. She passed with flying colors. Every day since then she has walked the downtown streets, following up on newspaper ads that look promising. She wonders if it was her lack of experience or how young she looked. Much like today, the interviews so far have not gone well.

She struggles to keep her spirits up despite the prospect of once again going home empty-handed. Capri sends money regularly, but Stella was saving all of it in a bank account that Rosetta helped her open in Abdul's name. As generous as her benefactors the Johnsons were, she longed to be able to take care of her family. She needed a good job that would pay her enough money to rent a place when Capri returned.

That last thought propels Stella forward with renewed determination. As she turns off Westmoreland Street, which runs from the east right across to the west of the city, she can see dark clouds over Tower Hill ahead. The sudden torrent that follows is unusual for this time of year. Stella ducks under the canopy of the Brown's Stationery Shoppe, beside the driveway leading to their gated compound.

The city's sewers sometimes became overwhelmed with the rushing water that ran down from the surrounding hills, forcing its way through streets and neighborhoods, and eventually emptying into the bay not far from where Stella sought shelter. These were not the little puddles in which children gleefully splashed about and sang their rainy-day songs. These waters could carry you away.

Stella and other pedestrians huddled under the shop front, squeezing in, to make room. They stand close, shivering and wet, looking on as lightning rip across the skyline. Soon, a dark-colored luxury car pulls up slowly to the gate. The sound of the rain drowns out the car horn, and Stella is not surprised that the gateman does not emerge despite the persistent honking. Stella can make out a passenger in the back seat. His head nearly touches the roof of the car forcing him to slump in his seat.

The honk changes to a startling blare. Stella hisses impatiently; she does not understand why the driver doesn't get out and open the gate himself. Resigned to the fact that her job hunting is over for the day, she only fleetingly considers that her clothes and newly done press and curl hairdo will be ruined, before she ventures out in the rain and runs over to the gate. The man-door is unlocked so she pushes it open.

Once inside she fumbles with the heavy bolt, finally managing to slide it open which causes the tall iron gates to swing apart. Her hair sags and her skirt clings to her thighs. The car eases through the open gates and crawls up the sloping driveway toward the garage. The driver leaves the engine running and jumps out.

"Yu titi!" he calls out to Stella.

She is not sure if she is more irritated by the driver's rude and thankless tone or that he addresses her as a girl.

"Na wetin?" Stella responds sharply, already turning to leave, anxious to get out of the rain. Her shoes are water-logged.

The legs and head of Mr. Brown emerge from the vehicle. Stella is beginning to regret her bold act; it dawns on her that she is trespassing. Lately, city residents have been on edge. Gangs, vagrants who dwell around the nearby King Jimmy wharf carried out home invasions. They set upon unsuspecting homeowners entering their compounds, holding them up for money, and other valuables. As a decoy, some of the attackers were rumored to employ a female accomplice who pretended to be in distress or otherwise distracted the potential victims to achieve the element of surprise.

In a panic Stella realizes the cost of being a good Samaritan is not worth losing the trust of the Johnsons once again. If she is even accused of being an accomplice, word would surely get back to Eric and June. She retreats toward the gate as the driver approaches. He continues to yell for her to stop. Bystanders at the gate look on curiously. Stella almost makes it to the street when she turns back to deliver a retort to match the driver's ungratefulness.

"Na di tɛnki dat?!" she calls out cheekily.

She feels herself going backward and flails her arms wildly, but not quickly enough to break her fall. By the time she realizes the heel of her right shoe is caught between the polished pave stones on the wet driveway, she lands with a heavy thud. Stella is conscious but closes her eyes as she takes a minute to survey for any sharp pain in her head.

"Lɔd a masi! i fɔdɔm!" She hears someone exclaim.

"Na faint i faint?" another asks. A few people have rushed over, one lady tries to lift her.

"Nɔ-na fɔ tek tɛm. Lɛf am fɔs!" another cautions, as they continue to debate whether to move her or leave in place.

Stella feels embarrassed and more than a little silly as she contemplates how to salvage her pride. She notices that the rain has stopped. The driver has now joined the group looking down at Stella. He hesitates, looking to his employer for instructions on what to do with the injured woman.

"Daniel," Mr. Brown addresses the driver while politely waiving the onlookers away, "Please, help me take her inside."

Osman, the chubby gateman, has made an appearance and sheepishly brushes crumbs from the corner of his mouth as he scurries away to attend to the gate shooing away the last of the onlookers. He returns promptly, hovering and clucking like a mother hen as the other two men carry Stella indoors.

ᗜᏙᗜ

Stella stirs as she is laid on a settee. She cracks her eyes open to see Mr. Brown looking at her with concern.

"You're awake," he says, his expression turns to relief.

She smiles weakly and tries to sit up, but he places a hand gently on her shoulder.

"Best to take it slowly," he advises kindly.

Stella nods and lies back down.

So far, Mr. Brown has sounded calm and pleasant, but Stella still mentally readies her defense in case she is accused of trespassing. She will explain that she took it upon herself to open the gate because she is a good Christian and she had been raised to do the right thing. In truth, she is more embarrassed than afraid. She entered the compound without really thinking and now she is inside these people's home, being cared for in a ridiculous charade that she knows she should stop but is not sure how to. She is shaken by the fall but otherwise feels fine.

"Daniel, bring me some water and call Missis please," Mr. Brown instructs.

"Yes, sir," Daniel replies, moving quickly to carry out the order.

Mr. Brown goes to open the windows that had been closed against the rain. Stella notices just how tall he is, as he gracefully moves about the room. She also takes a minute to look around the stylish surroundings.

The walls are painted a bright yellow and dark wood floors gleam. The furnishings are fancier than anything she had seen before. Stella imagined they had been bought at Décor Furniture on the west side of town or more likely shipped in from Europe.

The Browns ran a successful business and were well known and respected socialites in the city. Allan met his wife Elizabeth in her hometown Liverpool during his post-graduate years. After his studies, she emigrated back to Freetown with him. That much Stella knew.

"Psst!"

Stella turns around to look for the source of the signal and spots three small, coffee-brown faces peeking curiously at her from behind the end of the settee where she's still lying down. Before she can say hello, they scoot away when they hear their mother approaching. Stella cranes her neck to see where they disappeared to, but they are nowhere to be seen.

"Allan, what's the matter?"

Stella hears Mrs. Brown before she appears. She feels terrible because she can tell by the tone of her voice that the woman is truly worried.

"This young lady here—" Mr. Brown motions toward Stella, "helped open the gate because Osman wasn't around, and on her way out she had a nasty fall."

"My goodness! Is she a friend their's?" Mrs. Brown asks. Stella starts to speak but has to clear her throat.

"Oh!" Mrs. Brown exclaims, smiling nervously at Stella, "You're awake!"

"Yu dey yɛri?" she ventures in stilted Krio. She bends close, gesturing with her hands in a mime that Stella finds mildly amusing.

"Yes, ma," Stella responds with a weak smile.

Mrs. Brown asks her name and Stella responds, struggling to sit up at the same time. She suppresses a wince. She must have twisted her ankle because it throbs painfully. She hadn't noticed that earlier.

"Are you in pain, Stella?" Mrs. Brown continues to probe.

"I'm fine ma—thank you." Stella just wants to be on her way. She tries again to stand up and is surprised by a wave of dizziness that hits her, causing her to slump back down.

"Allan, I think we need to call the doctor!" Mrs. Brown exclaims.

"No, no I'm alright ma."

Stella leans back against the chair, just as her stomach rumbles audibly.

"I have been walking about town all day looking for a job, and haven't eaten since this morning ma, I just felt a little faint. I'll be okay, Ma."

Stella laughs nervously.

"You are poor dear!" Mrs. Brown groans, immediately rising from her perch.

"I'll be right back with some tea!" she says. "And we must warm you up. You'll freeze in those wet clothes!"

Before Stella has a chance to object Mrs. Brown has scurried out of the room. Stella in a panic think to herself that she really should leave now. Through the open window, the evening call of the muezzin echoes in the distance signaling seven o'clock. Ms. Rosetta, who had been so helpful since Comfort died, watched Abdul while Stella was out, and would feed him porridge for his evening meal, but the discomfort from her full breasts was becoming unbearable.

Once she got home, nursing Abdul would give her much needed relief. At the moment, her hurt ankle and sodden state made her miserable. *How could a bad day have gotten so much worse?* She wonders.

When Mrs. Brown returned with refreshments, Stella thanked her, gulping down the cup of tea as politely as she could manage and taking three biscuits from the expensive-looking china that had been placed beside her.

Stella's earlier visitors had returned. Their curiosity got the better of them now that the crisis appeared to be over.

"Psst, psst, psst!" came the urgent call from a corner in the room.

This time, the small faces were followed by arms and skinny chests, clad in matching green and yellow cotton gara shirts. Stella could not help but smile. The boys looked to range in age from four years to ten. With their initial shyness completely gone, they plopped themselves all squished together at the other end of the settee from where Stella sat. On cue, they chimed a 'Hello' and waited expectantly for her to reply.

"Hello!" Stella responded pleasantly, extending her hand toward the boy sitting closest to her.

"Una ow du o!" Stella added warmly in Krio before catching herself, unsure if they understood or spoke the language. One by one they shook hands with her. Stella was surprised when the oldest enunciating just as well as any child down the street, asked her a question.

"Wetin na yu nem?"

Stella replied, and in turn asked their names which the oldest whose name was Emeric, happily supplied. Before the boys could ply the visitor with more questions, their mother shooed them away.

"I should be going now, ma—" Stella starts to say, hoping she does not sound impolite.

"Certainly, but first, we must get you out of those wet clothes!" Elizabeth Brown proclaims, taking Stella by the arm and gently helping her up.

☙♈❧

As they climbed the long staircase to the upper levels of the house, Elizabeth asked Stella about herself, about the job search she had mentioned, where she lived, and who her people were. She expressed a happy surprise when Stella named June and Eric Johnson. Elizabeth and Allan knew the other couple well, had socialized with them often, especially at the Hill Station country club where the Browns spent much of their leisure time.

Stella knew them of course. She had served the Browns on several occasions when they attended June's soirees. It was not uncommon for domestic staff to blend into the background in the presence of their betters, as they topped up drinks, carried serving trays, and appeared not to listen when the topic of conversation invariably turned to local gossip or the politics of the day. Stella was used to this invisibility and did not blame the Browns for not recognizing her. She said nothing.

As they stood in Elizabeth's sewing room, Stella took in the items in the room. The tables and chairs piled high with fabric, garments in different stages of completion, a dress form, and an electric sewing machine like the one Ms. June owned. There was also an ornately designed antique foot pedal machine, which Stella stopped to admire.

"I was emptying some of my trunks to make room for the boys' clothes the other day when I found this dress. It should be just your size!" Elizabeth said, adding tentatively, "I hope it's alright."

She hands Stella the garment and ushers her toward a makeshift dressing room which has a full-length mirror leaned against the wall. Stella thanks Elizabeth shyly and accepts it.

After she climbs out of her soggy skirt suit, Stella slips on the dress, admiring herself in the mirror. The polyester fabric had a fashionable geometric print and precise stitching, better than any work she has seen at the local seamstress shops. Up until now, Stella has only seen ready-made dresses like this in the Patterson and Zirconia department store downtown when she window shopped.

Ms. June had been very generous and took Stella inside PZ to buy Abdul's christening clothes and crib. She would not have dared go inside on her own and only dreamed of being able to afford the expensive imported goods on offer there. She saved every penny of the monthly amounts Capri had been sending. That money was for Abdul's future, so he could have a good life. Stella did not doubt the Johnsons would keep their word and provide for Abdul's education, but Stella wanted Abdul to know one day, how much his father also sacrificed because he loved his son.

Elizabeth continues to chat about this and that while Stella gets changed. Stella makes genuinely understanding noises when Elizabeth explains how sad she is that her sons don't have friends in the neighborhood but instead are often teased and called "poor coral", a derogatory term for mulatto children.

The boys Emeric, Ethan, and Ernest had told their parents how street vendors, the regulars who set up their little box-stands along a section of the outside wall of the Brown's property and hawked roasted peanuts, peeled oranges, coconuts, and sweets to passersby, always came to their defense and chided the bullies.

When Stella is dress, they meet Mr. Brown in the main hallway. As Stella picks up her handbag from the table in the entryway where Daniel had placed it, she turns to face the Browns.

"Thank you very much for your help, ma, sir—" She nods in Mr. Brown's direction, respectfully avoiding eye contact.

"*We* should thank you, Stella, all this trouble you've gone through is because you were being helpful," Mr. Brown says kindly. "Daniel will drive you home," he says, and Mrs. Brown nods in agreement.

Stella feels uneasy at the offer. If she is seen in Mr. Brown's car there could be talk. The scandal of her being a young unwed mother living under the Johnson's roof had finally blown over, and the last thing Stella needed was more gossip. She had not been able to shake a feeling of guilt that her mother's sudden death was caused by a broken heart or from sheer disappointment in her.

Abdul meant the world to her and for his sake, Stella would do everything she could to keep her reputation intact. But it was late, her ankle did hurt, and finding a poda-poda would be difficult at this time of the evening, so pragmatism won the day.

"Yes, sir." She smiles. "Thank you, sir. Thank you, ma—"

Daniel was already waiting by the front door. Stella says good night and turns to leave. As she waves shyly to Mrs. Brown, three small hands peek out from behind their mother and wave back.

Chapter 2
Eric

Freetown

The military brass band took their position, ready to outshine the rival police band that played before them. It was a sunny morning in the capital and there was tremendous excitement in the air. Decorative buntings strung from the poles along the main streets of the city center lent an atmosphere of festivity to the fairgrounds.

The Recree was staged for the historic Independence Day celebrations. Invited guests milled about, trying to locate their assigned seats under the large white canopies arranged around a covered dais while scores of people crowded on balconies and rooftops of houses and buildings in the vicinity as far as the eye could see.

At the center of the grounds, the bodies of cultural dancers gleamed with sweat as they pounded their feet to the rhythm of djembe drums, and swayed provocatively in their raffia skirts, their bare chests adorned with ochre-colored beads and cowrie shells. They wore elaborately feathered and jeweled head gear that shimmered in the sunlight.

The white paint around their eyes, which mimicked the markings of the big cat, remained remarkably vibrant despite the sweltering heat. June turned to Eric but suppressed her bubbling excitement at the sight of his clenched jaw. Lately, he had been understandably tense. The lines on his forehead and bags under his eyes contrast the boyish roundness of his cheeks and chin.

On the drive down from their home in the hilly west end of town, even Sullay who was usually chatty, focused all his attention on the task of weaving through the narrow streets where traffic had been diverted by roadblocks, sensing that his master was in no mood for small talk. June pretended not to be bothered by the tension, and instead gazed out of the car window at the sights and sounds pulsating from the city. Momentous as all this was, they could not truly celebrate until the ink had dried on the document about to be signed, marking the country's new era of self-governance.

Although Eric kept the more insidious elements of his political battles out of their conversation, June knew enough from the terse telephone conversations she overheard from his library, and talk among the ladies at the club, to understand that the peaceful transition that they all anticipated, was being threatened. She was friends with the sister of Alan Cole, Eric's former classmate and now colleague down at the law courts.

Alan's sister told June how the recent sweeping arrests of individuals opposed to the colony's secession from the Empire had stirred up trouble. The threat of dissenters disrupting today's ceremonies was a real one.

Alan had arrived at the venue early, his lanky frame unmistakable as he waved to Eric and June from a row of seats reserved for members of their rank. The crowds were pressing into the field, and as more feet shuffled along, a fine brown dust settled on the folding chairs and June wondered how long her white gloves would remain pristine. She beamed as Alan leaned over and kissed her on the cheek. His grey suit looked brand new, and June did not miss the opportunity to gently tease the bachelor for having made an effort to dress up for the occasion.

"Wi swank tiday!" she complimented him with a smile. He grinned sheepishly.

As they took their seats, June looked around the tented area. She recognized acquaintances from the country club and nodded a greeting their way. June admired the dignitaries, especially the colorful gowns on display and the regalia of chieftains. The wives of the provincials had on traditional temle and lappas and wore thickly coiled headscarves.

The women of the Krio Descendants' Union also in attendance were dressed in their traditional kabaslɔt and wore checkered headwraps in a matching sky blue. The wraps were topped with beautifully crafted straw hats. They wore woven carpet slippers and carried their kotoku and a unique beautiful brocade scarf; the jojo lappa draped over one shoulder. The uninitiated would miss the deep symbolism of a lizard embossed into its rich fabric, and the parable of personal struggle borne by the wearer, with secrets known only to herself. Ɔl kondo lay in bɛlɛ na grɔn yu nɔ know ous wan dae at am.

June felt a swell of pride that her culture was being so elegantly and incomparably represented.

There were also the modern Krio ladies, looking prim and aloof, distinguished by their white gloves, Sunday hats and fancy linen frocks in a similar style to the rust-colored gown that June had on.

June's lace folding fan did little to prevent drops of sweat from settling on her nose. She was not focused on the heat, but instead admired all the splendor on display around her, even though she was aware that the pomp and ceremony belied a young society divided by politics and class—perhaps the most English of constructs.

June's family, the Walcott-Taylors were established in the pharmaceuticals business. As a young woman she understood now why her mother had stressed the importance of who she married. Eric, a Wallace-Johnson had been a more than desirable match despite his father's radical past. Eric's father had not been in his life for many years and his mother had died of malaria before he left home to pursue his studies. It had been a distant uncle of Eric's that arranged the *put stop* for June.

The *put stop* was symbolic bride price that signified their desire for June to no longer entertain other suitors. At the time, she and Eric were still in London finishing their university studies, but their families had eagerly conducted the ceremony in the absence of the prospective bride or groom; something the young lovers had found comical but were happy to indulge.

June and Eric were glad that both sides seemed satisfied, and the nagging questions about a wedding date ceased for a time. When they eventually came home and had their wedding ceremony at St. George's Cathedral, it was the talk of the town. The wedding reception held at the newly constructed King's Lodge had been attended by only a select few nearest and dearest friends, to the indignation of June's mother.

The sound of a steam engine broke June's reverie. The slow rumble of the train approaching the nearby Brook Town railway station announced the arrival of more travelers from the countryside, eager to share in the historic event. Just then, the band struck up the opening notes of the British Grenadiers' march, signaling the arrival of the Duke. The travelers were just in time to witness the formation of a guard of honor as a black Rolls Royce pulled up, and the Duke of Kent waved to the cheering crowds from the open window.

As the soon-to-be Prime Minister welcomed the Duke, June noticed the lines on Eric's face soften and his hunched shoulders slackened. She allowed herself to relax a little. Brigadier Mason unfurled the green, white, and blue flag, and hoisted it high above the white tents. June leaned back with a smile, ready to enjoy the remainder of the celebrations.

After much fanfare and parades, the new prime minister stood at the podium and started his address. Alan and Eric nodded enthusiastically along as Margai expressed his joy at the occasion that brought the nation together. Their admiration for the frail, grey-haired, well-spoken statesman was obvious.

"Work hard, for you are the future leaders of your country," he admonished.

"This new era will lay a foundation of traditions of which you will be proud. It will be up to you to uphold these foundations and to build upon them for the future. I pray for God's help and guidance on this historic day and in the years to come, and for His blessings on us all."

As he concluded, the crowds erupted in deafening applause with chants of "Margai! Margai! Margai!" that went on for what seemed an eternity. Sir Milton Margai gracefully bowed away from the podium, shook the hand of the Duke, and took his seat. His expression was one of solemn recognition that he had just made history.

৩৩৩

Their Ford Cortina was gleaming. Eric had started cleaning it himself following the morning ceremonies at the Recree grounds. Sullay was late for evening duty and Eric expected this was a result of the crowded streets flowing with revelers. Everyone was celebrating the country's independence, milling about, and causing traffic jams for miles along the downtown boulevards near where he lived. The crowds only thinned the farther you traveled away from the city center.

Sullay had walked most of the way to the Johnsons' house and was dismayed to see his master stripped to his undervest, trousers rolled up mid-calf, scrubbing the automobile's dusty tires. Sullay apologized profusely and once Eric left to have a shower, cleaned the car all over again in preparation for the Johnsons evening outing. As the car pulled out of the compound, looking almost brand new, Stella with Abdul tied snuggly on her back joined Mr. Johnny at the gate and waved excitedly at the rear window. June and Eric waved back.

As they settled in for the ride, Eric looked over at June and she returned his contented smile. He had complimented her as she applied the finishing touches to her make-up, saying she looked resplendent and making her blush. June was dressed in an emerald, green silk cocktail dress with a boat neck, was wearing her best pearl necklace, and carried a fashionable diamond studded clutch.

At her urging, Eric checked the inner pocket of his morning coat once more, confirming that the white and gold embossed invitation card had not been forgotten on their dressing table. They were both looking forward to an enjoyable evening, and Eric was especially eager to review the events of the day with his colleagues and their mentor Cornellius Campbell.

When Eric, Alan, and Emmanuel Pratt—'Imma' for short, returned home from their time at Holborn Law Tutors, the famous, or some would argue, infamous, Cornellius Campbell had invited them to his offices. Over a bottle of his finest whiskey, Claudius instructed the younger men on the responsibility of the mantle of decency and respect that was being passed on to them. They were examples of everything true and noble about a Krio man. He gave them advice on how to stay out of trouble and shared from his extensive experience navigating the increasingly tribalistic political landscape.

June was especially glad they were invited to the celebratory dinner hosted by the Hill Station country club. It was a signal that some of the most influential Krios in the judiciary approved of Eric. The car eased through the gates to the entrance of the clubhouse where it stopped to let them out before finding a spot to park and wait.

The club's main dining area had been transformed into a lovely cocktail lounge complete with green, white, and blue tablecloths and napkins, representing the colors of the flag of the new nation.

The party was in full swing as guests mingled, sipping cocktails and sampling from trays of olives, imported cheeses, and delightful-looking canapés. From the balcony overlooking the lush garden and manicured grounds, June noticed how the freshly white-washed lines of the tennis courts gleamed in the dying light of the day. The balcony offered a clear view of the coastline which snaked around the western side of the peninsula. A few other guests watched with June as the sun set over the Atlantic Ocean.

The dinner menu, imagined by a visiting chef from Singapore, promised delicious creations featuring prawns, sweet plantains, and avocados. June enjoyed a glass or two of sherry and planned to stay within that limit in case she needed to rustle Eric away at some point in the night if things got rowdy. The new prime minister would be attending the party, but word had spread that the popular trade unionist Robin Breton might also make an appearance.

Breton gained notoriety for attending the independence negotiation talks at Lancaster House in London, yet was the only member of the House of Representatives who refused the sign the independence agreement, citing knowledge of a secret defense pact of some sort between Britain and the colony which would favor the Krios. Eric planned to challenge Breton's preposterous claim and June could not think of a worse place for this to happen.

"Well, hello!" June recognized Elizabeth Brown's voice and turned around to greet her friend. The Browns had been seated at the opposite end of the hall and the two women had not had an opportunity to greet each other earlier.

The two exchanged pleasantries and decided that a walk around the grounds would be a nice way to stretch their legs and catch up. Toasts had been raised, there had been a few speeches, followed by dessert which was served uneventfully. With no sign of Breton and his people, June thought it was safe to slip away from Eric's side. He was engrossed in conversation and did not seem to notice her departure.

The two women chatted as they walked, their kitten heels clip-clopped on the asphalt. June complemented Elizabeth on her appearance. The English woman's blonde hair was swept up in an elegant bun and she wore a white silky affair, with a bold pattern of blue and green flowers. The dress had a mandarin collar and a slit on either side of the skirt.

June commented on Elizabeth's attempt to show support for the new nation by wearing its colors, making Elizabeth blush deeply. She responded that she suspected some of her countrymen might consider her dress statement a touch overboard.

They were still chuckling over recent gossip when June asked after the Brown's sons. She noticed her friend's hesitation.

"Is everything alright?" June inquired.

"Yes, yes, everything is fine. It's just that—" Elizabeth paused. "There *was something* I wanted to talk to you about."

June nodded expectantly, waiting for Elizabeth to spill the beans.

"Well, it's the young lady that lives with you," Elizabeth gushed.

"Stella?" June looked puzzled. "Did something happen? Did you hear anything?" she asked anxiously.

"No, no," Elizabeth interrupted, "not at all. In fact, she is quite lovely!" she paused.

"I don't know if she told you, but she came to our house—completely by accident," she rushed to explain, seeing June's puzzled expression.

"And now, well the boys won't stop talking about her. So, I—*Allan and I,* thought we would ask if you would mind terribly if we asked her to come and work for us, to help with the boys?" she finished breathlessly.

June thought for a moment. She had not been expecting this. She would have to speak with Eric of course but she was sure he would support her decision. Things had not been the same since Comfort died. They had all been saddened by the loss, but Stella seemed to carry a weight that made June feel inexplicably guilty. Maybe this would be a good thing.

Rosetta had taken up much of the household duties while Stella had continued to look for a job in her vocation without much success and Stella did not wish for the Johnsons to pull strings on her behalf. The Browns were good people, so perhaps this was the opportunity for a fresh start that they all needed but the proposition would need to be handled delicately so as not to offend Stella June beamed, taking the other woman by the arm as they entered the building. "Elizabeth, I think that's a wonderful idea!" she exclaimed.

Bo Town

Bisi's red docket and lappa were an eye-catching combination, and Eric did not fail to notice. He had felt the same stirring in his loins at the sight of June emerging from the bath, beads of moisture clinging to her glowing brown skin stretched taught over her pregnant belly. Eric knew he should change course, but Bisi was already half-way across the unpaved courtyard and it would be awkward if he abruptly turned on his heel and returned to his room in order to avoid her.

The compound of the United Methodist Church mission in Bo Town housed four guest bungalows that formed a square and overlooked a central court. A shrub-lined path between each house led to the main building and mission offices. A back room of the main house doubled as the cafeteria, and Eric knew from his time at the lodging that Bisi was probably heading there for breakfast.

"Good morning, sir."

Though her greeting, sparkling smile, and naturally pink lips were familiar, Eric still found them inexplicably alluring. He noticed how the red cotton fabric clung to the curves of her shapely hips and contrasted against her honey-golden complexion.

Eric paused. "Good morning, Bisi," he managed, in as level a tone as he could muster.

He shifted his briefcase to his right hand, thrusting his left hand in his pocket, and lengthened his stride. Mercifully, Bisi stopped mid-step and turned back toward her bungalow. Eric relaxed a little and continued on toward the aroma of freshly fried plantains.

The UMC mission house was a two-story concrete building painted a bright yellow, with ash wood doors and trim. In the four years since Independence, Eric's work had often brought him to the district courts of Bo, and he preferred the mission's guest accommodation over the bustling atmosphere at the handful of guest houses, and sole hotel in town.

Personally, Eric loved the mission house cook's famous breakfast of plantains and fish. Warm freshly baked loaves bought from the local Fula bakery were the perfect complement, excellent for sopping up the excess gravy served on the side.

Eric first met Bisi about two years prior when she stayed at the lodgings. Since then, they had chatted briefly whenever they bumped into each other. Bisi held a senior position with the reputable Barclays Bank, and her work involved frequent travel to the various provincial branches, mostly to provide training and mentorship to junior associates.

Eric had felt a strong attraction to the vivacious and intelligent young woman since they met. He resisted the temptation to try and get to know Bisi.

Eric loved his wife. He was a devoted husband, and he was excited at the prospect of welcoming his first child into the world.

Today, as usual, Eric exchanged pleasantries with the mission's head, Father Fred, who was leaving just as Eric entered the building. The locals had applied the paternal title to the Methodist clergyman from Leicester and although it was an ecclesiastical misnomer, it stuck.

The spacious interior of the house was almost monastic with its dark and silent halls. Eric noted as he reached the breakfast room, that the long table which sat twelve had only three places set. He hesitated. If he sat at the head of the table Bisi might think he was being typical chauvinist exerting his privilege.

On the other hand, if he did not take the seat and the third guest arrived for breakfast, they might be put in an awkward position. Deference to your betters was customary especially down there in the south, and the third guest, a junior colleague of Bisi's he'd met the day before, would be wary of disrespecting a man of higher status. Eric poured himself some tea from the thermos that had been set on the sideboard, opting to sit out on the verandah overlooking the missionary's garden, while he waited to find out who would eventually join him for breakfast.

He sipped the piping hot beverage, enjoying the serenity of his surroundings despite the occasional bleating of a goat tied to a far post, and the sound of chickens pecking about in the yard. There was an abundance of cassava leaf stalks growing next to a cluster of banana trees and he was already thinking about the sauce Mammy Yema would make them for lunch.

It was Saturday and Eric had only one meeting planned for the day. After a hard week of work, he looked forward to enjoying a leisurely afternoon before his return to Freetown the following day. The leaders in the Tikonko and Bumpe areas had welcomed him, but the communities around the bauxite mines were angry at Eric's efforts to talk to them about coming reforms. They had thrown rocks at his retreating car and in one instance, a man had brandished a machete.

Eric understood their mistrust. They felt betrayed by a government that failed to protect them from lopsided negotiations with the foreign holding corporation. Eric was there to help, but they saw him as just another big city lawyer trying to take advantage of their plight.

All his talk about their rights did not explain how they could change their situation. They had watched as almost overnight, the gated mining company campus with its gleaming buildings and modern amenities emerged and pushed aside the starkly contrasted rustic structures of the surrounding villages. Expensive new vehicles rumbled along the dusty highway passed their shacks on a weekly basis, loaded with the aluminum bearing ore, and headed straight to the barges docked at Port Niti.

Eric's driver was from the region and swore that the long-drawn-out greetings and small talk with the elders while sipping palm wine under a mango tree, were worth the effort towards forging alliance. Meanwhile Eric assigned his major undertaking the work required for the special status clause filings for Krios, to a junior partner.

The long days were taking a toll and sometimes the conversation faded into the background and Eric's mind wandered to home. He missed his time on the cricket field and certainly needed the exercise. His waistband had expanded considerably in recent months and June never failed to remind him.

June. Her time was fast approaching, which was why this would be one of his last times on the road until after the baby safely arrived.

"Penny for your thoughts?" Bisi's voice sounded warm and jovial near Eric's shoulder.

Eric's mouth felt dry, but he managed a reply, "Better yet, I'll give *you* a pound for yours!" She let out an adorably girlish giggle, her cheeks flushing lightly.

♋

Bisi took a seat to Eric's left at the breakfast table, while her colleague Joseph Sandy sat on his right. Mammy Yema was a matronly-looking woman who always had her head wrapped in a cotton head-tie. She served them herself, and they listened empathically as she complained about her arthritic knee. After breakfast, the trio stayed and chatted for a while. They talked about the rains; the new clock tower being erected at the center of the town and the prime minister whom Bisi revealed was a distant relative.

Eric was intrigued to hear more but checking his watch, realized he was running late for his meeting. Bisi and Joseph were themselves heading into town to attend a seminar being hosted by their bank's local branch.

With a promise to continue the story after dinner, Bisi waved goodbye saying, "See you later, Mr. Johnson!"

As Sullay maneuvered the Cortina along the main roads leading into Bo Town, Eric could hear the train sounding its arrival at the station. Sullay had cracked the windows open slightly since the air conditioner was broken, although his passenger did not seem to notice or mind.

Eric was immersed in the pile of documents spilling out of the open briefcase on his lap, and as they passed the bustling market at the Mile 91 junction, the driver quietly reminded his boss they should make a stop on their return. June had asked that they buy a bag of charcoal for the outside kitchen, and a bushel or two of the fleshy cassava tubers sold by the roadside vendors at the popular hub, known for their superior quality.

Eric could have taken the train from the Signal Hill station into Bo or on his other trips inland, but he preferred the drive. He and June decided they would put off buying a second car for now, and as she had stopped driving on the doctor's orders, it was no inconvenience to Eric. June was mostly on bed rest as she entered the latter part of her pregnancy and in the event of an emergency during Eric's absence, they had a list of friends ready to drive her to Netlands hospital at a moment's notice.

Overcrowding was not the reason Eric avoided the trains. As an independence gift from Britain, a few dozen new passenger coaches had in fact been added to the national consist. He avoided them because he would be forced to arrive at his destination along with the scores of European expatriates who made up the bulk of the passengers in the lounge cars or first-class.

Krios were increasingly scoffed at for pretending to be like the white man, and in many ways personifying the vestiges of colonial rule. Arriving at the central station alongside them could undoubtedly undermine Eric's efforts to change the perception among the people whose interest he and his partners were committed to protecting.

His law firm enjoyed some success, with Eric recently winning two cases in which he had represented workers dismissed unlawfully from the Diamond Mining Company out in the east, and the Pepel Iron Ore Mines up north. Through several witness interviews and a dogged hunt for evidence, Eric was able to prove that the men had been targeted for dissenting with their union but had stopped short of exposing suspected entanglements between union leaders and the company controllers.

Significant financial benefit and the recognition from these wins had put Eric, Alan, Imma, and other like-minded lawyers in the crosshairs of Breton and his supporters. Breton, a former union man was fomenting systematic antagonism toward the prime minister and promoting decentralization of political power. He established his newly formed political party as the official opposition, touting himself as the strong leader the country needed, to detach itself from the influence of a distant monarchy finally and completely.

This climate added a sense of urgency to Eric's trips. He buried himself in his work, meeting with as many paramount chiefs in the southern region as he could, to dialogue and to inform them of their rights. He was committed to opposing the policies that threatened to destroy the very foundation of their aspiring democracy.

ᎦᎧᎦ

One month later, turning off the narrow road on the approach to the Sunrise Hotel, Eric marveled at how modern and well-kept the grounds looked. His secretary Mrs. Jackson had called at the last minute to reserve his accommodation after she received Father Fred's message informing them that the annual UMC conference was being hosted at the mission for the week, with clergy arriving from all over the region to attend.

Father Fred had done his best to notify regular guests well in advance, but Eric must have missed the communication when he was there the month before. The head of the mission had apologized personally for the inconvenience and recommended the newly opened hotel a few miles from the Bo town center.

Eric did not mind so much. This would be his last trip before they welcomed their firstborn and after many long journeys on dusty highways, he was happy to exchange the hard cots at the mission house for more luxurious accommodation this one time. Despite their comfortable lifestyle, he and June saved money diligently. With typical Krio thriftiness, Eric maintained healthy investment accounts in Britain and believed in preparing for a rainy day.

Eric thought his mother would have been proud. She had brought him up in the old ways and would often say "if yu yams white, na fɔ kɔbar'am." It was wise to protect beautiful fat tubers growing in your yard from the prying eyes of neighbors. She, like many of her ilk, believed that only the so called provincials "put a hog head on the fence" for all to see when they had plenty. She would sniff distastefully at that thought, then continue extolling the superior virtue of modesty above all.

The recent completion of the Sunrise was marked with a much-publicized grand opening, and Eric looked forward to enjoying the modern amenities touted in the brochure. Eric was amused that Sullay refused his offer of a modest room and instead insisted no matter how distant, he could always find some relation that lived nearby and would be happy to put him up for a few nights.

Once they arrived at their destination, Eric made sure to give him enough money to compensate his hosts for their trouble. With Sullay being in his twenties and unmarried, uncommon for someone of his background, his family was happy that he held such a prestigious job. His starched white shirt and black trousers were always clean and neat. "Yu dɔn tɔn Krio man!" they jabbed, though they were well aware Sullay only dressed that way because the job required it, and not because he rejected his own traditional attire.

Mr. Lahai, the host and owner of the establishment, was proud that professionals from the capital were choosing to patronize his hotel, along with a growing mix of Lebanese, Pakistani and Ceylonese entrepreneurs, and British government officials with business in the region. Though the atmosphere was livelier than Eric preferred, there was an air of sophistication about the place which he appreciated.

It was one of only a few three-story buildings in the sprawling southern provincial town and the suites were spacious. Lightweight, gleaming white curtains over mesh screens allowed guests to enjoy a cooling breeze through open windows. High ceilings gave the entire place an airy feel, and Mr. Lahai ensured the wood floors always shone.

The host himself provided light entertainment during afternoon tea, plunking out jazzy tunes on the grand piano that adorned the huge dining room, while guests enjoyed imported biscuits and cucumber sandwiches served by staff that spoke English fluently.

Mr. Lahai's younger sister and business partner, Miatta, was studying in England and took the two-hour bus ride down to Piccadilly to purchase and ship the delectable butter biscuits served at teatime. She also supplied tins of Quality Street sweets, and most of the records which Mr. Lahai played at moderate volume on the gramophone set out on the terrace on Saturday nights, as the weather permitted. Davis' So What, Hancock's Maiden Voyage, and Simone's Nuff Said! were some of his favorites.

Mr. Lahai apparently hosted cricket tournaments which were quite popular, and he'd proudly informed Eric of plans to install a swimming pool and tennis courts on the grounds. Eric thought June might quite enjoy the place for a weekend. Perhaps they could invite friends to join them for their next wedding anniversary celebration after the baby arrived, he thought.

There had been an urgent and not entirely unexpected telegram for him in town earlier that day. The news it contained had Eric bursting to share, but he contained himself. Eric Johnson, High Court Judge. The words swirled around in his head, but he dared not say them out loud, only tested them to his own ears in a whisper. He liked the way they sounded. Yes, there was certainly much to celebrate.

☙♈❧

Dinner was tasty. Pemawi, a local dish, was made of sweet potato leaves simmered with hot peppers in light palm oil, served over perfectly cooked wild rice, and topped off with a sprinkling of benne seed powder that added the distinct flavor and texture.

It was a balmy night and Eric changed into one of his favorite casual dark blue safari suits and loafers to enjoy a leisurely walk around the gardens. The strains of the Righteous Brothers' popular hit could be heard in the background. Some occupants of the ground floor suites were out on their verandahs, one English gentleman sat alone smoking a pipe. A few feet down, a trio were engaged in spirited conversation.

You've lost that loving feeling, Eric hummed as he turned a corner on the path. He stopped; suddenly award of the electricity that started in his chest then slowly traveled lower. He was not sure if he had sensed her presence before he saw her, but there she stood. A rush of excitement bubbled inside. Bisi smiled at Eric in recognition, her pink lips parting delightedly as she waved him over. The incandescent lamp over the balcony ceiling bathed her in a soft light, and Eric was mesmerized.

The light breeze rustled the hem of her red satin dress, picking up the delicate scent of moonflower blossoms that hung in the air between them. Eric closed the distance quickly, and there was no need for words as he entered the open door to Bisi's suite.

☞♈☜

Freetown

June craved fresh fruit daily during her pregnancy. The half-dozen or so mangoes Sorie, the new houseboy picked from the tree in the back garden, never lasted more than a day. As she devoured them, the juice ran down her fingers. She would lick each fingertip shamelessly, to the delight of her husband.

June knew that in the privacy of their home, she could be child-like and even silly sometimes. Eric doted on her and encouraged her playful side, which most never saw. To the public, June Johnson was the perfect wife of the newly elected High Court judge to the Law Court of the Republic of Sierra Leone, and she played the part, effortlessly. Freetown high society knew her by name and recognized her for her grace, charm, and charity.

Eric and June attended a cocktail party at the national brewery the night before, and it had gone late. Eric was instrumental in identifying appropriate candidates for the board of directors, establishing what could be the first of many state-owned enterprises, so it had been quite an occasion. The brewery would provide a much-needed source of employment and revenue to further demonstrate that the regime's promises of financial and political capability held weight.

As the night had worn on, Eric occasionally sought out and squeezed June's hand, grateful that she was not complaining, although he knew her feet and back must hurt.

June slept in that morning and had just emerged from an afternoon nap, so she felt energized. She could hear Abdul playing outside.

"Kaytch am, kaytch am, kaytch am—" the little boy's voice rose in expectation and fell in frustration as he muttered to himself.

The sun set quickly this time of year, and darkness could fall quite suddenly. As the faint ringing of the market bells carried up from the city below, and she ambled over to the verandah to check on the boy playing by himself in the garden, June vaguely wondered whether Stella had returned.

Stepping out through the French doors, she sighed at the sight of the stunning view of the bay of Aberdeen expanding out toward the Atlantic Ocean.

June spotted Abdul, his shiny dark skin gleaming from ori; thick shea butter applied after his evening bath to protect his skin from the dry and harsh winds that blew most powerfully in December. He was crouched in the grass near a row of shrubbery, engrossed in his favorite pastime, chasing lizards. The red and blue reptiles scattered; scampering under bushes and up the nearby red hibiscus and yellow bell plants, startled by the *thwack* as Abdul aimed his stick and wacked the ground.

"Kaytch am!" he cried again, frustrated that his nimble arms and legs did not seem to move fast enough to grab hold of even one of the critters.

June, sure that the four-year-old would not be catching anything, decided to let him play a little longer. The Christmas holidays would soon be over, and he would be heading back to nursery school where his teachers were no doubt less accommodating of the child's newfound love for this strange sport. He probably also missed the Brown boys, June mused. They had been Abdul's playmates and 'adopted' older brothers for the first three years of his life after all.

June was glad that he seemed to have settled in well. When the Browns returned from their yearly holiday visit to Elizabeth's family in England, she made a mental note to invite them for an afternoon play date.

June waddled over to the kitchen to pour herself a glass of ginger beer. Stella always prepared the beverage just the way June liked it. Small, brown cloves of siminji floated on the surface, lending the spicy, sweet liquid a flavor that made it all the more delicious. Instead of sifting the cloves through her teeth, June searched the drawer for a teaspoon to scoop them with, realizing that she had left most of the silverware in a tray on the dining table where she had been polishing them before her nap.

A few older pieces from a set, two forks, a knife, and spoon remained in the back of the drawer. June retrieved them carefully. She ran her fingers over the inscription I.W.J., Eric's grandfather's initials were etched into each piece. Suddenly and seemingly without cause, June was flooded with a deep sense of loss for a man she had never known.

ဆၯဆ

"We should have been given more!" Eric huffed insistently. They were sitting out on the verandah at the King's Lodge. June had a wrap around her shoulders which she flung over her nose and mouth to protect against the cool night air.

Eric adopted the stance that democracy would falter and possibly fail if ethnic favoritism and political patronage were allowed to persist. So, he and other like-minded, highly educated, and influential Krios developed a plan to bring the members of ruling families among the protectorate chiefs to the side of equity for all.

June thought that Eric seemed pleased with their progress, and she had been understanding when his work took him up country for many months over the last few years. June noticed that Eric had recently been spending many hours mulling over the documents recovered from his late father's library.

A dry cough interrupted Eric's tirade, but he continued, "The Hut Tax war was meant to change everything, and now, they think by making me a high court judge, they can buy my loyalty. No!"

He stood up, pacing back and forth as his voice grew louder and more animated.

"These countrymen are greedy and ungrateful, why can't they learn from the example of the Gold Coast?"

June did not attempt to respond. She knew that when Eric launched into impassioned rhetoric, she was most useful simply listening. Besides, in the still of night when the compound and nearby roads had grown quiet, their voices surely carried. The last thing she wanted was to give anyone the impression that they were having an argument.

Lifting the weight of her pregnant belly with her left hand, she pushed herself up with her right and walked over to join him where he had flopped into the rattan loveseat. Placing a soothing hand on his back, June noticed Eric's vest was damp despite the dryness of the air and she wondered if he was coming down with malaria. He was stubborn enough not to complain if he had symptoms, and he hated to use the mosquito nets, so she doubted he had taken proper precautions on his recent trips up-country.

Eric calmed down somewhat. Turning to June he asked, "Does he think I don't remember what he did? What was he *trying* to do at Lancaster House?" he questioned incredulously.

June shook her head as she *tsk tsk*-ed in shared exasperation.

"I'm sure the Maroon Times would be interested to hear the information I've gathered on the bloody lot of them, including di Pa himself." Eric swung his arms in the direction of the city toward the domed Parliament building, a distinct feature of the city skyline, visible from their hillside home.

Although Breton's foot soldiers coopted the honorific as a way of referring to him, "di Pa" was a general term of respect for an older, usually accomplished and respected man. Eric and June could safely use it when discussing matters of a politically sensitive nature. They, as did others in their circles knew they must avoid uttering names.

Eric continued with his impassioned argument, "We fought, from all sides, for equal representation and now he wants to cut us out? Leave us in the shadows? Over my dead body!"

June tried to hush him, worried that indeed he would risk his health if he kept up the tirade. As Eric paced the tiled floor of the verandah, June couldn't help but notice the small rip at the seam of his vest. During his last trip to Bo, she had been sure to check all his vests and starched shirts that Rosetta laundered and had laid out on their bed. She must have missed this one.

♋

Bo Town

The former capital of the Protectorate was booming, and Mary Rogers loved her work there. After she finished nursing college, the United Methodist Mission had been pleased that she accepted their offer to serve in the southern area hospital. She was from the region and spoke the language. The relief that flooded the faces of the sick when they could describe their ailments in Mende always filled her with an enormous sense of responsibility.

Mary had met Fred, the young missionary from Leicester in England, almost as soon as he arrived in her town. It was right after the War, and they immediately struck up what would be a decades long friendship. Over the years, he learned to speak Mende albeit haltingly, and he and Mary made good partners. Most villagers were at first cautious of talking to the jengui, whose pale skin and slate blue eyes scared those that had never before seen a European up close.

Twenty years in, Fred was now very much a part of the community. Besides their work with the mission, which tried to meet the communities' spiritual, medical, and educational needs, the two had kept an extensive catalog of remedies from local wisdom passed on over the years. They had carefully curated details on how to prepare tinctures from the sickle bush plants, the sheku turay roots for malaria, and mambui, a favorite of the promiscuous farmer with many wives.

That morning, Mary started her hospital rounds as usual before the sun was up, knowing she would be on her feet late into the evening. The female ward was filling up quickly. The rains had come early and brought a surge of malaria cases. The trains had been less reliable lately, as many were diverted to servicing the mining routes in the east. In the wake of heavy rains, trucks, and passenger poda podas often lost tires or damaged their undercarriage as they dipped and maneuvered through large potholes on the up country roads.

Although the hospital pharmacy was still well stocked, she had sent a request to the capital for more medicine and supplies, anticipating the treacherous weather would delay the delivery. Setting aside her anxious thoughts, Mary concentrated on the day ahead.

As evening approached, she was looking forward to enjoying a hot cup of Ovaltine, thick with the creamy Peak milk she loved. She made her way down the last corridor of the female ward. Staff nurse Lucy had informed her that a new patient had an arrived earlier heavily pregnant and with a raging fever. Lucy was concerned.

"Sister Rogers, she looks familiar," Lucy had hinted.

"Oh, she does?" Mary inquired.

"Yes, I think she is the manager from the bank. She stays at the mission house with her colleague sometimes."

Lucy knew Sister Mary had a disdain for gossip, but she apparently could not help herself.

"I don't think she is married," Lucy continued, lowering her voice to a whisper, and glancing around furtively in case Matron was about.

Staff nurse Lucy had seen many patients over the years and a pregnant young woman without a husband or boyfriend was not uncommon. The older women, however, almost never came alone. Sister Mary was about to respond when they heard a low moan coming from the direction they were heading.

"Thank you for telling me, nurse Lucy," Sister Mary replied, already moving quickly toward the ward. She understood Lucy's apprehension. Without a husband or other family members around, a complication during childbirth became their sole responsibility, and the UMC mission was running low on funds to subsidize expenses beyond their free services.

Once in the ward, Mary headed toward the bed by the far window, where Lucy had placed the woman. Mary did recall the woman from the guest house. As she flipped through the hastily compiled medical chart, she also wondered why the woman from Freetown had traveled so far so late in her pregnancy.

Mary moved closer to her patient and could see that she was drenched in sweat. A yellow and pink gara lappa was all that covered her frame. As Mary approached, she could smell the telltale odor of birth fluids. The woman's contractions intensified, and as she clutched at Mary's extended hand, Mary noticed she was not wearing a wedding band. Going by the name on her registration card, Mary spoke gently:

"Bisi?" she said, pausing until the contraction that caused the poor woman's face to contort, had passed.

"Sister," Bisi's voice was strained and weak. She tried shifting her weight on the bed to get comfortable.

"Hush now," Mary said, rubbing Bisi's hand to soothe her as best as she could.

"My name is Sister Mary. We need to ask you a few questions if you don't mind so that we can help you."

This was not the best time to query her about where her family or the baby's father were, Mary thought to herself wryly, but she would need to obtain the details for a next of kin. The woman appeared to be suffering from malaria or worse still typhoid fever, and Mary knew they needed to attend to her quickly to reduce the risk to both her and the baby.

Before Mary could ask a question, another wave of pain shook the woman's already weak frame. Sister Mary and staff nurse Lucy's movements were quick and coordinated, having gone through this scenario many times before. They placed a drape over Bisi and started her on antibiotics immediately. They would not be able to manage her treatment on the main ward.

"Bisi," Mary spoke in between the woman's spasms, "we have to move you to the labor room. The baby is on the way. But you are also quite ill. You have a dangerously high fever that we need to control."

Mary's tone was quiet and urgent.

Bisi nodded, gripping the edge of the cot as more sweat broke out on her forehead. Mary rubbed her shoulders and coaxed her to breathe as the contraction crested. The other women on the ward who were awake, looked on and made sympathetic and encouraging noises as the two nurses carefully supported Bisi to her feet.

Lucy pulled the lappa under Bisi's arms and knotted it at her chest. Together they helped Bisi into a wheelchair and made their way slowly across the black and green tiled floor. Mary went back to pick up the woman's small bag of personal effects and joined Lucy on the concrete ramp, lit by pale lamplight in the dark of night.

When they arrived at the labor room, they wasted no time. Mary filled a wash basin to soak a face cloth and sponged the woman's pale face.

Bisi had been a regular patron at the UMC mission house in recent years, and though Mary did not know very much about her, she suspected the father of Bisi's child was unaware of her current state.

No matter how educated or accomplished she was, an unmarried woman and her child would be relegated to that unenviable caste of outsiders.

As they settled Bisi onto the birthing bed, Mary noticed with concern that Bisi's normally bright pink lips were grey and stuck together with dried saliva at the corners. Bisi's skin was alarmingly hot to the touch, despite the coolness of the air. The possibility that they were indeed dealing with a case of typhoid fever set off alarm bells in Mary's head, the entire ward could be at risk. She did her best to stay calm and focus on one thing at a time.

The baby was coming, and with each contraction, Bisi grew weaker. Lucy was busy getting hot water to fill the metal tub as Mary checked Bisi's dilations. The baby was crowning. She took Bisi's temperature, twisting the glass tube in the light to better read the mercury level. Her temperature was impossibly high.

Lucy soaked the face towel and continued to mop Bisi's forehead as Mary coached her through the next wave of contractions. Mary checked the pocket watch hanging from her apron seeing now that the contractions were a minute apart. Bisi let out a low grunt and gritted her teeth. She was deathly pale. Abruptly her eyes rolled back in her head. She was seizing.

"Lucy, fetch Father Fred, quick!"

By the time staff nurse Lucy and Father Fred arrived, they found Mary frantically attempting to revive the lifeless woman. Lucy picked up the hastily wrapped bundle from the nearby cot. A girl.

Lucy was cleaning the blood and mucus from the newborn's face when Father Fred's solemn prayer penetrated the stillness of the night.

"Lord Jesus Christ, deliver your child Bisi from all evil and set her free from every bond, that she may rest with all your saints in the joy of your eternal home, for ever and ever."

The amen stuck in Mary's throat, as she wept hot, silent tears.

Sister Mary cried for hours that night. What she had witnessed she would not soon forget. Once Bisi started seizing it was as though the life was sucked out of her. They watched as the spasms ended; her limp body having birthed the baby they agreed to name Angel.

Father Fred was stunned as they all were. When they talked quietly about what to do next, he had stuffed his shaking hands into his cassock so Mary and Lucy would not see how affected he truly was. He wrapped Bisi's body in the dark blue hospital sheet from one of the shelves, and placed the newborn in her mother's lappa, wrapping her carefully so her toes did not stick out before handing her to Sister Mary. Father Fred encouraged them to rest and pray. Surely in the morning, the Lord would help them decide what to do.

They had never been faced with an unclaimed body. The capital was a busy place and trying to find Bisi's relatives would be almost impossible without contacting the police. Sister Mary also suspected Bisi had intentionally avoided delivering her child where the cruel whispers and gossips could not mock her. Why else would she come knocking at their door so late?

The next morning, Sister Mary could not stomach breakfast. She went over to the nurses' station and fixed herself a cup of tea before she pulled out the bag Bisi had come in with. Mary thought she might look for clues as to a next of kin, or just someone to contact with the sad news.

Sister Mary was puzzled by the neat stack of letters, carefully penned and tied together at the bottom of the bag. They were all addressed to Mr. Eric Johnson, King's Lodge, Signal Hill, Freetown, and appeared to have never been sent. Sister Mary remembered Mr. Johnson from the mission house as well but had not realized he and Bisi knew each other that well.

She pulled off her apron, and unclipped her cap, setting it down and taking a seat. The task might take her all morning. Her rounds would have to wait. Bisi had taken her secrets to her grave, leaving Mary with the burden of finding out the truth about the baby now entrusted to her care. The responsibility of the situation was not lost on Mary, and she vowed to herself to bear it in sacred trust. She read the letters carefully, transfixed by the delicate script and the words on each page.

Chapter 3
Allison

Freetown

"Nothing, ten, twenty, thirty, forty—"

The five of us circling Finda are ambivalent to our defeat, and in fact we are enjoying her display of mastery almost as much as she is. The score continues to climb and Finda seems to be in no hurry to give up her winning streak. The game of acra is derived from a sport that originated in Ghana, called ampe. It is akin to the Chinese game known as rock paper scissors but is played using the feet. The player's opponents face her in a semicircle (the game is most popular among girls), and the object and skill are the ability to anticipate which foot the other players will put forward and do the opposite.

Each play can go for up to three tries and the player if victorious, continues to take on challengers along the line. The longer she can stay in the game, the higher her score. The players set the pace of the game according to the rhythm of their feet, accompanied by hand clapping. It was not uncommon for the tempo to increase to a near frenzy as two dueling players battled for victory.

If Finda keeps going, our cheers will soon attract an audience. Other class five girls sometimes joined in the fun and even the boys would take a break from playing gig, the game of hoops and sticks, and crowd around to cheer the winner on. I find blatant domination in any sport to be distasteful and somewhat embarrassing for all the attention it draws, but I enjoy the camaraderie, so I stick with the game and let Finda have her day in the spotlight.

The bigger the crowd grew, the more elaborate her moves became. First to the left and then the right, a dramatic spin of her green and white checked uniform skirt before her foot lands. *Two hundred!* Everyone goes crazy. Surely this must be a new record.

We went at it for what seemed like forever when somehow Eunice figured out Finda's pattern and caught a lucky break. Finda missed just a brief beat and then clapped again for a second count. Eunice was sweating and trying to focus as hard as she could, her face screwed up in determination. She matched Finda again. With the new record at stake, Finda twirled with more vigor and seemed to spend an eternity clapping down to the third and final play. On her count, Eunice flung out her right foot and Finda was about to as well. Then in a flash, she twisted around quickly and landed on her left.

"Foul!" the spectators cried in unison. Finda tried desperately to defend herself, but no one would hear it. Eunice had matched her third play and ended her reign as queen of the circle. Shamefaced but still adamant that she had not cheated, Finda conceded, and Eunice took her place. The tempo changed because Eunice liked to time her claps to a slower beat. I thought idly that the lunch bell should have been rung a while ago.

Since this was the end of the term, with nothing much to do besides preparing for the prizegiving play and Christmas parties, I guessed the teachers were not too concerned about us playing outside a little longer. As a new round of the game began, I begged out with my meager score of forty, which I could use in the continuation of the game after school if I chose to and headed in the direction of the outdoor school canteen looking for Ma Musu.

Many of my classmates ignore their packed lunches in favor of snacks. I like the roasted peanuts, guavas, and fried pastries the best. And like Mama, I love ginger beer, and especially enjoyed Ma Musu's version of the spicy sweet drink, half-frozen with chunks of ice inside. She used to sell the refreshment in reusable plastic bottles but after months of having to go around the school, looking in classrooms under desks and chairs to collect the bottles, she had resorted to bagging the refreshment in disposable plastic bags. My ten cents in hand, I find her under a tree by the path between the middle and lower schools.

The moderately sized primary school is known for its well-kept grounds. Its secluded location above the main Fourah Bay College campus on Mount Aureol is idyllic, with dense forest cover on all but the eastern face of the peak. The path that winds through the school grounds, offers a sweeping view of the seaport in the east, and the central area westward to Aberdeen bridge. Ma Musu notes the sweat on my brow. She probably witnessed the earlier action on the playground. She smiles and hands me two bags of ginger beer in exchange for the coin I hand her.

"Finda too sass," she says with a knowing smile that belies her pride in her daughter's prowess. I half-smile in response and shrug awkwardly.

I think her mother is right. Finda can be quite forceful. But on the other hand, it must be hard to not have parents well off enough to pay for a good education. Finda probably just wanted to fit in. Finda's father is a laborer. Ma Musu herself is not educated. Impressed by her industriousness she has become a trusted and beloved part of the community so the principal arranged for her children to attend school at no cost.

The bell rings and I wave goodbye and walk back to class. Ma Musu had offered me an extra bag of ginger beer for my sister, but I politely declined since there would not be enough time for me to give it to her. Jennifer was in class three and her teacher was very protective of her pupils. She did not let any of them wander around outside, not even at the end of the school day when the drivers lined up waiting to pick them up.

Those of us in class five and above were allowed to pick up our younger siblings, otherwise the children were kept until the driver or nanny came in to get them. Macabre stories of ritualistic killings and the mutilated corpses of young children being found had circulated through the city and in the newspapers for several months. These acts were rumored to be in relation to the approaching elections and had everyone on edge.

Our principal, Mrs. Roberts, watched all of us like a hawk. Although we were high up in the hills, away from the bustle of the city, the thick forest had beaten footpaths that led down to the east end of town where some of the notorious hunting and ojeh societies were based, so she was not taking any chances.

The rest of the afternoon was dull. My teacher Mrs. Cox-Jones was heavily pregnant and when we filed into class, she instructed us to read quietly or put our heads on our desks until the end of the day. I gave my friend Sam my second bag of ginger beer as I walked past, and he nodded his thanks. I slipped mine into my desk where it would melt faster, making it easier to gulp down when the teacher was not looking.

After Mrs. Cox-Jones had predictably fallen asleep in her chair, and my ginger beer was all gone, I crossed arms on my desk to cradle my head. The chirping sounds of birds and grasshoppers drifted in through the open windows and I silently rehearsed my lines for the school prizegiving play before dozing off as well.

The journey down to the capital city was a long and dusty one. Father Fred and Sister Mary Rogers had been traveling all day and were exhausted. Ongoing construction of the new grand highway commissioned by Breton's government meant there were long stretches of gravelly road and work zones which slowed traffic all the way from Bo Town center and well into the Masiaka region.

They had made a few stops on the way to buy snacks for Angella and soft drinks to cool off in the heat. Angella clutched her small portmanteaux close to her chest the entire time. The seats of the UMC mission's khaki-colored Land Rover were worn and the springs beneath them rammed into all their behinds, on the bumpy ride.

Since her birth, Bisi's daughter had been a ward of the church. Father Fred sent a telegram to notify the Barclays Bank Freetown branch of Bisi's passing. He arranged for an obituary in the Bo newspaper, suggesting they omit the next of kin section of the announcement to avoid any awkwardness. She had been buried in the far corner of the UMC parish cemetery with only Sister Mary, Lucy, and a handful of other staff attending, while Father Fred officiated.

Angella was cared for by her guardians at the mission and for over ten years, they had loved her and provided for all her needs. She was definitely an inquisitive child and gave Mama Yema a headache when she would chase after the chickens in the yard. But life at the mission house could be lonely for a child.

Angella was well ahead of her peers in learning and had been advanced from class 3 to 5. Sister Mary jokingly worried that if her teachers kept giving her double promotions, she would soon be one of the youngest students to enter university. Sister Mary loved the child's wit, wondering at times if she inherited it from her mother or her father.

Angela showed no interest in chores, preferring instead to devour the books on the shelves in Father Fred's office. She would read for hours until the lights or more recently the kerosene lamps, came on. Sister Mary hushed her up and shooed her away when she asked about her classmates that had been taken to

Bondo, a coming-of-age ritual practiced by many in the district, involving cutting female genitalia. When she noticed Angella's budding breasts against her cotton school uniform, Sister Mary had promptly bought her a set of camisoles for modesty.

Sister Mary never married, nor did she have children of her own, so she was thankful that God had seen it fit that she raised Angella. But she knew the time had come for her to give up caring for the child when the UMC assigned her to be matron at the district hospital in neighboring Serabu.

The wards there were more crowded there, and her days would be even longer. Most of her time would undoubtedly be needed to care for patients and manage her staff. She already felt guilty for not being with Angella as much as she wanted to; the little girl would soon grow into a young lady, and she needed to be provided with a proper family life.

Sister Mary had discussed Angella's future with Father Fred, her old friend in the faith. When she showed him Bisi's unsent letters, he had looked at them for a long time before saying, "Sister Mary," his tone was matter-of-fact. "I don't believe this poor man ever knew he had a child!"

Sister Mary had not tried to hide her derision at his use of the phrase "poor man."

"Well, you know what I mean," Fred mumbled.

"Eric Johnson certainly isn't poor!" Mary had shot back, insistently.

If anything, he was a lucky man, she thought. The letters Bisi had written were filled with tender words. Bisi had acknowledged the brief affair they had was wrong. She knew he would not return to Bo and had avoided any contact with him when she was in the capital. She had not expected to become pregnant. That was clear from her letters. A scandal was the last thing she wanted understanding that it could destroy Eric's reputation, his law practice and his career.

Sister Mary thought Bisi's words were wistful, and overly apologetic. Bisi had been an independent, professional woman. Mary was filled with sadness that she had not been able to save Bisi's life and was convinced that she could do better for Angella if there was a way to reach her father.

When they finally agreed on the plan, Father Fred made the call to Eric Johnson. They would tell him that Angella was an orphan who they hoped could attend secondary school in the capital, and they were seeking a benefactor to help with this undertaking. They would say that Eric Johnson had come highly recommended by the UMC mission as he was a respected patron and had young children of his own. They would express their confidence that his family would be willing and able to assist.

Father Fred's call was answered by Mrs. Johnson, and he was pleasantly surprised at how quickly she responded to the appeal. She needed a few days to convey the message to her husband and apologized that she could not give them an answer right away, Eric was terribly busy with filings and petitions.

A commander of the army, Brigadier David Lansana, had ordered the extrajudicial arrest of Robin Breton before the result of a recent election was announced. The attempted coup was quickly reversed with Breton reinstated as head of government. The brigadier had died while in custody and Eric was working day and night, reviewing evidence submitted in the inquest into the suspicious death. It was all over the news.

Mrs. Johnson returned the call within a few days as promised and gave Father Fred the good news. Their family would be delighted to take in this young girl in need of a home.

When Mary had told Angella that she would be moving to the capital city to live with a nice family, the girl's shiny round face had been filled with terror.

"But, Sister Mary, I want to stay here with you," she pouted.

In her usual logical way, Angella made her case for staying as Sister Mary listened patiently. She pranced around the room punctuating each reason with an emphatic wave of her arms.

"I will miss my friends. I will miss chasing the goats and chickens. I will miss reading Father Fred's books and I will miss you."

Then she rushed to Sister Mary, hugging her tightly around the waist and burying her head in the folds of her uniform, her shoulder shaking with sobs. The only other time Sister Mary had seen the child so sad was when they stood together at the graveside of the mother she had never known. Angella had fought back tears then as her guardian hugged her tightly.

Sister Mary nodded. Angella had never been anywhere outside Bo. Her life had been a simple one, revolving around the parish, school, and the mission house. She knew Angella was particularly excited about Christmas this year as Ms. Lucy promised she would buy her a bicycle. Sister Mary wasn't prepared for the sudden outburst of affection as Angella clung to her. Maybe it was not a good idea to send the child miles away from home to live with strangers after all.

Now gazing out of the dusty window of the Land Rover with the vivid orange of the evening sky overhead, she watched the child whisper a final goodbye to the mission and shut her eyes, probably trying to imagine what the people in her new family were like.

It was almost dusk when the dusty Land Rover pulled up to the gate of the King's Lodge. June called out to Stella to revive the dwindling coal pot and heat water for warm baths. After the vehicle had come to a stop, a lanky grey-haired man hopped out from the front passenger side, then assisted a rotund woman in a pleated grey dress as she also disembarked. Next, a young girl was helped out of the car. The ends of her neatly braided hair hung down past her shoulders and she carried a worn green leather case. She was clearly very tired and yawned, showing off small, closely set teeth.

When June emerged to greet them, the girl took a step back.

"Don't be afraid, Angella," Sister Rogers had assured the girl. "This is Ms. June. You will be staying with her from now on and she will take good care of you." Angella kept her case clutched tightly to her chest.

"Angella, welcome to our home," June had said with genuine kindness, as she guided the shy young girl by her elbow. "Come, let us go inside."

♋

Papa and Mama are hosting another dinner party tonight. It's Saturday morning and the bustling around the house started long before Angella, Jennifer, and I got out of bed. We could be sure Mama would have chores waiting for us when we did.

A dinner party meant there would be all sorts of tasty treats and of course jollof rice, my favorite. Slow-cooked white rice in a spicy tomato and onion base served with a rich beef and chicken stew. It was traditional Sunday fare but made a special appearance at every party Mama hosted and we were over the moon.

The tangy aroma of Mama's pepper chicken peanut sauce wafted through the doorway of the kitchen as our new house girl, Beatrice, no doubt would be pouring the marinade into a giant vat of freshly butchered poultry. We heard the sound of music coming from the verandah where Mama was pruning the roses and hibiscus in their flowerpots. She hummed along to the popular Miatta Fahnbulleh song "Kokolioko."

We girls shared a large bedroom with white and yellow floor tiles, the bright matching blinds which Mama had sewn had tiny pink flowers along the border and were layered over fine white lace curtains. Papa had taken down the mosquito nets mounted over each bed and put screens on all the windows of the house. Now able to move about freely, the three of us often crowded together on one bed, staying up and talking late into the night.

"Allison, Angella, Jennifer! Are you up yet?" Mama called out.

My mother loved her morning devotion. *Start the day with the Lord!* was a mantra she often reminded us of. She had a few other favorites.

Our younger brother Frank tried his best to skip out on the time together but no matter how long he stayed in the bathroom to brush his teeth or empty his apparently outsize bladder, Mama would just sit, waiting patiently on the living room settee until he appeared.

When Jennifer, Angella, and I emerged from our bedroom, still clad in our nightdresses, we found Mama in her usual spot. I did not mind our weekly devotion. It was a small price to pay in exchange for the freedom on a Saturday morning to get out of bed whenever we wanted and lollygag in our night clothes.

Mama's stories of her childhood–rising early, fetching water from the outside pump, helping in the kitchen, *and* having family devotion all before the crack of dawn sometimes sounded just a little exaggerated, but we were immensely thankful for her modern way of raising her children compared to other Krio households.

As I look across to where she sits on the sofa, I think not for the first time how beautiful my mother is. Our father's tall and imposing figure had been compared by our friends to the deadly Dr. Kananga played by a debonair Yaphet Kotto in one of the spy films we were too young to watch but saw the posters outside Odeon cinema. Our mother in contrast is like a delicate flower. Her skin's hue reminds me of the color of hessonite in the sunshine.

Although she had borne children late compared to many of her contemporaries, she has a beautiful figure. Her back is straight, and her breasts do not sag like the bare-chested women we see washing clothes beside the whitewater falls, along the road leading up to our house. She has packed away her assortment of expensive wigs and now sports a stylish afro. After forty, she began to develop faint lines around her eyes and mouth that only enhanced her elegant looks.

Jennifer is chatting away, and I wonder idly what I might look like at Mama's age when Frank finally shuffles in. He was a scrawny seven-year-old that Jennifer and I often fought with. He was good at using his elbows and knees because they were sharp, and he came over to the sofa and promptly wedged himself between the two of us even though he could barely get a thigh in. Angella loved the morning devotion as much as Mama did, as it reminded her of the times with Sister Mary at the UMC mission house.

Jennifer and I ease apart to let Frank in and then moved back to our original positions. Frank was pinned between our hips, and we can hear him grunt in discomfort. I tried to hide a gleeful smile.

"Serves you right, cockroach," I whispered under my breath.

Mama either did not notice or saw that Frank had picked this fight and decided not to intervene. She sighed deeply, bowed her head, and started with the Lord's prayer. Jennifer and I exchanged knowing glances before we each bowed our head. Once the prayer started, nothing short of a death would interrupt Mama, so Frank would not be able to protest.

Today's theme is forgiveness. We take turns reading a passage from the book of Ephesians. As we read, Frank nudges and squirms, his elbows dig into my rib cage, and I almost cry out. *Advantage Frank.* I would have to be smarter next time.

I tried to answer Mama's question about a recent instance where I might have chosen forgiveness, but my mind was blank. Despite the current horseplay with my brother, I did not think I'd been one to ever really keep a grudge. Jennifer on the other hand was at the ready, quick to recount an incident at school.

"Last week," she started to say, overly dramatically, "my friend Miatta took my twenty cents from my bag without asking me, and I couldn't buy groundnuts from Ma Musu. I found out later that she had been the one that stole it, but she said she had been very hungry. I was angry but now I forgive her."

She beamed as Mama nodded approvingly.

"Allison, Angella, Frank? Is there anything you can think of that you might want to forgive someone for?" Mama challenged us.

"I would like to forgive Allison for putting water in my crepe!" Frank blurted out, eyeing Mama to see her reaction.

"You mean, running shoes," Mama corrected him gently.

Mama was strict about our use of vocabulary and found it hard to hide her disdain when we interjected Krio words into our sentences. Frank had done it a lot in recent weeks and Mama had threatened to take it up with the principal at the school we attended. I heard her complain to Papa that maybe extending tuition and allowing less privileged students in, rather than the small group that had pioneered the school, was having a negative impact.

She would not let slip Frank's use of the colloquial "crepe," and she was similarly diligent when it came to people who called every nail polish Cutex and every vacuum cleaner a Hoover.

She spoke Krio when the situation was appropriate, but slang and incorrect vocabulary were particular peeves of hers. With dignitaries and important people often visiting Papa at home, she especially saw it as her duty to present well-mannered and well-spoken children. With the recent stunning referendum which effectively turned our country into a one-party state, we noticed that Mama had become a little stricter with us at home. As if she felt compelled to retain what diminishing control, she had over our world, while the world outside collapsed into itself.

"Allison?" Mama prompted, not about to let slip the offense for which Frank had so magnanimously offered me his forgiveness. *Rats!* I was busted.

I had been upset with Frank for getting into my diary and reading what I had written about Sam Koroma, my classmate from primary school. He made faces whenever I gave my extra ginger beer ice to him, but at other times his smile was shy and kind. It made me blush.

I liked Sam and he seemed to like me back, but also seemed to like a lot of other girls in our class. This confused me. Angella thought I was wasting my time pining for him, but I thought otherwise. After the school year ended, I rarely saw Sam anymore, so I poured out my feelings into my diary and was embarrassed that Frank had read it.

"Allison!" Mama's voice was sterner this time.

I decided not to deny the shoe incident or call it an accident.

"Sorry," I mumbled. "I was only trying to get Frank to stop bothering me—" my voice trailed, and I hoped my apology would be enough.

"You know better than that," Mama chided with a hint of exasperation. I knew she was right.

Angella feigned a small cough. Mama did not press the matter. We continued with a song from the Methodist Hymnal, then ended with a doxology.

☙ ♈ ❧

It was almost the end of the long holiday, so Mama already had our new secondary school uniforms made. Elizabeth Brown had sewn our uniforms since we were little, but I had still been embarrassed at the prospect that she would notice my breasts which seemed to have popped out overnight. Mrs. Brown had been nice enough not to comment, as she stretched her tape measure around my chest. Angella had them as well and we giggled as we undressed. There were other days when the stony lumps hurt, but we said nothing to Mama.

Papa called us together to talk about transportation arrangements for the school year. With Angella's arrival and the two of us older girls starting a new school on the opposite side of the city, the drive to and from the school presented a new challenge. Mama did not drive to work, and the British Council staff vehicle which picked her up every morning did not permit family members riding along. Traveling with her was not an option for Angella and me.

Papa still owned his old Ford and had just bought Mama a brand-new Fiat on their fifteenth wedding anniversary, but he didn't think it was safe for her to battle the daily traffic and take on the taxi drivers that zoomed at dizzying speeds up and down the winding route into town. Mama objected to hiring a second driver.

When Papa posed the option of taking the public bus to school Angella and I were ecstatic. I felt all grown up, and proud that he would trust I with such responsibility. When we were younger, we rode to school in the car with Papa as Sullay navigated the bumpy peninsular route up the mountain and through Regent and Leicester villages dropping us off before heading back down the hill with Papa to the Law Court building or to his chambers.

Papa never minded riding in the front with Sullay, unlike other well-to-do men who felt the need to sit in the owner's corner of their car at all times. Frank had sometimes petitioned to sit up front, complaining that Jennifer and I pushed and shoved him too much when he sat in the back with us. On days when Papa did not have reams of briefs and notes to look over on the drive, he indulged Frank's request.

Now with four rapidly growing children, road trips including Sunday afternoon drives with Papa were rare. We used to love the drive along the coastline, as we gazed out at the blue-green ocean waters while the tide brought mighty waves crashing to shore and the setting sun blazed over the horizon. One Sunday, Papa gently declined our pleas for a trip to Sans Souci the popular ice cream parlor, because we would not all fit in one car and Mama had a headache and could not drive the other car. We had gone back to our room deflated.

"It's all her fault!" Jennifer's gruff accusation surprised me.

I knew she was upset with Angella, most recently for accidentally using her face towel, but it sounded however like there was more to my sister's irritation. I waited for her to go on.

"Ever since she came, Papa stopped taking us to the beach for ice-cream. We have not been swimming. Allison, she eats with her hands and her farts are nasty," Jennifer declared.

"Jennifer!" I scolded. I felt disappointed. I wanted to be understanding, but Jennifer had been acting spoiled lately and I could not bring myself to agree with her. I saw Angella differently and wanted Jennifer to do the same.

"Why are you saying such bad things about her? She doesn't have a mother or a father. She eats with her hands because that was what a lot of the people around her did and just so you know, your farts don't smell nice either!"

"But I do miss our Sunday afternoon drives too," I softened my tone. "Maybe we could still ask Papa to take us next weekend?"

I tried to sound upbeat but knew that was unlikely. Papa was concerned about our safety and would never let us pile into a car without a seat for each passenger. He was upset when he heard or saw the terrible road accidents caused by speeding drivers along the peninsula roads. Taxis packed the passengers two and three people deep in order to get as many fares as they could. The traffic police had taken to accepting bribes and let them get away with it.

I wondered if Papa's cousin Aunty Loretta, Lolo, as we fondly called her, could take us on an outing if Papa and Mama were too busy. She was our closest family on Papa's side. She was beautiful and worldly, and we adored her, but sadly saw less and less of her as she was often traveling to promote her music.

For all my bargaining, Jennifer was not appeased. I left her to sulk and went in search of Angella. I was irritated with Jennifer but not angry. I felt I could never be angry toward my sister or brother. I could remember when each of them was born. I remember being in awe when they first entered my world.

Many Krio women still gave birth the old way, at home with the assistance of a midwife. Mama had not held to that tradition. Each of us had been delivered by Dr. Gooding at Netland's hospital; a new facility with shiny floors, private rooms and a matron with a uniform starched so much that it crackled when she walked.

I recalled the day Jennifer took her first steps. She and I had been playing on a wide straw mat spread on the ground with Ms. Stella keeping a watchful eye on us as she ironed and folded a mountain of fluffy white cloth nappies. I remember Ms. Stella's squeals of delight, and Mama's laughter and happy clapping when she rushed outside to see what the fuss was about and found her youngest child taking shaky but persistent steps.

When our brother came along the *pull na doh*, a traditional naming ceremony, was accompanied by a lavish feast complete with women dressed up in their kabaslɔts. They all had their kotoku from which emerged clean, crisp Leone notes which they carefully tucked into the folds of the baby's blanket as was customary.

Pull na doh was a time for celebration, with food, libations, and thanksgiving. Held on the seventh day after birth, it was the first formal introduction of a newborn to the world, to their religion, and to their community.

Papa and Mama never treated us girls differently from our brother, but that did not stop other people from offering special congratulations and gifts on the birth of their boy pikin'. It wasn't unusual for a boy to be valued as an asset, the principal heir, and the one who would carry forth the family name. The family would be assured that when he married, unlike the concern that women would embrace their husband's family and may lose touch with their own.

Somewhat different than others, my parents were less traditional and felt that a girl held as much worth as a boy and her birth was equally celebrated. In some families recently, women tended to maintain a strong connection to their family and faith, preferring to attend her home church and even hyphenating their surnames to reflect both families.

As children, we attended many other traditional ceremonies like Mama's younger brother's engagement, and Papa's great aunt's ten-year awujo and nyole. We often ate too many beans and Akara, sweet foora balls, and slices of fruit, and needed Mama's lemongrass tea to soothe the colic we almost always suffered from the next day. I felt a deep fondness for my little sister and brother and now that I was going off to secondary school, I would miss them.

Our morning drives had been fun, as we sang songs, traded Anansi stories, and did hot mental. They were smart as whips and I was always impressed at how well they kept up, as we tested each other's skills at solving math puzzles.

I always saved peppermints or bought an extra ginger beer to share with Jennifer at lunch time, and since Frank joined us in big school, he would come to my class for comfort and a pep talk if any of his classmates pushed him around. Jennifer proudly hovered around me whenever she could, just to show her classmates that she had a big sister willing to take them on if need be.

For the most part we were well behaved, but I did have a scuffle once in my final year. It was after school with a new boy in Jennifer's class. He had taken offense that she corrected his English and called us' too aristo'. Taken aback by his tone of disdain, I shoved the offender a bit too hard, watching with satisfaction as he toppled over his desk, smacking his lip on the edge as he went down.

We swore Sullay to secrecy, and the school mercifully did not report the incident to Mama, although I thought she should have been proud. I had fought for a cause she believed in, after all. Impeccable speech.

☙ ♈ ❧

"Eric, I think this will stir up more trouble!" Mama tried to maintain a hushed tone while she spoke.

We were gathered around the dining table doing homework or studying, but they both knew our ears had already perked up. Lately, Papa had caught me lingering at the door to his study after supper, peeking in as he combed through books and files. When he beckoned to me which he almost always did, I tumbled in and perched eagerly in the armchair across from his wide oak desk, plying him with questions about his day in the courtroom. Angella loved books, so she was always close behind, riffling through Papa's extensive collection while I chatted away.

The cause of Mama's particular concern was news of growing unrest in the Eastern districts as the president's divisive politics pit tribes and regions against each other. A country rich in vastly diverse natural resources was being manipulated into competing for the lion's share of multinational concessions and greased palms.

President Robin Breton had surrounded himself with cabals and syndicates, the most notorious of which involved illegal diamond mining operations by an elusive Lebanese businessman with shady associations, who had become the president's right-hand man, and sworn to protect di Pa with his life.

In his current sensitive position as a high court judge, Papa could still rely on the counsel of his trusted friends Alan Cole and Emmanuel Pratt. Matters of constitutional reform were of grave importance in the existing hostile and dangerous political climate. While Freetown still maintained strong echoes of its now fading glory, younger member states of the regional unions had been rocked by the assassination in Cairo of Anwar Sadat and looked to our small nation for leadership.

Once renowned as a seat of knowledge and deemed an Athens in its own right, Papa said Freetown should have been well equipped to traverse the chasm from a dying age into a new world of untold potential. Plagued by the student protests, frustrated calls for socioeconomic and legal reform were met with slogans and off-handed idioms, some notably coined by Robin Breton himself, inciting men's basest instincts by using the language of 'every man for himself'.

☙ᛦ❧

The day after June's frantic warnings, Eric did not find Alan and Imma in their offices when he arrived, so he continued up the stairs to his small office on the third floor of the colonial-style wooden building on the corner of Bathurst and Main Street. Eric spent less time here than before but thought it was important to maintain the private space even though he had a full docket at the Law Court. He dusted off his desk and opened the windows, letting in the sounds and sight of the sprawling cityscape.

Before long, it was almost lunchtime and Eric realized he had left his packed lunch in the car. Perhaps Sullay would spot in and bring it up. Eric could not spare the ten minutes it would take to sprint down three floors and back up again. June was very understanding about his long hours, but he still felt a pang of guilt for being neglectful. He had not had much leisure time with the children especially since the newest member joined the household and he intended to remedy this.

Angella was a delight, Eric thought, and the children had done such a good job of making her feel welcome. At times Jennifer had been gruff with Angella, but Eric would be patient. He was sure she would come around. He would take them to Sans Souci next Sunday.

The ice cream parlor on Lumley beach was the children's favorite. Better still they should make a picnic of it. The thought of June's usual picnic fare of roast meat skewers with peanut sauce, and Eric's favorite Akara and served with a spicy onion dip, had his stomach growling. Eric was about to head downstairs to pick up his lunch when the telephone rang.

"Eric!" June's voice on the other end of the line was unmistakably alarmed.

"Have you heard? The riots are starting again," she said.

Eric rushed toward the open window, almost ripping the telephone's extension cord from the wall socket as he pressed up against the side of the wooden shutter, trying to be inconspicuous as he trained his eyes on the street below.

"Where are you now?" Eric asked urgently, taking in the growing chaos of the scene outside.

"I am at the house," June responded.

"The children are here as well. We are all safe."

Eric felt a momentary relief. Within minutes, the usual hum of the city streets below grew into panicked cries. Sullay had appeared at the door looking sweaty and frantic. Eric gestured for Sullay to enter and lock the door behind himself.

June was speaking. She explained hurriedly "Elizabeth was at Mount Aureol when fighting there broke out. She knew I would not be able to get to Frank in time, so she picked him up. As you know, Jennifer had no school today because of the teachers' strikes, so I had the British Council vehicle bring me straight home."

"I'm worried for you, Eric." June continued, "You really should leave as quickly as possible. There were truckloads of SSD already assembling outside the State House an hour ago and only government or diplomatic vehicles were being allowed to pass. Some of the trucks looked to be heading up to the Fourah Bay College, but they will surely also be dispatched to Main Street. You must leave now!" June cried.

"I will," Eric assured her, trying to assess possible routes out of the city center, given the information June had just shared.

"Make sure the gate stays locked. I will see you soon my love," Eric tried to sound assuring as they ended the telephone call.

He moved to close the windows, but Sullay ran ahead of him, signaling to Eric to stay down so as not to be visible from the street below. Local vagabonds were known to use the chaos of the riots as cover to burglarize and vandalize office buildings and homes. Eric caught the smell of djamba in the air and he could hear the screams of people fleeing as the thugs marched closer, singing rowdy songs. The familiar crack of the ratlans rang out as they came down indiscriminately on whomever was in their way. The whips sounding like heavy raindrops on a tin roof.

Collecting his thoughts, Eric scrambled to gather his most important documents from the secret compartment behind a bookshelf in his office. He had notes and witness accounts of police abuse of detainees and sensitive documents obtained by a reporter from the Sierra Times newspaper revealing connections between the Interior Minister and a notorious diamond dealer.

The name of the Lebanese businessman had come up repeatedly in Eric's probing. Prosecution would be a long shot. It was unheard of for the police to arrest any friend of di Pa, but Eric hoped that with enough evidence, Chief Justice Macauley would have no choice but to hear the case.

Picking up an unmarked folder, Eric tucked it further into the recesses of its hiding place. It was an 'eyes only' dossier which if found in his possession would surely be grounds for a charge of treason. The document profiled a former corporal who had been cashiered from the army's signal corps and imprisoned for seven years at Pademba Road for taking part in a mutiny. The report reveals details of how the son of a Temne farmer and Loko mother who was born and raised in a remote village in the North until he joined the army in 1956. His release a few years ago barely made news.

It was now believed that his work as a photographer in the south and east of the country had put him in contact with some radical groups. The information Eric possessed was of the utmost sensitivity, alleging that the man in question and fellow collaborators were soliciting international support for an armed uprising to oust the government.

Eric was not surprised when the Chief of Police had paid a visit to his office twice in recent months. Neither meeting had been on the record, but both served as a warning. Flanked on either side by a red beret Special Security Division one officer, Chief Inspector Kamara had been direct. Word had reached di Pa that some 'Krio boys', hotshot lawyers with newfangled western ideas, were making trouble. The message was simple, cease and desist.

Sullay had the good sense to move Eric's car once he heard the rumblings of trouble. He had driven away a few city-blocks to the gated waterfront compound of Walcott-Taylor Pharmaceuticals, June's family's business. The gateman guided Sullay to park the car in a covered garage safely out of view among a fleet of delivery vans.

Despite Sullay's protests, Eric suggested they use side streets and alleyways to reach the compound and pick up the car. Eric considered calling Alan or Imma at home but thought better of it, as there was no telling who might be listening in. Mrs. Abigail Pratt, Emmanuel's grandmother had almost lost her house some weeks back in a suspicious fire that started in the middle of the day.

The fire brigade mysteriously did not receive the call even though the station at Tower Hill was within shouting distance. Neighbors had scrambled to put out the flames and luckily no one was harmed. The story was propagandized by media sympathizers of di Pa, as another example of why the remaining traditional Krio settler's wooden houses instead of being heritage sites, were an eye sore and a hazard and should be torn down.

Eric led the way down the narrow unlit back stairways. He halted abruptly at the final landing with Sullay crouched close behind. There was a banging sound and muffled conversation coming from the front office. They waited until the noise faded into silence, punctuated by the clanging of a heavy bolt.

When he thought it was safe, Eric slowly cracked open the connecting door startling Mrs. Jackson his longtime secretary. She quickly regained her composure and held a finger to her lips nodding pointedly toward the front of the building. She had been able to convince the group that had come banging on the doors looking for 'di big boss', that she was alone except for the security man out front. After haranguing her for money they eventually left, but through a corner of the window curtain, they saw a few stragglers were still hanging about outside.

The three of them remained quiet, sitting on the floor for cover. Another hour passed before the commotion outside finally died down. At Eric's urging, Sullay reluctantly surrendered the car keys to him and promised to see Mrs. Jackson safely home before himself heading home to find his family.

Mrs. Jackson left Eric with the snacks she had bought earlier that day, insisting that he would need to keep his strength up. She promised she would call and update June on the situation, the moment she arrived home. Eric locked up behind Mrs. Jackson and Sullay, and quietly made his way up the stairs and back to his office. Any thought of hunger had long departed but he settled down on the floor and numbly chewed on a benne seed bar as he contemplated recent events. In a word, it was chaos.

Eric crawled quietly over to his desk and pulled out the almost empty bottle of whiskey from the drawer, he drained the contents into a glass and sat back, sighing wearily. There was legal and political pressure from the few vocal dissenters that had not been imprisoned or killed, and there were organized protests sending a clear message. A recent attack on Breton during a convocation ceremony when students had pelted him with half eaten oranges and stones, angered him.

Di Pa's response had been to weaponize disgruntled and unemployed youth, who were as disenfranchised and frustrated as everyone else. The thugs gathered at the party offices where they were plied with cheap alcohol and drugs and along with the secret police, the SSD, stood ready to be activated on di Pa's command. Increasing waves of unrest rocked major towns and small villages alike. Eric wondered how long the situation would go on before things hit rock bottom.

Mrs. Jackson must have reached home by now Eric thought, as he leaned back against the wall and closed his eyes. It was going to be a long night.

☙♈❧

Chapter 4
Angella

Freetown

Papa is in his study working late as usual. Mama sent Frank to bed after the episode of Ultraman ended before the start of the 10 o'clock news. It is Frank's thirteenth birthday tomorrow and I doubt he will sleep he is so excited.

Angella and I stay and watch the news with Mama. Jennifer lingers even though she is clearly sleepy. She is captain of the junior division volleyball team, and this being the week of the annual inter-secondary school tournament she's quite exhausted at the end of the day and promptly curled up on the rug by Mama's feet after supper.

Angella and I lounge on the settee and after the news ended, we gossiped while Mama crocheted. She was making booties and blankets for the Women's Fellowship Drive to support the Princess Christian Maternity Hospital. I listened as Angella recounted an incident that had happened in her class involving two of the newest Namibian refugee students that started attending our school the week before.

I had seen the girls in the chapel, one had skin as dark as coal and the other had a caramel complexion like Mama. The dark-skinned girl had long naturally wavy hair and the other girl wore her hair in a plump afro. Since most of us had our hair relaxed and braided to allow our school berets to fit properly, our fascination was more with their hair than their strange accents.

Neither Grace nor Nothando smiled much. They kept their heads down and sat in a far corner of the compound during lunch break. They were boarders at the school and the other boarders rumored that they didn't speak much there either, only whispered to each other in their own language.

"Mr. Sawyer was passing out the tests," Angella started to say, "when he got to Nothando, Mbalu and Constance started to chant 'Nothando, the kondo' under their breath which made the other girls giggle."

I tried not to laugh when she said that. Rhyming a name with the colorful lizards that scrambled about the schoolyard was funny.

Angella continued, "Mr. Sawyer demanded to know who had started the teasing. We knew we would all be made to miss lunch as punishment if no one owned up."

"So, what happened next?" I asked curiously.

"I told him who did! Named names," Angella spoke with a defiant expression.

Jennifer had perked up and echoed my surprise.

"Ay!" Jennifer and I exclaimed in unison.

Mama told us not to interfere in other people's business, which I always thought was ironic, considering Papa's entire career had been about 'other people's businesses.

"What happened then?" I probed.

Angella told us that she had pointed out the culprits to Mr. Sawyer, ignoring the eye rolls and angry stares she received from them in return. She had saved the rest of the class from missing lunch and didn't feel bad that the girls would receive their due punishment of weeding the large garden at the top of the school drive or cleaning toilets. We all chuckled nervously at the thought. None of us had ever gotten in trouble since we started secondary school and we were sure that Mama would have worse punishment in store for us at home if we ever did.

"Mama, what do you think about that?" I asked.

Even though she was busy with her work, I knew Mama had been listening to the conversation.

"That was brave of you, Angella," she said after a brief moment.

"War is very bad," she continued pensively, "those girls have lost their parents, their homes, everything. I cannot imagine what that must feel like. Teasing them because their names are unfamiliar to you is wrong," she paused. "There is an old saying 'rain nɔ dey fɔdɔm na wan man doh mɔt!'."

We had heard that saying before. I had dared myself to think beyond the axiom and the result was the same messy outcome. Even if the rain *did* fall only at one man's door, sooner or later his neighbors would have to deal with the overflow or be swept away.

"We are fortunate to have peace in the Republic now, but what would happen if we had a war and had to take refuge in a strange country far away from the home we know?" Mama looked pointedly at us, and we all stared back at her, the weight of her words sinking in. Angella frowned and I shivered at the thought. Mama was right. I was glad Angella had spoken up in class. Even if I disagreed with her reasons.

As we contemplated Mama's question, I felt sad that I had not done more to befriend the girls. They must miss their family and friends. I could not even imagine life without Papa and Mama or my brother and sisters. Mama sighed and gave us a wan smile before returning to her work.

It is my turn to share my story, so I tell them about the incident with my substitute teacher Miss Mansaray, who for the life of her could not pronounce the word 'utensils'. I had slyly found ways to ask her questions that caused her to repeat the word.

This had the entire class giggling throughout the lesson. I demonstrated for my current audience, mimicking Miss Mansaray's pronunciation 'yun-tesils' which had Jennifer and Angella in stitches. Even Mama could not hide her grin, the weight of the earlier conversation having lifted. After we had quietened down Jennifer whispered another '—yun-tesils!' Another eruption of raucous laughter ensued, leaving Jennifer and Angella rolling on the floor and me in tears.

After we recovered, we kissed Mama goodnight and went to bed. Jennifer promptly fell asleep with Angella close behind. As I watched Angella's eyelids grow heavy, I was thankful to have a loving family and my new best friend. Thoughts of Frank's birthday party crept into my mind, and I looked forward to helping Mama bake her mouth-watering pound cake, saturated with butter and nutmeg. It was one of my favorites.

The next morning, we awoke to the sound of Mama humming. The rhythmic sound of sweeping in the yard was unmistakably Abdul, who always did six long strokes followed by a short tap. I could hear Papa about the house, instructing the house boys on where to set up chairs and tables. The party was going to be a lot of fun.

Although we joked and fooled around, pinched food from the serving trays, and smudged the red fizzy Vimto drink on our lips to look like lipstick, Mama was grateful for our help. Beatrice was not very experienced in the kitchen, and Stella was sick with a bout of malaria. Mama had sent her to her quarters after giving her chloroquine tablets and a bowl of pepper soup, insisting that she rest.

Frank's party would be filled with awkward teenagers unsure of their breaking voices, sprouting odd-looking facial hair, and with newfound attraction to girls. Nonetheless, Allison, Jennifer, and I loved the opportunity to play hosts to our baby brother's classmates and friends.

As we prepared King's Lodge with party streamers, balloons, and fresh flowers, Abdul smiled and winked at me whenever he walked by, and Angella teased me mercilessly for it. She loved the idea of star-crossed lovers and was always comparing Abdul and me to romantic stories in the Mills and Boon novels she and Jennifer loved to read.

"No way!" I denied emphatically. "I am not interested in being one of those women who need to be saved by some prince," I scoffed.

What I did not admit to her was how much I did like Abdul. I especially looked forward to laundry day. Miss Rosetta had developed arthritis in her hands and was increasingly unable to carry out many of her household duties, so Abdul assisted with the task. I would eagerly wander down to the bottom of the garden and sit on the low concrete ledge next to the pump where Abdul scrubbed and wrang the heavy sheets.

Except when Mama called me inside with a hint of firmness in her tone, Abdul and I would talk for ages about the latest James Hadley Chase novel we had both read. His lean muscles glistened in the sun, and I looked on, mesmerized as he swirled the heavy household linens in soapy water and rubbed them vigorously along the washboard. I never admitted this secret delight to Angella or anyone else. I kept it all to myself.

෫ၣႇ

It was Tuesday and like most Tuesdays that I can remember, Papa attended the Steward's meeting at Cathedral church. Since his meeting starts at 6 o'clock and is only a few streets away from the office, he usually sends Sullay off for the day and drives himself home. On his way, Papa always stops at Mountain Lion bakery on the corner of Bathurst Street, where Mama Sally the proprietress always has hot, fresh rolls of sweet bread waiting for him to pick up.

We all looked forward to supper on Tuesday nights. Sweet bread lathered with grape jam imported from Harrods in London. Mama discovered a long time ago that marmalade and marmite were wasted on us. The bread and jam made for a special treat, and Papa chuckled in amusement as we wolfed down the food as politely as we could.

Later that week, Mama told us that Miss Rosetta would not be returning to work at King's Lodge after the holidays. Mama was not surprised. Her health had been in decline for some time. Rather than collect wages for sloppy work, she preferred to take her leave. We knew this had been a hard decision for our long-time housekeeper.

We were all attached to her and relied heavily on her quiet dedication. She had washed my first nappies, and Frank's confirmation whites. She kept the King's Lodge as immaculate as Mama demanded, cleaning and scrubbing, waxing, and polishing, and never complaining. We were all saddened by the news of her health. She was fiercely proud, and I guessed her departure had more to do with not wanting to live off my parent's charity when they offered than stay, even though she could no longer work.

We would miss her terribly, Abdul and Miss Stella most of all. The two women had a close bond and Miss Rosetta had been like a surrogate mother to Miss Stella and like a grandmother to Abdul after Mammy Comfort passed.

Mama gave Miss Rosetta a nice send-off party, and we showered her with gifts doing our best to make her feel special that day. Miss Rosetta's niece had come to accompany her back to Goderich and Papa arranged for Sullay to drive them. There were tears all around as the last suitcase was stuffed into the trunk and the car pulled slowly out of the driveway.

That evening after supper, I sought out Papa hoping to ask him some questions that had been on my mind.

"Papa?" I ventured, being sure to wait at the door of the verandah, not wanting to disturb him if it was not a good time.

The others had gone to bed, and I had heard the familiar BBC world service theme signaling the end of the news broadcast.

"Yes, Allison?" he raised his head to look at me.

"Come," he signaled.

"Papa," I said, "If Miss Rosetta chose to stay with us but she could not work, would you have let her live here, and still paid her?" I ventured inquisitively.

"Of course, my dear," Papa leaned forward as he replied. "Miss Rosetta, and for that matter, anyone who stays here at King's Lodge is considered part of this family!" he concluded.

I nodded with relief. Papa had always encouraged my curiosity and as I grew older our conversations grew less childish and more incisive. Both my parents asked me on recent occasions about my thoughts of a career once I finished secondary school. Mama would have preferred that Papa discourage my interest in Justice and the Law. She feared her 'intelligent' and 'compassionate' daughter would become a victim of the vicious attacks many Krio lawyers suffered to their character and their person, especially in recent times.

I am in awe of brave men and the trailblazing women like Frances Claudia Wright, 'West Africa's Portia'. Frances was the first Sierra Leonean woman to be called to the Bar in Great Britain and to practice law in Sierra Leone. She survived a shipwreck in North Africa and lost all her possessions but persisted and returned home to become a formidable personality in the judiciary. Nonetheless, the number of seats held by Krios in the legislative council had diminished drastically since 1961.

"Papa, why did the people in Angola have to fight for independence? What does a civil war mean? Will there be fighting here in our country if the citizens are not happy with President Breton's actions?" I chose my words thoughtfully.

He switched off the radio, rubbing his forehead wearily.

"I hope not, my dear," he replied to my last question first, turning to give me his full attention.

Papa started relaying the story to me, about how the Republic gained independence from the British and how laws and policies in the protectorate had changed over time. I had heard some of the history before, but I loved hearing it again. Every narrative had bits of new detail, adding to what I learned. I hung on Papa's every word as he explained.

The cause of unrest in our country was much the same as Angola's. Power struggles were almost inevitable when nations were in transition, and it was always innocent citizens who suffered. In Angola, two former anti-colonial guerrilla movements were being manipulated in a surrogate Cold War battle, with Cuba, the Soviet Union, South Africa, and the United States as its protagonists.

I imagined the villagers and all the people who had to leave their homes. I imagined Grace and Nothando going days without food, running for their lives as rough, dangerous men with guns strapped to their backs mounted attacks from camps deep in the jungle. I tell Papa about the girls, and he shares my sentiments that it is a good thing our country can provide them refuge.

As Papa and I talk, Mama joins us, and I cannot help but notice her look of pride as she observes the teacher and the student. She had come to shoo me to bed, but she lets me stay a few minutes longer. Relaxing into her favorite chair I watch her breathe in deeply, enjoying the scent of the heavy jasmine blossoms that hang in the night air and listening to us as she sips from a glass of her favorite Harvey Bristol cream sherry.

♋♈♋

Mount Aureol — Freetown

A nervous energy and the smell of sweat hung in the air as Abdul and the other young men and a handful of young women crammed into the dorm room five floors up in block-C. The power was out and a kerosene lantern in the corner of the room stood unlit. A candle stuck to a saucer illuminated the room and Abdul thought it might last another hour by which time he hoped they would be released from the gathering.

The narrow bunks squeaked as tightly packed bodies shifted around to make room for other arrivals. They all had class the next morning, so Abdul had pressed Mo, one of group's leaders to keep his instructions succinct.

"Welcome, comrade Ali," Mo grunted as a giant of a man sauntered in.

More students arrived, and the gathering spilled over onto the balcony. Mo cautioned for quiet. It was easier for their voices to carry into the night. Without any formality, Ali launched into plans for the 'No Work, No School' campaign. The student leaders had started the Awareness and Participation for the People of the Republic movement (APPR), out of frustration and a desire to make the voices of youth heard in the call for political reform.

They had grown in number and gotten bolder each day. They started protest marches from their university campus up on Mount Aureol, down to the State House. As time went on, they were joined by dissatisfied members of teachers' unions and petty traders.

Their mission was to raise awareness among the working poor, of the mismanagement of the country's resources under the leadership of Breton and his government cronies. The first few marches were not well attended, and the police put an end to the gathering within a short time. They continued to organize, plastering lamp posts and walls across the city with flyers, defying the calls to stop the protests.

More and more people paid attention and the next protests were better attended, better organized, and nearly made it to the foot of the enormous landmark Cotton Tree in the center of the city, a stone's throw from the president's offices at State House. They were gaining traction and Mo was excited.

As the discussion turned to the route for the next march, tensions in the room rose. The police had engaged the *raray* men; delinquent slum youth, to infiltrate the crowd and create chaos. These men usually had a criminal history and could be dangerous. The raucous they caused gave the police an excuse to wantonly use tear gas and batons on the crowds of otherwise peaceful protesters.

Di Pa had commissioned a unit of officers, the SSD, who had already driven through campus a number of times that afternoon. A state of emergency had not yet been declared, but Mo knew they needed to move quickly before it did.

"I think we should start in front of State House, then move down to the Cotton Tree and head west this time," Mo suggested. There was some ascent from the group.

"And then what?" Ali questioned.

The fork at Kroo Town Road junction had split the protesters two weeks prior. When the police vans arrived, those that had taken Sanders Street received the worst beating and many were arrested including Ali. Those who had stayed on Kroo Town Road were able to run into to the market and hide under the bridge. Moving away from State House rather than toward it did not seem to make sense. Others in the group nodded in agreement with Ali's question.

Mo hesitated, then started to speak. "We could take Pademba Road this time," Mo stood as he spoke. "That way, we can rally the secondary school boys around Circular Road and Berry Street, go past the prisons, and then take Jomo Kenyatta Road to his residence. They think we may be heading for the State House this time, so if we go to his residence, he won't be ready or expecting us!" he finished confidently.

Ali was considering the proposal. He dropped his head thoughtfully. His left hand was covered with a soiled bandage from the wrist up to his fingertips. He rubbed at it slowly. An almost meditative calm had descended on the group. There were no established hierarchy so natural leaders had emerged in the months since they first came together.

Where Mo was of medium build, sinewed, and moved with an air of cunning, Ali was a hulking mass of muscle and his very presence commanded full attention. The others gazed at the candle in the center of the room, waiting for their de facto leader to speak. Abdul could feel the sweat tracking a path down his back.

A door slammed down the hall and they could hear a girlish giggle from a student making her way back to her hostel, the heavier footfalls of her male companion in time with the clicking of her heels. Ali's bushy brow furrowed at the sound.

"Thank you, comrade. We will go with your plan," he spoke directly to Mo. To the rest of the group he said, "We will meet at Model junction. 8 o'clock in the morning. Remember to bring your handkerchiefs for the gas, and wear two or three shirts. Any questions?"

There were none. Abdul moved outside with the dispersing group, chatting briefly with some old classmates before doubling back and squeezing his way toward the emptying dorm room.

"What if they arrest you again?" Abdul asked his friend in a hushed whisper when the two of them were finally alone on the balcony. He looked pointedly at Ali's hands, still severely burned from his recent torture and beatings while being held by the police. The cigarette burns had formed jagged circles of purple and yellow scarred skin.

"If they do, so be it," Ali responded with a shrug.

His hands were shaking slightly as he lit a cigarette and rested his forearms on the railing. Mo had joined them and startled Abdul with a hiss through clenched teeth.

"They will kill you, Ali!" Mo warned his friend tersely.

Abdul had often wondered how this half-caste with a Mende mother and Libyan father ended up in their movement. His father's country had problems too, but they at least enjoyed immensely greater prosperity. He did not need to join this fight.

"We need to get stronger and better than them," Mo whispered forcefully.

"Why don't you want us to ask for Papa's support?" he continued, sounding insistent.

Ali pulled himself up to full height as he turned to face Mo.

"When the time is right, we will," he replied. "When the time is right."

They all went back into the dorm room and Ali turned on his transistor radio. Not surprisingly the BBC hourly news was reporting the latest developments in the region but none of them were prepared for what they heard next. The Organization of African Unity had applauded the handling of the recent violent clashes by Robin Breton's newly installed puppet and successor.

When he heard the announcement, Ali let out a grunt of frustration and kicked a wall repeatedly, breaking one of the glass slats in the window. As it crashed to the floor, the commotion brought Mr. Hunter, the hall warden running, with his flashlight swinging in the dark. He stared at the mess and at the young men then quietly told them to make sure they cleaned up the shards before he turned around and left.

When things calmed down, the trio continued talking into the night. The country was still reeling from the ruinous expense of hosting an OAU summit it could not afford. It had all worked in di Pa's favor of course. He had many eating from the palm of his hand and currying favor. Although he was no longer president, he was still scoring political points as some sort of elder statesman.

Mo had been encouraging Ali to reach out to experienced and respected members of the old guard, known to disagree with Breton's regime. In some ways, Abdul always suspected Ali wanted his help seeking support from Mr. Eric, but he waited for Ali to ask him directly. Ali frequently mentioned that having prominent lawyers and members of the judiciary supporting their cause would be an advantage. Still, when Ali quoted I.J.W. and his exploits, Abdul remained silent. Mr. Eric had not sent him to university to join youth movements.

Abdul was a skilled footballer and as far as Mr. Eric was aware, the many weekends Abdul did not return to King's Lodge were on account of his many amateur football competitions, not organizing student activism. This side of himself was a secret he kept even from Allison. She had pleaded with Abdul to see him play. He hated disappointing her, so he had taken her with him to a few games, begging forgiveness for the rest. Mr. Eric was very generous to him and Aunty, as he called Stella even though she was his mother. They would be heartbroken to know that he was mixed up in this dangerous business.

Mo had returned to the balcony and was smoking a cigarette. Ali picked up the thermos at the foot of his bed and shook it gently, confirming it still contained rice pap. Abdul looked on as Ali poured the warm, tangy balls of sticky rice porridge into his mouth, eyeing Abdul the whole time.

"Is your uncle in town?" he asked, wiping his mouth with the bottom of his shirt.

Abdul knew the meaning of the pointed question. Ali was as aware of Eric Johnson's recent vocal opposition to Breton, perhaps the time was right to form more powerful alliances.

Setting aside his initial unease, Abdul replied, "Yes. Yes, he is."

♋

Freetown

I wake early to the sound of the muezzin's call to prayer rising up from the heart of the city, floating on a thin haze of mist, and echoing across the plateaus surrounding our house on Signal Hill. It is Saturday, which means helping in the kitchen which I love, and Jennifer detests.

I am impressed with my contemporaries who have mastered the art of single-handedly cooking our traditional foods. The ability possessed by my mother and such women, to add a dice of this, a pinch of the other, and end up with the same rich and complex flavors created by our great-grandmothers, is something magical to me. My busy college schedule would have been a reasonable excuse to duck out, but I am willing to learn, and Mama is eager to teach us. Men want wives who can cook well, she would say with a sly smile.

I could have made a case for women's liberation and their right to have as much freedom from the kitchen as men did, but I knew my mother well enough to understand that such comments were merely pragmatic. Growing up, I had overheard enough of Mama and the aunties gossiping about women who lost their husbands to mistresses or their mothers not least so due to their poor skills in the kitchen.

Uncle Robert, Mama's younger brother had grown quite a big belly in the past year and was happy to blame his new wife for the added pounds. He would rub his mountain of a stomach proudly, boasting 'di gyal sabi cook!'

Nyanga, the 'gyal' in question was a Mende lady from Pujehun who as the story goes had stunned Robert off his feet. They met just a year before at a Christmas party thrown by one of his old Grammar School friends when he came to visit from Pepel. He was chief engineer at the mines, and we only got to see him a few times a year.

We had all heard the virtues of the alluring Nyanga extolled long before we ever met her. He praised the delicate beauty of her 'opin teet', 'cɔt neck', and 'kak wase'. Perhaps in another culture, a gap tooth, neck rings, and an ample bottom were all features a woman might seek a surgeon's blade to correct but according to our currency of attraction, these were all assets.

I would eye myself in the mirror and wonder what sort of husband I might be able to snag with only two out of three of Nyanga's assets. My behind was as flat as was my chest. I supposed my 'bɔl yay' counted for something, as I often received compliments about them. It was yet another feature best translated as bug-eyed, which was not only a thing of beauty but also meant *the apple of one's eye*. I could understand why western ways could be so confusing to our people, so many things appeared to be upside down.

Angella and I often took turns looking at our images in the mirror. Sharing what parts, we liked about our looks and which ones we thought we would like to swap. Angella's eyes had struck me the most when she first came to live with us all those years ago. Very much like mine, they were bright and piercing and had the ability to make an inscrutable subject squirm. Papa said we would make effective judges.

When we were young Mama used to say Angella was a precocious child, which had her promptly running off to hunt through the encyclopedic volumes in Papa's study to find out exactly what 'precocious' meant. Angella was curious and also a bit of a worrier, so Mama always answered her curious questions in a patient tone, the corners of Mama's full lips turned up lightly in amusement.

Miss Stella keeps a watchful eye as I do my best to 'turn the foo-foo', struggling to balance the heavy pot over the fire. The starchy ball is heavy and requires significant effort to stir and smooth out any lumps as the paste thickens.

"You mustn't worry so much, Angella," Mama says. "Neither you, nor Lili, nor Jenny will be joining any secret society."

Angella has lately been concerned about talk of girls and young women going missing, believed to have died after initiation ceremonies. Angella believes she left the mysterious world of secret societies behind when as a child she was brought from the countryside to live in a big city. She was disturbed by the stories. Fearful as she was curious about a world known to her only through whispers and in the shadows.

Jennifer is just walking into the kitchen and looks confused then alarmed at the snippet of conversation she hears.

"See, I told you there is nothing to worry about," I reinforce Mama's assurance to Angella. Handing over the foo-foo pot to Miss Stella, I nip a piece of dried fish from the heaping plate on the kitchen counter. Anticipating that Mama's hand will follow mine with a playful swipe, I move quickly, popping the salty morsel into my mouth as her fingertips miss me and land on the table with a tap.

"We're living in modern times now so the days of grabbing young women and forcibly initiating them are over. And anyway, if anyone tries anything, I'll be ready for them!" I counter, raising both my fists and grinning cheekily to get Mama to smile.

"Allison Regina Frederica!" Mama declares, "What has gotten into you today?"

Mama turns to face me, hands on her hips. She has taken to wearing the traditional print dress on weekends. This one was s a casual version of the kabaslot. It had short sleeves, a knee length skirt, and deep side pockets hidden between the pleats and folds. Mama loathes any talk of violence and especially thinks that fighting is unladylike and certainly not something a young Krio woman should contemplate.

"Just joking, Ma!" I say, giving her a disarming peck on the cheek and yanking Angella's hand as we beat a hasty retreat. We have finished our chores for the day.

"We're going out now," I call out as we run out of the kitchen before Mama can pin us down for details.

"Ah!" Mama sputters with exasperation, "Where to? It's almost lunch time."

Her voice trails behind us. We are already out of earshot. After a quick change of clothes, we head out of the gate, our pockets jiggling with just enough coins for transportation and snacks. It is track and field championship day at the new stadium downtown, and we wouldn't miss it for the world.

♋

The crowd goes wild. Tillay is ahead by mere inches with David close behind, pumping his legs as hard as he can. As they barrel toward the finish line, the cheering fans nearly overrun the track despite Coach Jones' attempts to block them.

"Tillay! Tillay!" The chants were out of beat with the pounding of his feet on the new tarmac. As he pushed past the tape the cheers turned into a deafening roar. Angella and I held hands tightly and screamed just as loudly as the rest. My ears were buzzing, and my heart raced. The officials hurriedly cross-checked their stop clocks, but Coach Jones' grin said it all. The numbers up on the board included a brand-new African record, and three others were well within the qualifying times for the upcoming world junior athletics championship in Rome.

I was incredibly happy for Tillay. His mother, Aunty Duro was Mama's second cousin. Aunty Duro had reservations about her son's athletic pursuits, so we all knew this win would mean a lot to him. According to our aunt, she was worried sick that Tillay's schoolwork would suffer because he often stayed out late training and competing.

"E fɔ lan buk!" Aunty Duro had lamented. She'd dreamt that her son would be educated, not a star athlete.

At nineteen years of age, Tillay was much taller than his peers and had gone from a waif of a boy to a bundle of muscles with hair on his chest. Aunty Duro's worry was compounded by the rise in the number of young ladies calling on the house telephone for her son, whom she promptly dressed down and warned not to call back.

As we made our way down toward the field, I hoped this victory would change Auntie's mind and that she would become more supportive of Tillay. As spectators and friends high-fived and patted each other on the back, the announcer was squawking something inaudible into his megaphone. The hundred-meter dash was the final event of the day and with dusk fast approaching, the throng of mostly students started making their way down from the stands.

The awards and medals would be given out soon. As Angella and I near the tunnels that led out to the track, I spot Abdul running toward us. His shirt is untucked and sticking to his chest, wet with sweat.

"Tillay! Tillay!" Abdul chants as he joins us, pumping his fist in the air and beaming. The three of us continue, crossing the tracks to the area where the field events are wrapping up a lack luster day. Unfortunately, triple jump and javelin had not elicited the same level of euphoria as the sprints. We inch through the crowd and approach the makeshift perimeter around the podium.

During our secondary school days when there were no strikes, the competition had been held during the week with heats for the various events taking place mostly in the afternoons. Teachers were frustrated at the number of students who either left school early to attend the games and support their friends or just did not show up to class at all. As the final day of the competitions approached, the near-empty classrooms forced some teachers to give up all together.

After much debate, the Ministry of Education and the Ministry of Youth and Sports agreed that having the final day of the championship on a weekend made more sense. Requiring the students to show up in uniform was received with mixed enthusiasm. From our vantage point, we had seen the stands peppered with the checkered purple, green, and blue dresses of the schoolgirls and the white shirt and khaki shorts of the high school boys.

One of the few times Angella and I had ever dared to skip school had been for such an event. When Mama found out that we had dodged Sullay, hopped in a poda-poda and made our way to watch the heats, it had been a rare occasion on which she greeted us at the front gate with her bundle of long rattan canes, and whipped us all the way up to our bedroom, chastising us about obedience and virtue the entire time.

According to Mama we had acted like vagrants and threatened to sully the family name. What would people say? Her admonishments had been rhetorical, and we bore our punishment in silence. Over time Mama let us socialize more, but I could tell she was pleased that Frank and Jennifer preferred to spend their free time with friends at Aqua, the local boating club with limited membership, rather than at such large public events.

As the medals are awarded, friends and supporters sing and chant the names of the recipients. When it comes to the men's 100 meters medals, I excitedly grasp Abdul's hand. I feel him gently squeeze my hand and turn to look at him, but he continues to stare straight ahead, a small smile dancing on the corner of his lips. I grin and squeeze back, and his smile widens. Not for the first time, being close to Abdul makes my heart skip a beat and I feel like a hundred butterflies are carrying me to the clouds.

When the floodlights snap on and the ceremony ends, we have to hurry. Papa does not mind us being at the stadium but once it gets dark, he worries for our safety. As we exit, we see groups of young people still scattered outside the perimeter of the grounds. While most of the city is plunged in darkness from the frequent power outages, the stadium generator hums away, and surrounding lampposts bath the area in a fluorescent halo.

Hawkers are trying to sell the last of their ginger beer and cookies, and shy young suitors egged on by friends are making their final moves before everyone will eventually have to clear out onto the poorly lit streets. I nestle my head into Abdul's shoulder ignoring the pointed look from Angella as we make our way home.

♋♈♋

I awake just as the night sounds fades into silence and all in the household is still. Climbing quietly out of bed careful not to disturb anyone as they sleep soundly, I feel my way by the dim light that filters in underneath the curtains. I try not to crash into anything as I cross the wide space to our bedroom's balcony. Stepping outside, I fold my arms against the dewy chill of the early morning air. Final exams have just ended and so have the many nights of studying and quizzes. The past few years flew by like a whirlwind.

Angella and I had fought desperately to stay awake those nights. When Abdul visited, he brought us bitter kola nut. It was supposed to have enough caffeine to do the trick, but neither Angela nor I could manage more than a nibble. It tasted truly awful. The National Power Authority rarely supplied power these days, so we studied by gas light. When the gas was not available to buy, we lit candles that were dim and strained our eyes. The smell from kerosene lamps made Frank ill so we did not use them around the house.

Mama promised that we could stay on the campus for our final year, and I was looking forward to it. Roommates were assigned through a ballot system, but Mama knew the matron of Lati Hyde hall, the popular female dorm, and made sure that Angella and I would room together. 'Tatu ɛn Yawa' Miss Stella named us after the folklore twins that went everywhere and did everything together. We were thick as thieves.

I breathed in deeply, enjoying the crispness of the morning air. I was surprised to see Abdul out in the yard carrying a hamper and walking toward the laundry shed.

After he finished college, Abdul insisted he wanted to join the army, and as much as Papa had reservations and Miss Stella was tearful and upset, Mama was surprisingly supportive. She thought the armed service would be a good fit for Abdul. That had only been a year ago, but it already felt like a lifetime. Before that when Papa learned of Abdul's involvement in the student protests, he had been surprised but not angry. Papa ordered him to leave the group immediately.

We only heard snippets of how events had unfolded. Apparently, Abdul's mentor, an agitator named Mo had approached Papa and sought his support for their cause and Papa had turned him away offering little in explanation for his reluctance to align with the youth movement. Abdul did not like to talk about those times despite my pressing questions. Instead, he distanced himself from any further activism and vigorously turned his attention to completing his studies, finishing out his final year with distinction.

Mama felt sure he would do well and climb the army ranks quickly. She saw joining the military as a sign of maturity and discipline. She prided herself in having some part in that. I was eager to hear about Abdul's training and recent tour. Mama noticed the long hours everything under the sun. So far, she had said nothing, but I sensed her disapproval.

Abdul came to visit Miss Stella as often as his schedule allowed and always helped her with chores when he was around, as he appeared to be doing this morning. I watched him carry the hamper containing their sheets and clothes to be laundered. Miss Stella only did domestic work for us part-time. Some years back, she had started working at the Brown's Stationary business. They had expanded and welcomed an office administrator they knew and trusted.

Elizabeth Brown adored Stella since she had gotten to know her. Not only did Stella raise Abdul alongside Elizabeth and Allan's sons in the early years, but she still checked in on the boys as Elizabeth did with Abdul. The young men were great friends and Elizabeth often extolled Abdul's respectful manner. Abdul was gentle and very generous, traits which Elizabeth felt her sons were not naturally endowed with but picked up from him. Elizabeth was still one of Mama's closest friends, and her affection for Stella only brought our families closer.

Back inside the bedroom, I slip my hand underneath Angella's bedcovers and yank her big toe.

"Hey, wake up! Wake up, sleepy head—your future husband is here," I say in an exaggerated whisper.

Angella groans and rolls over, peeking out of the covers. She cocks her head to one side; a sly smile is on her lips.

"You mean *your* future husband," she chuckles.

"You know he really likes you," she mumbles, stifling a yawn as she stretches.

"And I can tell you like him too; I saw you two, all over each other behind the boys' quarters." She makes a kissy face. I scoff and roll my eyes, unsuccessfully attempting to hide a smile as I leave the bedroom.

☙♈❧

Big Faya was a slender man whose name belied his physique but not his voice. As the members of the dance band set up their instruments on the back lawn of King's Lodge, we busied ourselves in the kitchen taking instructions from Miss Stella as we sorted through enormous baskets of vegetables.

Papa had just been appointed to the supreme court and a celebration was in order. Earlier that day, the sound of gumbe drums approaching the compound had drawn us all outside. Much like the griots in other West African cultures, gumbe music was used to tell the story of our people through songs.

The country had just lost a legend in Ebenezer Calendar, the most famous gumbe musician of my parents' time, but we had Dr. Oloh. Neighbors gathered around as Dr. Oloh, and his milo jazz band sang songs. Using simple but eloquent rhymes they sang in Krio, extolling 'Pa Johnson' and his exploits, and praising 'Mammy Johnson' for her beauty and grace. In appreciation, and as was custom, the musicians were showered with money by the hosts and onlookers.

Gumbe would not be complete without the interplay between the harmonica and vocalist, which was mostly male. The unmistakable thrumming of the bata drum was the heartbeat of gumbe music, with the triangle and other percussive instruments rounding out the sound. Mama had ordered the gates to be open to let the musicians in. We stood opposite the drummers, cheering and clapping as Mama and the older women danced inside the circle. Gumbe dancing, one of Mama's favorites, was a conservative form of West Indian calypso dancing, with movement mostly of the hips and feet.

Once the gumbe music takes over, dancers often improvise with duels to see who can 'go down low', or men demonstrate their skill by balancing an empty beer bottle on their head or chest as they move to the music. Unable to resist the beat, we shimmied our hips and shook our shoulders, but we were too shy to enter the circle of dancers.

The music set a celebratory mood as we all went about the final preparations for the party in honor of Papa's appointment. Abdul had set aside six of the dozen or so chickens he was meticulously beheading on the wood bock in the shed. Sullay off-loaded a piglet from the back of the lorry that had just arrived, and a few ladies from the canteen at the British Council were stacking charcoal into wide metal grills and setting wooden logs centered in the middle of three stones, ready to be lit.

Papa and Uncle Allan were staging a makeshift bar on the walkout, and Mama fidgeted with the tablecloths, seat cushions, and window curtains for the umpteenth time as Aunt Elizabeth put the finishing touches on her special trifle recipe. Tonight, was a big night.

As the day had approached, we all felt a sense of pride and excitement. For a moment we set aside the inherent tension in the message being sent by Papa's appointment to the highest court of the land. He was one of the President's most vocal opponents, and this gambit only raised the stakes. If Papa was concerned, he did not show it.

Recently, we had been teasing Papa and Mama of how affectionate they still were to each other whenever we found them cuddled on the settee or exchanging loving looks over breakfast. It felt like their marriage was being renewed. Mama hinted we would all be traveling to London for the coming long holidays and might even extend the trip to France and Switzerland, giving her and Papa time for the honeymoon they never had.

Frank was a pimply teenager with a sweet tooth, and all he talked about was buying as much chocolate as he could fit into his suitcase. Angella and Jennifer joked about what we would do if we ended up at Buckingham Palace and had the rest of us in stitches as they attempted to outdo each other's made-up royal African courtesy to the Queen.

Recently, we all took to holding our teacups with the little finger pointed high in the air, with Mama looking on and shaking her head in exasperation. Angella had lived with us for many years now, but this would be our first trip out of the country since she joined our household.

I had not given much thought to passports before then, but a few days prior I had heard Mama on the phone with someone from the UMC Mission. Her voice was tense, and she waved me away and shut the door to the study as she talked. Curiosity got the better of me and using a trick we mastered as teenagers, I carefully picked up the handset of the phone in the living room only to hear the conversation winding down.

Mama and the person on the other end of the line discussed Angella's birth certificate. It would be sent by courier as soon as possible as Mama needed it to apply for Angella's passport. I carefully set the receiver down as the call ended. The prospect of visiting the U.K. again was thrilling, and I prayed the papers would be processed quickly. My heart filled with pride at how generous my parents were. Other families might leave a ward at home, but that seemed unthinkable to Papa and Mama who treated Angella as one of their own.

The band had everyone on their feet as they played hit after hit. White-gloved servers carrying silver platters passed out delightful edibles to the guests. The ladies sipped on sherry and rosé wines, while the men having had their fill of Star beer had turned to whiskey. The mood was light, and we hung about the periphery and enjoyed the party late into the night. Papa even allowed Angella and I a glass of sherry earlier in the evening, we felt very mellow.

Recent times had been trying for Papa, as he faced immense pressure to turn a blind eye to constitution violations by the country's executive branch and the new head of state handpicked by Robin Breton. Breton had by this time, firmly established himself in history among the likes of Mobutu Sese

Seko or Ferdinand Marcos. We were proud of Papa, and we all loved seeing him celebrated by his peers and friends.

Even Frank who often sulked and complained when we had guests, was busy trying to beat Abdul at a game of Ludo in the parlor, spinning his dice on the board and finding ways to get his plastic pieces into the sanctuary at the center of the board as quickly as he could. The live band had switched up the tempo and were playing all the popular hits. The band's selection was almost as good as our favorite disc jockey DJ Solo's. Angella, Jennifer, and I sang along and tapped our feet to the music.

"Would you just shut up!" Papa's voice came from the direction of the garden.

The band stopped playing altogether and everything was hushed. Mama looked shocked by Papa's outburst. From where I stood at the double doors, I could see Uncle Alan and Uncle Emmanuel were already moving toward Papa, sensing they should try and restrain him. Papa took a step back almost losing his balance. Mama was close and grabbed his elbow, gently removing the sloshing glass of whiskey from his loose grip. He was facing a man I did not recognize and who seemed somewhat embarrassed.

The man shook his head derisively and immediately turned to leave. Angella joined me at the verandah door, and we guessed that Papa's outburst had been aimed at the stranger with the ebony skin, broad nose, and suave demeanor.

Mama looked visibly shaken but she laughed off the disturbance and made some light joke about Papa having had one too many. Big Faya took her cue, and the band struck up a lively version of S. E. Rogie's hit 'My lovely Elizabeth', which got everyone back on their feet, clicking their heels and swaying their hips to the beat. We would later learn that the man my father had a row with was the eldest son of di Pa. Albert Breton was said to be privately opposed to his father's blatant corruption and intimidation tactics but was seen by some like Papa, as a hypocrite and an enabler of his father's corruption.

Albert had studied economics in London and upon his return home had struck up a friendship with Uncle Alan. They often shared meals at each other's homes, but Papa complained when Alan attempted to draw Albert close, inviting him to join that most sacred circle which was their cricket team.

Papa had relented, probably because Albert batted exceptionally well, and Papa was happy for the opportunity to take back the title from the reigning Old

Edwardians team. Junior, as most people called di Pa's first-born son, had the same commanding presence of his father and his looks attracted the attention of many eligible young ladies, but he remained single.

Alan confronted Albert about rumors that he had been the one that advised the current regime to accept the crippling terms of the International Monetary Fund's recent structural adjustment programs, but Albert casually denied those claims. He also dismissed talk of his company's trucks being spotted late at night plying the smuggling routes from the small diamond mining towns and crossing the southern border.

Papa apparently became incensed at the party when Albert suggested that justice was served in the recent summary execution of six men, including Gabriel Kaikai a high-ranking police official, for an alleged coup attempt. I wondered why Uncle Alan was friends with the man, surmising he had followed the old maxim of keeping your enemies closer. I hoped for his and Papa's sake the strategy did not backfire.

Chapter 5
Abdul

Freetown

"Are you sure we should go inside?" Angella's voice trails anxiously.

We wait for the traffic policewoman's signal before crossing the street. Angella and I are on our way to the local YWCA to watch a variety show, which is popular entertainment on any day. The cinemas mostly show repeats of old Indian films with no subtitles, and we are bored of them. Sometimes there are theater productions, which we love.

The Mount Aureol Players' production of Bobo Lef, an eternal coming of age tale penned by the inimitable founder of the group had taken the country by storm. There was also a wave of historical, and social commentary, which bore the marks of protest art. This may have been the inspiration for another new dynamic theater company, Freetong Players, that debuted their work a few weeks prior.

Variety shows remained a staple of live performance in the city. Tickets to the live events were cheap, complete with refreshments for purchase. Loud music pulsates through the packed hall as the DJ spun countless hits. The flashily dressed announcer introduces the acts; male, female, solo or in groups went up and mimed popular songs, tells jokes, or show off the latest dance moves to the appreciative cheers of the crowd.

Angella had done much better with her punk hairstyle than I could, and she sported it proudly. Miss Stella had painstakingly applied the popular Dark and Lovely hair relaxer for Angella. She had smoothed the sides up to match the picture of Madonna that we showed her, then sprayed liberal amounts of a holding spray to the spikey peaks in the middle, using hair pins to try and keep them in place. Angella's hair texture cooperated with the manipulation but mine was rapidly wilting with the heat and sweat from my scalp as we had sat in the cramped taxi earlier.

We hopped off at Congo Cross roundabout and took another taxi over to the YWCA, which was close to the city center just across from the stadium. We were keen to see the two youngest Brown Brothers' new break dance routine, sure they would win their competition hands down. Abdul had told us how hard they practiced. Dance was still just a hobby for them, but recognition from local shows like this could mean the big time.

The line into the YWCA snakes around the block, putting us right at the entrance of the popular Countdown night club. As though on cue, Papa's cousin, one of the singers at the club, spots us and calls out, "My goodness, Allison, Angella, is that you?"

She envelopes us in hugs, and we fidget shyly as she coos, "You ladies are more beautiful each time I see you."

Our aunt is ever the charmer and something of a celebrity. Every now and then a passing driver toots their horn and waves. She always waves back. Angella is in awe and has gone silent as she does when she is nervous. I do most of the talking, answering Lolo's deluge of questions about how we have been.

"You haven't come to the house in so long, aunty. When will you visit?" I ask.

"I've been extremely busy darlings, but soon." She smiles warmly, placing a hand on each of our shoulders.

Angella finally speaks, "Papa says you're recording a new album?"

"Ha! Tell my cousin he should be worrying about this country's crazy politics, not my career." Despite her huffiness, Lolo is pleased Papa takes an interest in her.

She explains how much she regrets missing the recent party in Papa's honor. She is keenly aware of how precarious things are for him as he often stands in opposition to the government.

"Where are you two off to anyway?" she asks.

As we tell her about the variety show, we see her partner Abe who owns the nightclub coming outside. He locks the doors to the building and walks over to us. We exchanged hellos.

He has brought Lolo's handbag with him, and she fishes around inside it distractedly as the line moves and we inch closer the entry of the hall.

"Here, take this, please," she says, handing each of us a sizable note.

"For a snack or transport," she insists when we demur. We take the money, thank her, and leave, turning to wave before we round the corner.

Once inside, we could see the hall was packed, the music blaring. A group of our friends from college had arrived early and saved us good seats. We laugh and chat excitedly together, heckling the really bad acts and running up to the stage to shower small bills and coins on the good ones. We snap our fingers to the beat of Tina Turner and Madonna, singing along to lyrics we know by heart.

After the show, we walked out into the late afternoon and meandered through throngs of young people. We bought ice-cold Fantas and meat pies from the vendors lined up outside and played it cool when a group of guys that had been eying us finally sent one brave representative over to the spot under a mango tree where we sat. Whatever courage the young man had possessed had wilted significantly by the time he crossed the stretch of grass.

He licked his lips, avoiding eye contact as he glanced back to where the other guys leaned against a fence. They were ribbing each other and teased one cool cat in particular. The Cool Cat rested his elbow casually on the fence post, appearing unphased by their jokes. He adjusted his collar, stiffening it up around his neck, then proceeded to take a comb out if his pant pocket and slicked down the sides of his jerry curls, eyes hidden behind dark aviator glasses.

My friend Ruth stood up and eyed the messenger impatiently "Did you want to say something Prince?" she asked.

Prince gestured toward me sticking his hand in his pocket and taking it out to reveal a note, as he mumbled incoherently. I felt a little sorry for the scrawny young man whom I knew from church. I looked across at Cool Cat over by the fence post, he had raised his head just then and was nodding to me with a cool smile. Eddie Robinson was good-looking, and he knew it, but his reputation for breaking girls' hearts put him firmly in the No-Go zone for me. Ruth promptly grabbed the note, and Prince scurried off.

We all clamored around to read it, musing over the childish, flowery proclamations of love and devotion. We were doubled over with laughter at its verboseness. By the time we came up for air Cool Cat and his crew had vanished.

On the drive home, I thought how funny it was that for all my derision of suitors, I had never been kissed, and only one person came to mind when I did imagine my first kiss. Maybe Angella was right, and Abdul and I were star-crossed lovers. Other than silly antics like today, men did not harass us. Pensively, I reminded myself how fortunate we were to have escaped from unwanted sexual encounters heard of from our fellow female students.

Unscrupulous and predatory professors were rumored to be taking advantage of the widening income gap, threatening female students with failure unless they greased their palms with money or provided sexual favors. Many female students resorted to wearing trousers on campus, or wearing shorts underneath their skirts when they went to the library or labs, to protect themselves against being groped.

The university authorities at first took a laissez-faire approach, claiming the reports were due to the rising sugar daddy culture and blaming the victims. The stories had recently started to make the front page of the newspapers, forcing the University senate to take up the matter.

Academically speaking, my final year proved to be the most rigorous. I was one of only two female students in the engineering department and cringed at the thought of my marks ever following lower than my male counterparts. Besides Wilfred Williams, who was considered to be a genius, I knew I was as smart if not smarter than any of them.

I had my whole life ahead of me. Enjoying the cool evening breeze brush my now wet strands of hair against my forehead, I savored the memory of meat pies, soft drinks and camaraderie shared with friends.

☙♈❧

The steady flow of sympathizers in and out of King's Lodge continued for many days and Mama looked about to crumble under the weight of it all. I urged her to take it easy. At times like this, I lamented the disdain Krios often showed toward other tribes for living with many of their extended family under one roof.

The nuclear nature of the Krio household was a disadvantage, especially now. After the mourners went home, an almost deafening silence threatened to swallow us up and was broken only by Mama's sobs which carried through the house in the middle of the night when she would awake to an empty bed and the fresh realization that Papa was gone.

Papa had no siblings, so Uncle Robert did his best to fill the void. Aunty Lolo had stayed at the house with us for almost two weeks. She was the one who went throughout the house, covering all the mirrors and turning any photographs of Papa face down as was custom. She had brought her domestic help to assist Miss Stella as we prepared the seventh day awujoh cook. We ended up with so much food that neighbors and even the bisa-bodis, curious passers-by who stopped at the gate to inquire which 'big man' had died, were given packages of food to take home.

Soon Lolo had to leave, but she would return for the feast on the fortieth day which would be an even bigger event given Papa's position in society. Mama and Papa's friends were incredibly helpful, especially Elizabeth and Allan Brown whose entire family was always around to lend a hand or a shoulder. Jennifer's and Frank's university friends and Angella's and my work colleagues all offered us their tireless support.

Some days all I do is replay the events of that day in my head. Angella and I had been in the west end of town. She was starting an internship as a law clerk with a juvenile justice non-profit, and I was a junior draftsman at Davies and Davies architects. I was surprised to receive a call at work from Alan Cole and knew something awful had happened when he asked that I immediately get hold of my siblings and meet him at our home. He had almost seemed relieved that his frantic call to Mama did not get through due to a fault at the Signal Hill exchange.

Frank and Jenny were at their college dorms and it took almost no time at all to gather in our living room. Uncle Alan looked ashen, and his hands shook as he grasped Mama's hands. He had stopped at home and picked up his wife who had her arm around Mama's shoulder. We listened in shock and horror as he explained how Papa's body had crashed into the street traders below his third-floor office window, scattering their wares into traffic.

He had been fully clothed, necktie neatly knotted, a smashed bottle of Johnny Walker beside his lifeless body. On descent, his head had wedged between two aluminum tables while his torso hit the concrete, cracking his ribs, and breaking his spine. The coroner's initial assessment would state that Papa's crushed kneecaps had not resulted from the fall, but those findings never made it into the final report.

When death visited our home, the tragedy hit us hard, but our grief was closely followed by outrage, which Mama did her best to contain until after the funeral. Eyewitnesses claimed that they saw uniformed men enter the back of the building on the afternoon in question but no one followed up this investigative lead or stepped forward to confirm or deny. Alan and Emmanuel closed the chambers for several weeks and hired a second watchman to guard the back entrance both day and night. Although there was no sign of a struggle, or that Eric's office had been searched, Eric's law partners had not guarantee the perpetrators would not return.

After the funeral, Mama spent more and more time in her bedroom. Stella moved slowly but deliberately around the house, checking that everything was in order before checking on Mama.

After graduation, Allison and I had moved into a downstairs extension Papa built to afford us our privacy. In the weeks after Papa died, we spent much of our time back up in the main house. Mama needed us. Jenny and Frank returned to school to finish out the year, doing their best to get back to a sense of normalcy. Abdul was around a lot, though I knew he would be gone again, deploying to the war front. The government grossly underestimated what they thought were a ragtag bunch of radicals, and the fighting along the southern border was escalating by the day.

We all did our part to run the household. Uncle Alan instructed Abdul and Sullay on how to turn the newly installed petrol generator off and on, letting it run just long enough in the evening to keep the fridge and freezer cool, run the standing fans and allow time for Miss Stella to do some ironing.

Mama had given strict instructions that no food should be accepted except family and trusted friends. Instead of declining the baskets of food still being brought to the gate by well-wishers, some with a political connection, Miss Stella wisely accepted the food with a smile, disposing of it well after the visitor had left which at least made the neighborhood stray dogs quite happy. When Mama was well and ready, we prayed she would show her face. For now, we had to keep our situation private. We did not need any rumors of a crazed, reclusive widow living in King's Lodge.

In the weeks that followed, Mama opened up in ways she had not done previously, asking me to stay with her as she went through the papers in Papa's office, something she had not done in their thirty years of marriage.

"I have never touched any of the papers in here," she apologized between sniffles.

"We kept no secrets from each other, but we still had our traditional way of life somehow."

The distracted episodes were common, and I knew I had to be patient. Sometimes the lapse was mid-sentence. Other times, once the sobbing started, I knew she may never finish her train of thought and I would need to pick up after a few days. She told me she had maintained a British savings account where she deposited the sum of an inheritance left by her parents and income from her shares in the Walcott-Taylor business. In essence, money was not of concern.

However, her current account, like most of ours, was dwindling rapidly since the president declared an economic state of emergency. The price of everything skyrocketed and hard currency was scarce.

Mama showed me a rice bag hidden in the recesses of their wardrobe. It was for emergencies. As the financial decline worsened, residents in the big cities had started stashing bank notes under their mattress. The rice bag was a clever switch. I gasped at the neatly packed bills. Mama and I agreed she should save the funds for the most extreme emergency since the austerity measures would likely last a long time.

The current conditions were aggravating the unemployed youth around the country, and we avoided listening to the BBC West Africa broadcasts when Mama was around, partly because it might remind her of Papa, but also not to increase her anxiety.

The academic year ended, and Jenny and Frank came home. Angella and I tried to be positive but the sense of tension that hung over the house was palpable. Our jovial teasing and joking at dinner time was replaced by a solemn quietness.

With Mama retreating into herself, I did my best to ensure that everything around the house was taken care of. The cost of living was increasing exponentially, and I became shrewder about the purchase of food and other essentials, to minimize waste. Miss Stella had been ahead of me there and started hoarding the meager produce she could find at the near empty market stalls.

Mama tended the vegetable garden faithfully and was happy to bake bread and cakes for the house because it took her mind off the grief. On some days, I found her with hands clutched tightly in her lap, the tears falling in rivulets between the creases on her cheeks and did my best to comfort her. My heart ached with worry, but I could not show it.

Despite Mama's objections, I made the trip into town with Sullay early one morning hoping to help him in securing much-needed fuel. The outcry over the doubled price of rice, oil, and sugar were compounded by near-constant power outages which sometimes lasted for weeks.

The yellow taxis revved their engines in annoyance each time private or expatriate vehicles flashed a chit and were signaled to the front of the line by the station attendants who manned the pumps. There was a hodge-podge of cars, motorbikes, lorries, and commercial trucks, even some people on foot, carrying plastic or metal jerrycans which served as makeshift benches as they waited. The tension rose between the attendants and disgruntled customers and Sullay shifted uncomfortably in his seat.

I was lost in thought when I heard a loud thud and our car violently jerked forward. Sullay hissed in irritation, swinging open his driver's door and hopping out to investigate. The driver of the taxi that hit us was an elderly man who apologized profusely, clearly shaken by the accident.

"Sorry sir, sorry sir!" the man repeated, switching to "Sorry ma! sorry ma," when he approached the front and saw me seated inside. Sullay returned to report there was barely a scratch to the bumper. I waved, politely acknowledging the man's apology as it dawned on me the man was probably reacting to the license plate on our car. JD SPC 1, the official designation on Papa's government issue jeep. Mama had not been ready to deal with it yet, but perhaps it was time we contacted the ministry and arranged for the return of the vehicle.

Sullay admonished the old man to have the brakes on his rusty taxi checked but agreed with me that we should let it go. It was not entirely his fault, and it did not help that everyone was on edge these days. We were also finally next in line at the pump, so a long exchange was not worth the risk of missing our spot.

Just then, a luxury car with dark tinted windows pulled up in the adjacent line, edging in and cutting off the customer at the front. The driver disembarked and hailed for service. He was dressed in a khaki safari suit with a white undervest visible through the open buttons of his shirt. He wore dark glasses and military-style boots. In response to this brazen act, an angry mob erupted, pouncing on the driver, and attempting to wrestle the nozzle from the hands of the attendant. Others banged on the windows and trunk of the car in frustration.

The driver beat back the attack, then reached into the vehicle and emerged with a polished black revolver which he leveled at the attendant's head. I held my breath. It was the first time I had ever seen a gun in real life. A hush fell over the place.

"Move!" he bellowed.

The mob melted away as the stunned attendant filled the tank, sloshing petrol on his feet as he struggled to stay calm. When he was finished, he kept his eyes down, weakly accepting the notes handed to him, and shoved them into his satchel uncounted. With a final glare toward the crowd, the driver climbed behind the wheel and sped off. My hands shook long after we were miles away and almost home.

ॐ丫ॐ

The Northern Province

Saidu Kargbo hurriedly shoved his keys into the back pocket of his thread bare jeans, looking out toward the lecturers' residences in the distance for any sign of movement since Abdul and Ali often arrived unannounced. Saidu had not succeeded in getting the male students to stay behind after classes the previous day.

He guessed many of them were nervous because Principal Turay appeared to have grown suspicious. The usually soft-spoken head of the college frowned, his deeply line forehead creasing further at Saidu's current request to leave the building unlocked so that students repeating their exams could access the lecture rooms.

"But Saidu, we don't have any tests for at least another six weeks," he argued.

"Besides, you know the ADB rep wants the carpenters to come in and start work soon. It would be a hazard."

"Ah, yes, sir! Sorry, I forgot, sir," Saidu slapped himself on the forehead and tried to sound light-hearted. Dr. Turay looked relieved that he did not push the matter, making it one less thing for him to worry about.

"Remember," Dr. Turay said, wagging his finger in the air as he turned to leave, "all eyes on Bumbuna!"

Saidu returned the older man's smile wryly and watched him depart. Abdul would be disappointed that he had failed, but Saidu was not worried about him. Ali was the one with the temper. He hid the dark bruise from his last encounter with Ali's fist by letting his beard grow out. They would expect Saidu to have completed preparations for the visit from Foday and Charles and would expect him to gather a sizable group for the meeting at Bumbuna College. He had not succeeded at either assignment. The repercussions would be grave.

Approaching the two-bedroom bungalow from the rear, Saidu was careful to avoid his two younger sisters who were sitting on the verandah playing hand games. He knew Musu, their mother, would still be at the hairdressing shop where she worked. Friday hairdressing appointments were never short. He packed his few possessions into a sports bag, making sure to leave nothing behind. If anyone came looking for him, his family could honestly say they had no idea where he was.

"Ali, go ahead and hop in the truck. I need to get some sugar cane for Ms. June," Abdul calls out. They are in the back of a lorry a few miles away with other passengers and have pulled into the Mile 91 truck stop to refuel. It is almost dusk, and the driver is anxious to complete the next leg of the journey.

Ali had insisted that they go to Bumbuna College to make sure that Saidu had men ready for their Commanders' visit, and was unaware of how disgusted Abdul was, at the betrayal he had just witnessed in the provinces. Abdul saw the movement for the ruse that it was a guise for self-enrichment, looting, and forming what could prove to be a very dangerous political structure. He knew enough from the few times he spoke to Mr. Eric that such a group could bring down the republic and end in more bloodshed.

As the driver revs the lorry engine and the apprentice shouts for passengers to board, Abdul saunters down the market lane casually picking up bundles of sugar cane and haggling with the sellers.

"Hurry up man!" Ali calls out, tapping his foot in irritation.

Abdul's heart is racing but he continues to walk calmly away. He hears the lorry driver and Abdul arguing, "If you want to find him, you need to get off now!" the driver says irately.

"Mek wi go nɔ!" shouts one of the men.

"Place dey dark oh!" another complains.

Seeing his chance, Abdul ducks behind an omolanke which is piled high with firewood, and he walks alongside the cart and waits for his chance. It soon comes, and he darts down a dirt path and disappears into a nearby thicket.

Back at the lorry, Ali cranes his neck and calls out again for Abdul. Unable to hold them back any longer and unwilling to lose the last ride up to Bumbuna, Ali slams the side of the vehicle, signaling to the driver to take off. Abdul watches with relief as the lorry pulls away. He will catch a ride to Freetown when the trucks come by in the morning he thinks, as he slumps down in his hiding place for the night.

The next day, after hours of travel, the other passengers lulled to sleep by the rhythmic turning of the lorry's wheels on newly tarred road, Abdul massages his cramped leg as he savors the memory of Allison's broad smile when she had last whispered in his ear not to stay away too long. She had allowed him to kiss her deeply then, giggling when they both eventually pulled away to catch their breath.

"So that is what suck tongue is?" She'd mused with a cheeky grin, "I like it!"

Abdul had playfully grabbed her by the waist and whispered in her ear about other things he would like to teach her. She swatted at him, mortified and mesmerized all at once.

Allison told Abdul that more distant relatives were showing up at King's Lodge each week, asking for food, or money for rent or to pay for a funeral. Times were beyond desperate. He knew his own mother rose early and went down to Thursday market at King Jimmy wharf. She liked to say she was strong and told him not to worry about her, but Abdul couldn't help it. He had heard the same stories all across the country.

Skirmishes erupted in the market over traders' price gouging essential commodities. Street traders bought bags of sugar from the Syrian and Lebanese shops and packaging it into smaller plastic pellets which were more affordable if you only had pennies in your pocket and were clearly ripping people off.

Some market women who had been caught lining their tin measuring cups with wax were beaten and stripped, their wares capsized and trampled.

Allison told him about her mother's problems with her library staff performing poorly. People were distracted and exhausted from trying to eke out extra income by night tutoring or selling homemade ginger beer and finger food to make ends meet. Civil servants spent most of their workday petty trading in the government buildings, hawking everything from fish cakes and roast chicken, to watches and shoes.

Unmarried and without children, Abdul had not been allocated the same rations from the army as those with dependents. Still, he had spoken to the captain of his company about getting some supplies for his family. The president was an ex-military man and made all the right noises about supporting the troops on the frontlines, but in reality, soldiers were starving, and some resorted to looting and raiding just as the rebels did. All this while rumors of piles of cash covered in plastic wrap and stored in secure rooms in the president's private residence continued to circulate.

The president's Lebanese business partners had become skittish when the consultants reviewing the IMF agreements started sniffing around the central bank, and government revenue reports. So much money was being pilfered, taken out of the country in the form of raw cash or diamonds, an entirely new vocabulary was created to describe this raiding of the coffers. These scandals were known in the national and international media as Vouchergate, Squandergate, and Milliongate.

With the unrest escalating, soldiers were now engaged in guerilla warfare out in the provincial districts close to neighboring Liberia but complained of grossly insufficient meals and poor grade equipment. Compounding the crisis was an increasing number of defections and so-called Sobels, or soldiers turned rebels. Abdul's Captain was a buffoon who had no self-respect. He was one of the few who thrived as the rest of the nation crumbled. His moon-shaped face shone with excess, and his protruding belly strained over his near-invisible belt buckle.

Abdul felt rage boil up inside, but he would have to keep his feelings to himself for now. It was important that he get to King's Lodge to warn them. With Mr. Eric gone, he had a responsibility to keep them safe. At times like this, he thought about his father. Abdul never met the man whose last name he bore. He was five years old when Capri Kamara and nineteen others aboard the *Elorrio* drowned when the ship foundered in the Tyrrhenian sea six hundred kilometers from the Valencian coast.

As the truck rolls closer to the capital, Abdul can see the lights from the hills just beyond Waterloo. By the time he arrives at the barracks, he knows what he must do.

♋♈♋

Freetown

As the sound of gunshots repeat in the distance, Abdul shouts instructions to everyone in the compound to take cover and stay low.

"Allison, listen very carefully to me," Abdul says as he presses my hands tightly together.

"You need to talk to Miss June. The city won't be safe for much longer, you should leave as soon as possible." As he speaks, his grip on my fingers tightens until I can feel them tingling from the slowing blood flow. We were standing outside the workers' quarters at the back of the King's Lodge compound, the early morning sun reflecting off the windowpanes was blinding.

I squint against the glare as I process Abdul's words and try to make sense of everything that is happening. When Abdul announced his decision to join the military, I had cried every day for weeks, not because I was scared then, but because my heart ached, and I would miss him. Now, I am scared.

Ever since Papa was killed, Abdul had played the role of the man in the house whenever he was around, even though Mama would not acknowledge or admit it.

With the sudden rattle of gunfire going off in the city, it was clear the violence had escalated.

Abdul gave instructions to Frank and Pa Foday, the gateman to secure the compound and lock all the gates. Afterward, we huddled together in the boy's quarters to avoid stray bullets. Mama did not join us but instead took shelter in the storeroom with Frank, pulling the steel door shut behind them. We tried to catch a signal on the radio, but there was just static on all frequencies. We had stayed still for what seemed like hours while the sound of sporadic shots and returning fire rang out. Suddenly, there was silence.

Miss Stella kept trying her pocket-sized transistor radio and after several attempts caught the somber notes of marshal music on the national broadcasting service frequency. It was about an hour later when we heard a new sound. It was the hum of horns blaring in the distance.

We looked at each other in confusion as the volume of the hum increased to a shout. We ran around to the side of the house where Mama was already at the kitchen door.

"Abdul, are the rebels here? What is that sound?" her voice was shrill with panic.

"No, Ma. They have advanced but not this far yet. Our troops took a hard hit near Taiama junction earlier this week, so they are still some ways away. For now."

"It must be something else then," Frank looked thoughtful as he spoke. By this time, the whole household had gathered in the yard.

"I will go and check, Ma," Abdul assured Mama. I could sense Abdul's unease around my mother. She had changed so much in the year since Papa died, had grown extremely distrustful of everyone outside of her immediate family. Telltale signs of sleepless nights showed on her face. Some mornings her breath was still heavy from sherry. Abdul eased away and avoided eye contact with him. He noticed how Mama had changed but did not speak of it.

I was as surprised as everyone when Mama went into the house and quickly returned with keys to the brand-new Toyota Hilux. She handed them to Abdul.

Recently, out of the blue, a driver from the Law Courts had come to the house and unceremoniously demanded the keys to Papa's official vehicle.

"Good riddance to bad rubbish!" Mama had screamed and thrown an empty sherry bottle as the car pulled away.

That left us with only Mama's Fiat which frequently broke down. In such uncertain and tumultuous times no one was able to arrange a car payment through the bank. So out of necessity, Mama had bought the vehicle from a dealership on Wilkinson Road, paying in cash.

Abdul got into the car, and I hopped into the front passenger seat. Before Mama could protest, Angella and Jennifer hopped in the back, and Frank climbed into the open cab. As we descended the slope toward Congo Cross, I grew increasingly worried about Frank, out there in the open, and called out to ask if he was okay. He gave me a thumbs up. He was fine.

By the time we reach the bottom of the hill we have slowed to a crawl. The shouts we heard from the top of the hill had turned into a deafening roar. Throngs of people poured into the streets and all we can see for what looked like miles was a sea of bobbing heads. The old and the young alike, women with infants wrapped in lappas and secured to their backs, people of all ages and stations had joined their voices to the sound of clanging pots and pans, and car horns blaring.

This was not a riot or a rebel invasion, but a welcoming party. A mass exodus from war-ravaged parts of the country had converged in the capital. The people were demanding an end to war. We stopped the vehicle unable to move forward or back. Abdul got out and the rest of us followed.

"Lili?" Frank called to me from his vantage point on the open bed of the truck. "Where do you think they are going?"

I stood there, mesmerized, as throngs continued to mill past us.

"I don't know, Frankie. I don't know," I called back over the din.

🙖♋🙖

Kambia District

I had read about the Greater and Little Scarcies rivers which ran along the northern part of the country bordering Guinea but was unprepared for the breath-taking beauty of the surrounding countryside. I would miss the bounty of the mixed fresh and salty waters, with their barracuda, bonga, snapper, and mackerel, oysters and crayfish. mackerel, their oysters, crayfish, and lobster. We spotted emerald cuckoos, and owls, little swifts, and hawks as we made our way towards Kambia.

Sullay boasted that many of his people from the north were experts at navigating the twenty-mile span and knew the waters like the backs of their hands. In the heat of the sun, I felt a bittersweet anticipation at the promise of the Atlantic Ocean breeze greeting us as we approached the point where the river emptied into the yawning deep.

We left Kambia town on foot to Madina junction, where we were loaded onto a truck and transported to another village close to Kukuna. The river carried us slowly and steadily forward, as gentle waves lapped against the sides of the dugout canoe we had been in since the night before.

As Abdul explained, the events a few days before at Bumbuna unfolded in such a manner that he knew he had made a mistake. When he and Ali arrived, Ali had given him the manifesto that Sankoh their 'leader' was said to have written, and he was sickened by the things it contained. After seeing armed men and boys brandishing AK47s looting and burning villages, and committing heinous acts of mutilation against innocent people, he could no longer tell apart soldiers from rebels.

Both groups seemed more interested in raping women and seizing raw diamonds from small time miners in the villages surrounding the diamond district, than restoring democracy. Abdul had made his escape into the bushes aware that he would now be targeted by Ali, Mo, and their group. He was a soldier, not a rebel. He needed to make it clear to his superiors that any ties he may have had to Ali and Mo had been cut. It would be risky reporting back to the capital, but it was the right thing to do.

Abdul described to me how his sense of pride returned once he put on his uniform again despite it being stained with sweat and blood. And then the frustrated action of a handful of young army corporals had overthrown the regime of the last three decades quickly and decisively and was touted as one of the few bloodless coups in the continent's history.

For the rest of us, a military coup meant rule by decree. The National Supreme Council of State was the final authority in all matters and promptly suspended the constitution. The airports were closed, and soldiers were granted unlimited powers of administrative detention without charge or trial. For Mama that was more than she could take.

Abdul had told us to keep going and not look back. We secured as much foreign currency as we could on our persons and in our shoes. I had stored all the birth certificates in my handbag. Mama held our passports. We had some local currency on hand but were cautious about purchasing food from the villages. We relied on fruits we could pick on the way, reserving the tins of sardines and luncheon meat and, packets of crackers for emergencies.

None of us spoke French or Susu, and so we relied on the signs Abdul had told us to watch for, to help us identify those who would be likely to help us. We were headed for neighboring Guinea.

Abdul thought we had little time left before more waves of people trying to flee, moved to the north as well. The boats that ferried the refugees across the river were dangerously overloaded. Some of them capsized, drowning everyone inside. He had arranged for a smaller canoe to transport the four of us, while Mama and Miss Stella would come along with two of Emmanuel Pratt's sisters on a bigger fishing boat.

I looked around, feeling afraid but mostly sad. I was unsure of what to expect once we landed. I had barely eaten that day and my stomach growled noisily as the taste of bile rose in my throat. I couldn't sleep in the canoe, and neither could Frank, so we kept vigil while Angella and Jennifer nodded off. We could see the shoreline in the breaking dawn. The canoe slowed. The fisherman expertly tapping the sides with his paddle to guide it in. As we stepped out of the boat, I raised my head and that's when I heard it, barely a whisper carried on the breeze. It was the unmistakable sound of Papa's voice.

"Allison, take care of your family. Take good care."

Chapter 6
Allison

Washington, D.C

The air conditioning is broken again so we are in for another sweaty night. I glance at my watch. Angella and I are sitting on one of the benches scattered around the edge of the u-shaped housing apartment complex on 14th Street. From that vantage point, we can see the early signs of transformation merge with the once scattered landscape of burned-out husks and other drab buildings like ours, run by rapacious slumlords.

Luxury condos and fixer-upper types are cropping up, and the financial crisis that had driven the city below so-called 'junk status', looks about to turn. Congress had intervened and put the city under the power of a federal control board and the most controversial mayor in its history is finally on his way out.

It's going on seven o'clock and Aunty Khadi will be waiting for us to eat dinner together. She is probably anxiously pacing the balcony and chain-smoking, the latter of which I have repeatedly urged her to give up.

Aunty Khadi is not our relative but in the past five years, we have become family. She is as plain speaking and stubborn as she is caring and kind-hearted. She took four strangers into her home as part of the United States government refugee resettlement program, and for that, we would forever be in her debt. Khadi would tell friends that she took us in because she wanted the extra cash given to hosts in the resettlement program, but we know she appreciates having company, and the family she always longed for.

She was a young woman, just about to start Bumbuna Teacher's College when her father, a widower was appointed Chargé d'affaires of the newly opened embassy in DC and moved with her to the United States. Prior to that, she had only ever lived in a small town with little knowledge of the ways of people from a different culture or ethnicity. She said unreservedly that she had picked the four of us from the list based on our last name because of the reputation Krios had for being respectful of elders and for being discrete.

Angella and I often sat outside in the park in silence, each lost in our own memories and thoughts. Aunty Khadi had done her best to make us comfortable, but the time was coming for us to make our own way. If the jobs we applied for came through, we agreed to save up for the deposit on a townhouse as a priority.

When we first arrived, Jennifer surprised us all when she decided to no longer pursue medicine but instead said she would go into business and marketing. She had done exceptionally well and secured an internship for the summer. Frank had the hardest time adjusting of all of us but was starting to get on his feet. He was volunteering at the local library and was half-way through his English degree.

Without the proper documents, Angella and I were required to return to undergraduate level studies. We flew though our courses as quickly as time afforded between working odd jobs, so graduating cum laude had been gratifying for both Angella and I.

Years ago, it was hard to imagine how we could all fit in the tiny apartment. It was a far cry from the King's Lodge and the life we once knew. But it was a palace compared to the refugee camp. I tried not to dwell on all we had lost, Papa, Mama, family, friends. Abdul.

It is too painful to think about now. When the repatriations started, I had been reluctant to add our names to the list of asylum seekers but had not been able to wait any longer. Word came to us daily that the camps on the southern border had been overrun and the rebels were once again pushing north, hoping to cut off the capital in the west, and force the government to surrender or make some type of deal. They were holding the whole country ransom.

Once we left the capital, Abdul had arranged for a truck to pick up Mama and Miss Stella. Frank had wanted to stay with them, but Abdul thought we could move faster through the back roads on foot, while the older women were transported to the Kychom jetty.

I remembered Papa's stories about his travels to that part of the country back when he worked to rally the chiefs in the north. Papa had described Kychom to us. A village perched high on a rugged cliff overlooking the majestic river below. Coconut trees lined the water's edge and tree branches swayed lazily in the breeze.

The farmers and fishermen had been friendly to him and had viewed the impassioned Krio boy from the capital with curiosity. They'd plied him with bags of coarse, locally grown rice, cassava and groundnut that Mama often had to share with her workmates down at the British Council. Papa declined the bigger gifts of goats and chickens, but he loved the fish, which they would catch from the river soon after he arrived, carefully drying it out and smoking it over low wooden flames for days until it was time for him to leave.

There was no sign of Mama or Miss Stella as day after day we waited for news from them. The camp grew more crowded, and food and water became scarce. Frank had frequent bouts of malaria and Jennifer nearly died when a wave of cholera swept through. When our names came up on the list for resettlement, I was relieved but pleaded with the UNHCR director of the camp to keep our family together. We did not have our passports which were with Mama, but we had our birth certificates.

"What are your names?" the camp director had asked when we presented to her for what felt like the tenth time.

"Allision, Angella, Jennifer, and Frank," I replied.

"And your surname?" she continued brusquely, not looking up from the stack of papers on her desk.

"Johnson," I said quickly, throwing Angella a sharp look before she could protest. Her surname was Macauley, but I was determined for that not to be the reason we would be separated. We did not have our passports and I lied that our birth certificates had also been lost. Angella said nothing. I stole a glance at Jennifer and Frank, but their expressions were blank. We shared a silent understanding that we would do whatever it took to make it out of the place together. It was what Papa and Mama would have wanted.

Through the makeshift door which had been rolled back on the tarpaulin tent, my eyes were drawn to a toddler rolling in the mud. Her mother sitting on the ground next to her stared into the distance, looked dejected and too weak to pick up the infant. Our parents had set an example for us our whole lives in giving generously to charitable causes and to those less fortunate than ourselves. I had never before known what it felt like to depend on the generosity of strangers.

Despite the overwhelming humidity, Aunty Khadi refused to open any windows while we waited for the building superintendent to send a utility man to our apartment. She was paranoid after a recent wave of shootings. Innocent bystanders were getting caught in gun battles between what the police were calling feuding gangs, and even up on the fifth floor, she was not taking any chances.

The two standing fans that Aunty Khadi bought on sale at work are angled strategically in the hallway, and wisps of cool air thread through the open bedroom doors as the blades swivel past. When we enter the apartment, she raises her hands up and greets us with a welcoming smile, and "Alhamdulillah, Alhamdulillah, Alhamdulillah." To which we respond, "Ameen."

Aunty Sallay is at the house. She and Aunty Khadi are best friends and from the stories we've heard over the years, they have been there for each other through thick and thin. During the early years in Washington D.C., Khadi took on the full-time job of supporting her father as his personal assistant, putting her education on hold.

After her father suddenly fell ill and had to return home, her boyfriend proposed, and Khadi accepted, moving to New York to be with him. Her father would be looked after by relatives back home, so she was happy to stay in America with her husband. Steven Koroma was a brilliant young man from the same town as Khadi, their families were friends and a personal recommendation from Khadi's father had not hurt Steven's chances of landing the assignment as Ambassador to the United Nations.

Steven had always been popular with the ladies, but Khadi felt secure in the marriage and was willing to turn a blind eye to his indiscretions. She had grown accustomed to moving in diplomatic circles and loved her bourgeoisie expatriate lifestyle in the cosmopolitan city. She quickly learned from the other wives that it was normal for their husbands to have a little fun on the side.

They had no children, so she busied herself being a good wife. She dressed well, was articulate, and dedicated herself to Steven and his career, hoping wholeheartedly that her friends had been right when they assured her with the platitude that since "Khadi had the ring, Miss Doublet could have the man." They had been wrong.

The marriage unraveled as her relationship with Steven drifted further apart until eventually Miss Dubuslut, as Khadi called her, got both the ring and the man, leaving Khadi angry and alone. She learned that Steven was having an affair with a flashy debutante from Louisiana and before she knew it, it was too late. She was too angry and tired to fight him.

She was too humiliated to ask for help from her family nor could she bear the thought of trying to find evidence to support an infidelity claim against Steven. I smiled when I heard the story, not because of her misfortune, but because of what Ms. Stella would have said to us proudly, "Fri po bɛtɛh pass tayt jentry."

Aunty Khadi embodies the Krio proverb. She appreciates peace over plenty. She left Steven and his new lover. Her heart was hurt but she was determined to keep her pride intact.

The little money she had set aside soon ran out. On the brink of homelessness, she left New York and moved back to DC where she met Sallay by chance at a laundromat. Khadi was surprised at the kindness the other woman showed toward her, offering to help because she was someone from the same soil even though they were complete strangers.

"Men who leave our sisters for these afro women are useless!" Sallay had declared with disgust.

Forced to fend for herself for the first time in her life, Khadi had received a rude shock upon realizing the only types of jobs she was qualified for. A secondary education from a distant part of the world meant very little to employers in America.

Sallay had been intent on finding a suitor for Khadi, but after a few years, it was clear to Khadi that many of the single men around them were already supporting two or three children, or were simply more interested in finding someone to help foot their bills and not in a hurry to play the role of breadwinner or knight in shining armor.

"It isn't easy," Aunty Khadi often reminded us. "Education is the key that will open many doors and give you a better life." She'd looked around the cluttered apartment as she spoke.

We'd heard her say those words often, and each time I felt she sounded less convinced herself. I longed to assure her a time would come when she could once again afford life's luxuries. I wanted to believe that. The peace of plenty mantra sounded hollow.

When she was braiding Jennifer's hair, or when she and I prepared meals together in the cramped kitchen, Aunty Khadi would grow wistful as she shared stories about her time back home. One night soon after we had arrived, we were all crowded around her kitchen table, Frank and Angella using overturned milk crates for benches as we ate dinner. Aunty Khadi fondly recalled how different life would have been for her back home, how knowing the right people in the Republic would almost guarantee you a very lucrative job in the public service sector.

"Di Pa was a crafty man," she said, shaking her head as she recalled his infamous wile.

I bristle at her mention of the former president, a man who I feel was personally responsible for my father's assassination and the destruction of my beloved country. I hold my breath, wondering what she will say next. Fortunately, she rambles on about di Pa's betrayal of the former vice-president, who happens to be Steven's uncle. She is alarmed at how easily politicians change allegiance. I am relieved that she is not harboring any sympathy toward Papa's killers, and I feel able to breathe again.

Aunty Khadi's room was at the far end of the narrow hallway. Angella and I shared the small bedroom next to hers. Frank slept on the pullout sofa in the living room but kept his clothes and personal items in our closet. We were able to fit a single bed in the small storage space across from our room, to make a bedroom for Jennifer. I was a light sleeper unlike the others, and some nights I would awaken to hear Aunty Khadi crying quietly through the thin walls separating us.

One night, after she had been sobbing for an hour, I ventured into her room, "Aunty Khadi?" I whispered. The crying stopped, and I hovered at the door and waited as I held the door ajar. As my eyes adjusted to the dark, I heard her sigh heavily.

"Yes, Allison, come in," she beckoned.

I could make out her form on the bed. She pulled her legs tightly up to her chest, breathing deeply as she appeared to be using all her might to stop from wailing out loud. My heart was heavy as I looked at her. Mama had been like this after Papa was killed. Grief took a firm hold of her and she was nearly swallowed up by it.

For days, Mama would lay in the bed that she and Papa had shared, only getting up to wash herself, and barely eating any food. During that time, I would go and sit quietly with her. There were no words spoken, only her pain filled the emptiness. As she lay there, unable to sleep even after her third or fourth glass of sherry, I would gently rub her feet and then her hands, with her favorite English Rose scented oil that she bought from Yardley of London whenever we went to England in summer holiday. It helped calm her down and she would drift off to sleep.

I went over to Aunty Khadi's dresser and looked for the Churai incense oil which she used during her Maghrib prayers. As I gently rubbed her hands and feet with the oil, she talked to me about her life before we came to live with her. After the divorce from Steven, unable to find a decent job, depressed and desperate for relief she walked into the Social Services Administration and applied for assistance.

She sank into a deep depression, and the anger and sadness threatened to overtake her. She had started smoking cigarettes. Her late mother would be disappointed since the Qu'ran was clear about keeping your body pure, but she hadn't seen the inside of a mosque in years and wasn't ready to give up the calm nicotine brought to her.

Aunty Khadi had been able to secure a subsidized housing unit, and Sallay helped her find some furniture and a mattress at the Salvation Army a block away. The sight of the two African women balancing a mattress on their heads all the way back to the apartment had drawn a mix of amused and disdainful looks.

Since that day, Aunty Khadi learned to sacrifice her pride when pragmatism demanded it. She started taking night classes at the District of Columbia College of Arts and Culture in order to obtain her general education diploma.

After Aunty Khadi passed the exam, some of her former confidence slowly returned and she applied for her first proper job. She had to persevere, fighting hard not to let rejection sink her back into depression. When she finally landed the cashier position at the new Hecht's Department store on Florida Ave, she cooked a huge pot of cassava leaves for herself, loading it with enough beef and chicken to feed an army.

She had never been much of a drinker, but that night she continued her celebration with cigarettes and an entire bottle of Mateus wine. A splitting headache the next morning was enough to make that her last run with alcohol, but she continued to smoke.

Aunty Khadi eventually drifted off to sleep, and I sat at the foot of her bed for a while and watched her as you would a child. As her shaky tearful breathing settled, I felt a pang of longing for my own mother. I knew Frank, Jennifer and Angella felt the same, although they each had found ways to cope since our lives were ripped apart.

In the years after the refugee camp in Guinea, I had done my best to be the big sister, but I am uncertain how much longer I can be strong for everyone. Memories of the awful conditions, the raids by rebels fighting on both sides of the border as they sought food and water, memories of the maiming and beheadings, of the assaults, still haunt me. I tried to shut my eyes against those images and now all I see is Mama's face. I miss her.

We had lingered at the border for days hoping that she and Miss Stella would soon turn up. We had not seen them since we split up at Kambia. Frank had wanted to stay with Mama then, but Abdul thought we could move faster through the back roads on foot. It was a race against time. The numbers of displaced around the border villages having grown and caused an increased sense of unease.

We were heading for the crossing that would take us to the Guéckédou settlement. There we hoped to secure places for our family and Mama's travel companions only to discover that Guéckédou had been over run. The UNHCR was diverting new arrivals to Madina. When Mama and the others did not arrive, we reluctantly crossed into Guinea, following Abdul's instructions on which way to go. We had no passports, and I could only pray we would be allowed to stay.

Now in this new country, with a new home, a new 'mother', and a new life, our main entry point into the system is through education. We protested at being set back by two or three academic years. Angella and I particularly were confused that we could not simply sit for graduate exams to establish our qualifications. Instead, we were required to take undergraduate level classes and earn credits from an American university if we were to have any hope of pursuing our chosen careers.

Colleges and schools were all shut down during the war, so we did not have any documents to prove our academic credentials. Much of the capital had been ravaged by fire, many people were brutalized and tortured when the rebels invaded.

The country was in the grips of an all-out civil war. Every other day, one of us would go to the local library and use the computers there to search the internet and print out Voice of America, BBC, or Deutsche Welle news stories of events. The local stations we caught on the small television in the apartment, made no mention of the civil war in a small West African nation. We tried calling King's Lodge no one ever answered the phone.

Sallay often remarked at how lucky Khadi was to have gotten such 'good people'. She told us stories about other refugees who had not fared as well, their sponsors eventually canceling the arrangement which forced some to be repatriated to the Gambia or Ghana. The good news was that refugees who resettled in those African countries were thriving. That made me glad. I would not wish life at Guéckédou or any other refugee camp on even my worst enemy.

♋

During the summer months, none of us felt like going indoors early just to watch repeats of game shows on television or end up listening to Aunty Khadi chat with her friends on the phone. The apartment offered very little privacy. She succeeded in cornering me earlier that day with juicy gossip about the funeral of one of her *osusu* members. The deceased, a hefty lady by the name of Julie Lewis, tragically died of a heart attack. Her abrupt demise hadn't stopped her family members from preparing an enormous spread at her repast.

Mourners had apparently capsized a table as they clamored for take-out containers to stuff food into. I learned my lesson the hard way after a bout of food poisoning almost landed me in the hospital, so I shied away from bringing food home from those events. Aunty Khadi suspected some of the younger women who were busy with young children or worked multiple jobs, cooked dishes weeks in advance as their contribution to the potluck.

Tamru Selassie, a bushy-haired Ethiopian with scrawny legs and a hint of a mustache has brought a small stereo outside and sets it down on the bench a few feet away from us. Lately, he and some of our other neighbors have outdoor the gatherings that have become a full-blown tailgate party with burgers on the grill, drinks, and dancing competitions; the eskista versus jola, the ndebele versus soukous.

Once he shows up, it is going to be hard to draw Angella away. Despite her denial, I have noticed the flush in her cheeks whenever Tamru speaks to her. His deep dimples are charming and catch a lot of the girls off guard, but he only has eyes for Angella. I enjoy nights like this because they offer us a welcome escape from our cramped apartment.

Jennifer had been snobbish in the beginning, but she soon gave up the airs and graces of a forgotten life, gradually sharing her insecure and shy side with Aunty Khadi, who teased it out of her by regularly praising her. Aunty Khadi always had something good to say, whether about Jennifer's intelligence or how pretty her thick shoulder-length hair looked.

Eventually, Jennifer even let Aunty Khadi style her hair the way the African American girls in the neighborhood did, blow drying and pressing it until it was shiny and bone straight.

I was happy that Jennifer was making friends at school and in the projects where we lived. After a life of being insulated from the harsh realities of the world, where having chauffeurs and house staff had been the norm, the shock of life in the refugee camp and adjusting to this new life in America had taken a toll on all of us in one way or the other.

Mama had taught us to always be respectful toward elders, but in the early days, Jennifer had barely spoken to Aunty Khadi. She would grunt a greeting to our host before leaving in the morning, and stayed out all day at the local library or explored the bus routes using the weekly transit passes we received as part of our resettlement allowance.

Aunty Khadi was patient and continued to praise us for our good manners, never complaining about Jennifer's behavior. Eventually, Jennifer had softened and become more accepting of our plight. She expressed gratitude toward Aunty Khadi, and showed more cheer, laughing at Aunty Khadi's jokes and offering sweet gestures. Last summer, Jennifer took a bus ride all the way up to Silver Spring and returned with a bounty.

A new African grocery store had opened up there, and the bags filled with coca yams, dried fish, red palm oil, egusi, and bags of fresh potato leaves she returned with, had brought Aunty Khadi to tears.

The only time we saw Aunty Khadi truly furious was one day, mere months after we moved in. She had been tidying the living room and found what I thought were a handful of small rocks. They had rolled into the recesses of the fold-out sofa, which doubled as Frank's bed.

Aunty Khadi paced the cramped apartment, muttering to no one in particular and I stayed out of her way, contemplating how to handle this new development with my brother when he returned. Aunty Khadi knew exactly where he got the 'rocks' even before she interrogated him.

Mouse, who lived on the first floor of our apartment complex was the self-professed king of the block. Frank had been taken by the young man's confidence and charm. He was indeed regal looking. His hands dripped with diamond studded rings, and he wore a wreath of platinum around his neck.

When Mouse and his posse are stationed in our building's entryway, I stall in the stairwell or use the fire escape to avoid running into them. I wasn't really afraid of them, but I didn't look forward to getting caught in crossfire if the turf war between street gangs came to our doorstep.

A lot of the neighborhood kids looked up to Mouse and from what I heard he was something of a Robin Hood; spending a good portion of his profits to fund free daycare for single parents who had to work, and sponsoring a makeshift meals on wheels program which was a lifesaver for seniors in the community who were willing to turn a blind eye to how he paid for it.

The night she found the 'rocks' Aunty Khadi wailed in Temne and tore at her headtie, leaving Frank stunned and chagrined. By the time we were able to calm her down, Frank had seen the error of his choice. The temptation of earning fast money by working for Mouse was strong but Frank knew he was not cut out for that life. The evidence left behind for Aunty Khadi to find was proof that Frank would surely make a sloppy criminal.

He packed up the 'goods' to return to Mouse and we all had a laugh about it later when the tension had eased. Despite my humor, that day was a sobering reminder to me that we were in a desperate situation.

When we first arrived, Aunty Khadi was unable to hide the shock on her face and burst into tears, hugging our gaunt frames and tending to our swollen feet. I had stood in front of the bathroom mirror for a long time, my own reflection was unrecognizable except for my eyes, and the haunted sadness I saw terrified me. The nights were hardest. We were all plagued with nightmares. Angella worst of all.

She suffered from spells during the day too. They started during our final days at G camp. She would stare into the distance for time on end, unfazed by what was going on around us. Sometimes her muscles spasmed and her arms swiped about, stabbing at an unseen enemy. Whenever that happened, I learned to approach her cautiously, singing the words to *Abide with me.* The old Anglican hymn was one of Mama's favorites and had brought us all comfort during those dark days.

In an episode soon after we moved in with Aunty Khadi, Angella grabbed a knife from the kitchen and ran around brandishing it as she stared blankly ahead. Terrified, Aunty Khadi, Jennifer, and Frank locked themselves in the bedroom. I was also afraid, but I ignored it, instead closing my eyes and singing. I started softly at first but by the time I reached the last verse, I had forgotten my fear and was so wrapped up in the words, I barely noticed Angella had stopped in her tracks. She dropped the knife and slumped down on the floor in a sobbing heap.

After we settled in, things improved, and we had some good times. We would gather around the dining table and tell old folk tales or run Ludo championships. Aunty Khadi loved the popular board game. I could see how happy she was that we were all together; the family she always wanted and never had, and the one we truly needed to help us move past the horrors we'd endured.

As we set up the Ludo board and got ready to choose the color of our game pieces, I picked out the green one and my mind went to Abdul. Green was his favorite color. I recalled him sitting across from me when we played the game together; his eyes glinting with affection as he watched me squeal with glee every time I rolled a double six.

There was no way we could work enough hours to afford our education so whenever we discovered a new scholarship opportunity, Aunty Khadi contacted Steven her, "useless ex" as she referred to him, to help us with the applications since the language and terms were quite complicated and difficult for us to understand.

Though he hinted at having used his position to pull a few strings, Aunty Khadi dismissed Steven's mention of dinner at the apartment, knowing full well her signature cassava leaf sauce was the motivation behind his request. Aunty Khadi was immensely proud that each of us obtained some form of grants and scholarships. Angella and I at Catholic University, Jennifer and Frank at Howard University.

ജYജ

The stranger standing at the counter has a smirk on his face that I try to ignore as I take the next order. I know most of the regulars who come in for their first brew of the day, but I have never seen this man before. He is dressed in a navy blazer, white button-down shirt, and jeans. As Angella would say in her best Bronx accent, he 'smells like monay'. He studies the menu lazily. His smirk is starting to get on my nerves. I have a pounding headache from being up early for days in a row and am feeling less than my usual patient self.

"I'm sorry, but are you going to order something?" I say, trying not to sound too harsh.

It's Monday, and the line running through the store's front doors has not shortened since we opened. When we started this job, Angella quickly proved to have a knack for the beverage machines and was whipping up drinks on our first day of training. Abigail, one of the baristas, saw her potential and took Angella under her wing. I am lost when it comes to the drinks and could not tell you the difference between a flat white and a latte. I am trained to handle the cash register, so I find the job of taking muffin or bagel orders significantly less daunting than the elaborate beverage concoctions.

This morning we are both stressed. Angella is singlehandedly running the coffee machines because Abigail is off with a colitis flare-up, and I am doing my best to keep up, between working the cash and making sandwiches.

"Yes, I would like a black coffee, one of the small ones." He motions to the cups displayed on the back counter. He has a crisp English accent.

I cannot help smiling, seeing he doesn't know the names of the different drink sizes any better than I do.

"You know you aren't doing a very good job," he says, as I punch in his order.

I stop; fingers frozen on the screen in front of me. I am taken aback by his words and unsure if I should respond.

How did he know I hated taking coffee orders? I think in a panic. I glance at him nervously and he holds my gaze, smiling deliberately.

Feeling flustered and a little confused I can sense Angella behind me before I hear her voice.

"Well, Sir! You aren't doing a particularly good job of placing your order and getting out of the way! You are holding up the line, Sir!" she spits out the last word caustically.

The line is backed up and spilling out on the sidewalk now and I know if we don't get things moving, Corrine will undoubtedly be watching from the back-office camera and come out to admonish us soon.

The man is no longer smiling. He shoves a five-dollar bill toward me and before I can give him his change and ask what name to scribble on his cup, he walks stiffly over to the end of the counter to wait.

Angella hisses long and low as she picks up a small cup. She scribbles something, fills it with the steaming dark liquid, and walks over to the end of the counter. The stranger goes up to her and she hands him his coffee. After he reads what she's written, he raises his eyebrow apparently humored, before snapping on the lid, turning on his heel, and walking out.

Later, when I asked what she wrote, she replied, "Have a nice day," with a shrug. I wasn't entirely sure I believed her. On days like this, I was grateful for Angella's ability to be both assertive and compassionate, in a way that reminded me of Papa.

We got this gig some weeks before graduation. Aunty Khadi had urged Angella and me to be at the door with our applications in hand before the new location on the corner of Georgia Ave and Eastern even posted a hiring sign. The owner, David Gregory, had greasy hair, drove a bright yellow Maserati, and had a penchant for chihuahuas. Like him or not, he had hired both of us, so we were thankful for that.

The baristas and some of the other employees speculated about where our boss got the money to open this location; his fourth Starbucks in the DMV. We heard that his real name was Davit Gregoryan. Business savvy, hard work, and a strategic name change had propelled him from humble immigrant beginnings to the success he now enjoyed.

He started with his first Starbucks near the University of Maryland, College Park, and had never looked back. Corrine, his general manager was a skinny blonde woman who oversaw the daily operation of the shops. She boasted that David was expanding business down the 14th Street corridor and would be there when the so-called urban renewal started. To his credit, his timing was genius.

David's wealth did not translate into generosity. He was utterly shrewd, and our paychecks proved it. Regular full-day shifts were exhausting especially because Corrine kept the shop consistently understaffed. After our final exams, Angella and I became full-time employees. We were up at five am, six out of seven days a week.

On most days it was almost ten hours before we finished cleaning the kitchen and the tables, locked up the shop and walked to the bus stop a block away. Despite a rambling and barely intelligible pep talk on orientation day when he had enticed us with the promise of bonuses for the cleanest store of the month, we grew suspicious over time. No matter how late we stayed behind, scrubbing, and polishing the shop, a bonus never materialized. Abigail who had worked there longest confirmed this was just a ploy to keep us on our toes and encouraged us to take the leftover cakes and cookies home as a reward.

After a long week at work, Saturday nights were relaxing and fun. Since we had started working full time, Angella and I went dancing at the Kilimanjaro nightclub once a month and we loved it. Entry was a little pricey, so we waited till it was Ladies' night when we could get in free. Concentric patterns from colorful disco lights swirled around the dim smokey lighting inter swirled in around the darkened lounge which was tastefully and plushily furnished in purple and gold. The people, the music, and the food, all reminded me of the best things about Africa and home.

Although Aunty Khadi did not truly object, she worried whenever any of us was out late. She was also skeptical of those in the diaspora community who put on a show of wealth.

"You don't have to go to every party, oh!" she asserted with a knowing sniff. "Some of them just pretend to be well off, but half of them clean toilets at night just to drive a rented Mercedes." She sucked air sharply through her front teeth to show her disapproval.

Aunty Khadi was not a strict Muslim, but she was culturally conservative. She was adamant that we not become *too American,* which was a sentiment I often heard among the diaspora community. Ironic considering the whole purpose of our immigration to a great extent was to become American. No one ever defined what being *too American* looked like or how it was measured, but rest assured that once you got there, our people let you know.

Aunty Khadi was more concerned that we continue the customs which to some might seem mundane but remain the cornerstone of much of African society similar in some ways to what I observed when I first visited the southern United States. The greeting was sacred, it spoke volumes about your background and your upbringing. We were all adults but would never invite a friend over, especially not of the opposite sex without first informing Aunty Khadi. We cleaned the house and washed up after ourselves.

"Students or not, you are not living in a dormitory," she reminded us of when our schedules became busy with classes and work. This was still her house, and she expected to maintain her standards. On the weekends Jennifer and Frank often went to the movies while Angella and I preferred going dancing. If Aunty Khadi suspected we drank while we were out, she never objected or questioned us. We did have a beer now and then, but the DJ at Kilimanjaro had us dancing all night so by the time it was last call any alcohol we had consumed was gone in our sweat before we got home.

Tamru's father owned a taxi which he allowed him to use on weekends. We convinced him to pick us up when the nightclub closed and since he was sweet on Angella, he would wait patiently outside the club to give us a ride home. On Thursdays, he hung around the first-floor elevator to check if we would need a ride and could not hide his disappointment when Angella said she couldn't go out because she was busy studying or had to work.

Tamru was a sweet guy, but I feared his gentle demeanor and personality might irritate Angella. It was clear they liked each other but I resisted the urge to say anything. Angella had little patience for soppy behavior so Tamru would just have to take a chance at some point and let Angella know how he felt. For now, they eyed each other, unclear how to express the awkward attraction between them.

I loved going out as much as Angella did but any money we earned would need to be used thoughtfully. Angella and I talked late into the night about our grand ideas of buying a house in Silver Spring where we could all live, of getting newer, nicer clothes, a car for Aunty Khadi, and the family trip to Las Vegas that she wistfully talked about.

Aunty Khadi thought too many of 'our' people lived in Silver Spring and that we should look for a place up in Frederick where a smattering of new developments was popping up. I had been to Silver Spring a few times, most recently to a summer cookout, and I liked the area despite Aunty Khadi's misgivings.

We started job hunting soon after we graduated and hoped that being alumni of Catholic University would give us an edge. Angella was looking for a position as a paralegal while she resat her bar exam. She had been frustrated to fail on the first attempt, but I assured her with more confidence than I actually felt that my salary would be sufficient to sustain us for now.

During my research, my hands actually shook when I saw the number of zeros at the end of the salaries for an architect at the peak of their profession. I allowed myself to feel hopeful for the first time in a long time. I had four interviews lined up in the coming weeks and they all seemed promising.

We were not interested in joining the cliques of young people known for driving fancy cars while living in rundown apartment complexes in some of the roughest neighborhoods. We had a plan of working hard and earning enough to go back home when the war was over. When we were eventually able to afford cable, Angella and I spent countless hours following updates on the conflict at home and hoping for good news.

☾♈☽

The day I received a crumpled letter bearing the blue and white insignia in the corner my hands shook so much, I almost couldn't get it open without ripping through it. I retrieved the folded piece of paper from the envelope and immediately called the local telephone number on the back. After selecting for language and purpose of my call, I did not have to wait long before someone on the other end of the line announced that I had reached the UN High Commission for Refugees.

"Ma'am?" The voice on the other end of the phone line had sounded kind after I asked whether the sender of the letter could be contacted. I braced myself for disappointment.

"All I know is that the letter arrived among correspondence from a nearby UN peacekeeping base. A joint division was working to clear a former camp near the Guinea border, and someone called in a favor. We don't usually deliver personal mail," she added.

She waited silently as I digested the information. I told her I understood and thanked her for her help.

"Have a nice day." She sounded apologetic.

I had been in such a rush when I first read the words on the page, then hurriedly called the UNHCR office, it was not until the second and third and fourth reading when the words were no longer a blur and I had calmed myself, that it dawned on me.

Some way, somehow, Abdul's letter had found me! The glimmer of hope turned into a smoldering ember when I saw that Abdul had included a post box number in Freetown. His letter explained that the post office was not functioning, but he wanted me to have a way to find him when things returned to normal. I was beyond happy. This was something I could hold on to.

I sat in a corner of the kitchen reading the words over and over till I memorized his every word. I feared that Abdul had been captured by the rebels. I had heard stories of others who had been held hostage and used as leverage in the rebel group's negotiations with the government. I believed in my heart he was safe and would eventually be released. It was a story I told myself to cope with the months of not knowing.

The letter was dated almost six months before. Abdul did not go into detail about the situation on the ground, there was enough of that in the news. He hoped to God that the letter would find me. He had gotten lucky when a Ghanaian officer agreed to take the letter along with his outgoing mail. He was safe and well. He hoped my brother, sisters, and I were well too.

He had been moving around the country a lot, was no longer on the frontlines but instead was being drawn into the leadership ranks of the National Provision Ruling Council. They struggled for legitimacy in the eyes of the United Nations who did not look kindly on a military junta, regardless of its altruistic ideology. The rebel war was still raging, and the refugee crisis was as desperate as ever. He spent every waking moment trying to find his mother and mine, but it was as if they had vanished. He encouraged me to take heart.

As I was unable to send mail back, I wrote letters to the UNHCR and the Embassy in Guinea, cutting and pasting a new date every six months before taking them to the post office. I finally tracked down a phone number in Ghana where the West African program coordinator was based. He sounded sympathetic when I eventually reached him.

"Ma'am, we have searched all our records and we do not have any information on June Johnson or Stella Metzger having arrived at the Guéckédou or Forécariah camps in 1992 or any other year after that," he said.

In the silence that followed, I knew that the man on the other end of the line had chosen not to give voice to my worst fears, that they had been captured or worse. As deflated as I felt after the call, I knew I couldn't stop trying even when the answer was always the same. That was three years ago, and as the weeks turned into months and one season faded into the next so did the hope of seeing my mother again.

☙ ♈ ❧

The Y2K frenzy was well underway, and it had Aunty Khadi worried sick. "I don't know anything about this, oh!" she lamented, placing both hands flat on her head as a sign of her agitation.

On weekends when Aunty Khadi worked double shifts, one of us would help out by making her bed and tidying her room. She had always kept cash under her mattress, but Jennifer commented, and Angella and I agreed that the stash of envelopes stuffed with fifty and hundred dollar bills had grown considerably.

Aunty Sallay lived in a townhouse in White Oak, and she had cleared out her garage to use as extra storage. She even purchased herself a deep freezer to be able to store the beef, oxtail, and lamb she'd gradually accumulated from the Halal store in Silver Spring where she shopped. *Better safe than sorry* was the advice Aunty Khadi repeated as we helped haul boxes of canned goods, packs of soap, paper towels, gallons of oil, and lots of bottled water she had purchased into Sallay's garage.

Beneath the tension and fear of the unknown, I could feel a growing excitement. The turn of a new year and a new millennium promised a world of possibility. After five years of slogging away and trying to set our lives on a sure course, I finally felt like we were getting close. It was strange graduating at the same time as my younger siblings, but that did not matter. I was just grateful we had made it. If all went as planned, we would soon be entirely independent. Frank was eying a two bedroom further north in the Germantown suburbs.

Jennifer and her friend and sorority sister Christine Maddox were soon to be flatmates; they had secured a swanky place in Georgetown and their lease started in the spring. Angella and I had paid the deposit on the townhouse in Wheaton and our move-in date was confirmed. We invited Aunty Khadi to move in with us. The place was quite spacious with two bedrooms and a den which I would have been happy to take but Aunty Khadi declined, promising instead to visit often.

We knew she would miss having our company, but it was clear she could use some privacy. For a few weeks now I had heard her whispering and giggling on the phone to someone late in the night. The way she sounded saying hello to the caller was a dead giveaway. At other times she came home from work calling out a happy hello and wearing a broad smile on her face. As she walked about the apartment humming softly to herself, I remembered the way Miss Stella had teased me.

Abdul's battalion had been in the provinces for about three months and when the day came for his return, I had washed my hair, scrubbed my feet, and put on my best shorts and t-shirt. Miss Stella was passing by and saw me waiting patiently by the front gate so I could be the first-person Abdul saw when he came up the driveway.

"Love so bayberaybay," she teased.

Her gentle acknowledgment of our deep passion for each other was encouraging to me, and I returned her smile shyly. I had been determined to kiss Abdul when he arrived, and I knew the security post by the front gate wasn't visible from the kitchen window where Mama was likely to be on a Saturday. Aunty Khadi definitely had a glow. I learnt that some lovers like Aunty Khadi and I wear our hearts on our sleeve. She hadn't mentioned anything to us, but she had all the telltale signs of being lovestruck and I was happy.

Jennifer, Christine and a handful of others at the top of their graduating class had been offered jobs by Christine's father. The insurance industry was advantageously positioned in the millennium madness thanks to the pioneering work of Edward Yourdon. Charles Maddox was confident in the fail safes his team had implemented for their clients. Charles came from a long line of insurance magnates and his eye was currently on black-owned banking, his big play was to scoop up brilliant young talent to spearhead the venture.

There were also the apocalyptic predictions which I tried to avoid but was curious about all the same. Angella posited that if the world ended and Jesus Christ returned regardless of the outcome, she was still stuck with her bar exam. She found either prospect upsetting. When she wasn't studying, she would sit out on the balcony, zoned out with her headphones on and her portable cd player blasting Mozart's Symphony no. 5, one of her favorites.

Frank majored in English and despite Aunty Khadi's doubts about job prospects, in the age of computer technology his chosen field of Library and

Information studies was a long way from the card catalogs of Mama's Day. The way Frank saw things, the possibilities were endless.

The approach of the new year brought waves of nostalgia as I remembered the services at Cathedral Church in Freetown. As young children, we were excited to stay up late, but we always ended up falling asleep before midnight. As we got older and were able to stay awake and participated in the watch night service.

Minutes before midnight, with churches across the city packed and overflowing, a solemn quiet would descend as congregations reflected on the year's end. The names of those who had died that year were read, psalms were sung, and silent resolutions were affirmed. At five minutes to midnight, the lights in the church were switched off and the church bell was sounded with every passing minute. The booming voice of the clergy called all to prepare for the new year, then at the stroke of midnight, the bells chimed, the lights came on and the sound of loud cheers went up around the city.

There were hugs and handshakes as everyone sang, "Appy new year mi nɔ die oh! Tɛl God tɛnki for di life oh!"

We took turns with Uncle Emmanuel's family in hosting the celebrations. Star beer flowed freely, and our parents played the latest hit songs on the cassette player, followed by oldies on the record player. Pepper soup containing 'all creatures great and small' was the main item on the menu. The clear broth was delicately flavored and chock full of pig's feet and cow's feet boiled for hours until the bones were soft enough to chew down to a pulp, and gummy slices of premium tripe.

When we hosted, Mama would start breakfast just as the dark sky slowly peeled back to reveal a warm orange hue. She made big fluffy omelets with fried green tomatoes and plenty of hot coffee.

Exhausted as we all were, Papa and Uncle Imma would leave early to pay their respects to the dead. It was New Year's Day ritual that Papa kept faithfully no matter how much he drank or partied the night before. Having only dozed for a few hours at best, they would drive to the cemetery on the other side of town to 'talk' to their mothers, and grandfathers buried there.

Families went to share the good news with the departed that they had made it through another year. As per tradition water and new bottles of the deceased's favorite liquor were poured at the graveside. Some people were chatty while others stand silently; their conversations only heard by those they pour the libation for.

It took Papa a few hours to make it across town and back, but when we heard his car coming up the driveway, we knew it was time to get up and get ready for another New Year's tradition. A day at the beach!

ᎦᏤᎦ

Washington DC

It was only a few weeks before New Year's Eve and I was waiting for the bus to work when my eyes were drawn to a row of fliers plastered along the inside of the bus shelter. Pastor and First Lady Akintayo of the River of Life Ministries were inviting one and all to join them for the 'Millennium MegaFest! An all-night praise celebration to usher in the first in many years of extraordinary prosperity and bountiful abundance!' the blazing letters promised.

I resisted the pang of guilt I felt for not making plans to go to church. Angella had asked if I was interested in going to the New Year's Eve party at Kilimanjaro but I was ambivalent. I decided I might look around for a midnight service, not with the inimitable Pastor and First Lady, as entertaining as that might be, but perhaps the tiny Episcopalian Church up the road from the apartment.

My mind drifted to Abdul. I wondered where he was and what he was doing. I had discovered how to listen to BBC Africa from my computer and according to the latest news, the United Nations Mission to Sierra Leone (UNAMSIL) had been fully established and were trying to work out a peace deal between the rebels and the government. For the chance to find our mother and for Abdul's sake, I prayed that they would succeed.

The lunchtime crowd had thinned out considerably when I saw Smartass again. It was the name Angella gave to the customer who had received the sharp edge of her tongue once before. His well-tailored blazer, white button-down shirt, and black lace-up shoes appeared to be a signature and I recognized him instantly. It had been a while since the incident and I tensed up, worried what he was going to say this time. We weren't terribly busy. Angella had cut down her shifts to prepare for her exam, so she wasn't working that day, Abigail was working the coffee machines.

As he walked over, I racked my brain for a witty retort in case he said something silly again. I was in a fairly good mood and hoped it wasn't about to be ruined by his royal smugness.

Up close, I noticed for the first time that he was actually quite handsome. The angles of his cheeks were well aligned, and he had a strong chin with a faint dimple in the center. His mustache looked freshly trimmed and his teeth were bright white as he grinned.

"Hi. I'm Carl. Carl Wellesley-Coker." His voice was a deep baritone.

"Oh," I responded. I had been startled by his introduction and by the hand he was extending over the counter toward me. His gaze held mine and he smiled a softer smile this time and my heart skipped a beat.

Carl bought a black coffee and took it to a corner table where he set his laptop down and soon appeared to be lost in his work. I don't know if I caught him looking at me or the other way around, but our eyes made contact a few times.

He smiled and I blushed, busying myself at my station. When my shift was ending, he started to pack up his things. It was only once we were walking outside together that I realized he had been waiting for me. We said an awkward goodbye and I turned to walk toward the bus station. My head was a mess of unfamiliar feelings.

Realizing where I was headed, Carl jogged up to me and offered to drive me home. It wasn't just his nice clothes and manner, but my instinct told me I could trust him, so I said yes.

He entered my address into the TomTom mounted on the dashboard and we took off. On the ride home, we talked about various things from the news. Before long we were sparring about Y2K, the topic of the day. I asked for his take on the scenario where the internet crashed, and we debated that for a while. He asked how long I'd been in America, and I told him.

As we turned onto 14th Street, I casually mentioned the war, but his response didn't seem particularly interested or up to date on news of the conflict. Talk of forced amputations or entire villages burned down did not seem appropriate to the conversation so I stuck to telling him about my family and our arrival in the US and about Aunty Khadi.

"So, she is Temne?" he asked.

"Yes, she is. In my opinion, Krios don't interact enough with other tribes, so I am glad things turned out the way they have for us."

"For such a small country we have way too many tribal divisions," I complained.

Carl told me he was born in Sierra Leone as well, but his family emigrated to America when he was two years old, and his family spent a number of years in Britain when he was a teenager. They had not maintained ties to the country, and he barely understood Krio let alone spoke the language. That being said, with so many of immigrants, diplomats, and refugees–living in DC, and scattered across the states, he recognized the unique accent when he heard it.

I asked Carl what he meant that first time we met when he said I wasn't doing a good job. He explained he meant I wasn't hiding my accent very well and that I shouldn't try.

"You have a way of sounding your 'r's. It's a dead giveaway!" He chuckled. "It took me a moment to be sure with you, but then I overheard you and firecracker talking and I recognized the Krio words."

Carl said he loved to hear me speak because my accent sounded musical, and when I gesticulated with my hands, I reminded him of a maestro. I almost gasped out loud when Carl's hand brushed against mine as he changed gears. It happened again when he reached into the glove compartment for a stick of gum, which he almost always had in his mouth.

We saw each other almost every day after that. We talked about Sierra Leone, and I shared what I knew of the politics, corruption, and the "diamond resource curse" that Papa had often talked about. Carl gazed intently at me, taking in my every word.

"Fascinating!" he would interject, with a smile that took my breath away.

I had introduced Carl to Angella soon after our first drive together and I had been seeing him for about four weeks before he met Aunty Khadi when he stopped by briefly a few days before Christmas day to bring me a gift. The leather-bound diary was the most beautiful item of its kind I had ever owned, I thought, as I had brushed my thumb over the luxurious covers. I felt embarrassed as I apologized for not getting him anything. He graciously reassured me there was nothing to be sorry about.

After Carl left, I was surprised that Aunty Khadi did not press for more information about him. Angella still thought he was a smart ass and out of my league and told me as such. This made me laugh. I had not expected Angella to react any differently as she was always overly protective. I tried to convince her she would change her mind once she got to know him, but she maintained her usual skepticism. I wasn't sure if Carl even thought we were dating and didn't know how to broach the subject with him. Angella had no advice to give.

"Just ask him what his intentions are," she said back-handedly.

But every time I meant to ask him; I lost my nerve.

Carl and I had never been out together with other people, and besides a peck on the cheek when he dropped me off at home, we hadn't had a proper kiss. Angella thought he was probably too embarrassed to let his mother, or his friends know he was dating a refugee from a housing project.

"But he doesn't really have friends!" I retorted.

Carl was not a big sports fan, but he loved jazz and promised to take me to a live concert if I was interested. He could not understand what we found appealing about nightclubs but was willing to give it a go sometime. He rarely talked about anything outside of his work. Carl was a financial analyst and an executive vice-president at the Wells Fargo corporate office down the street from the Starbucks where we first met.

"Be careful. Maybe he is a serial killer or some psycho," Angella warned. "I don't like Smartass and I don't trust him either," she said, rolling her eyes.

The rides home with Carl had become an almost daily occurrence. Sometimes Angella rode with us, but she had changed her shifts to better fit her study schedule, so I saw less of her with each passing week. A few days before New Year's Eve, as Angella and I worked our last shift for the year, I told her Carl had said he had a surprise for me.

"Well, it's not much of a surprise if he's already told you about it," she said sardonically. She had a point, and I couldn't help smiling. I asked Angella if she would come along with us after work.

"You love birds go ahead," she said, retreating to the back to empty the trash before I could respond or stop her. In a way I was looking forward to being alone with Carl, so I let her go. Carl was right on time and waiting in the parking lot when I went outside. I hopped into the front seat curious about what he had in store.

"Today, my dear Allison, I am going to give you a tour of the other side," he declared with a grand wave of his hand.

My heart raced with excitement, and I had the familiar feeling of butterflies in my stomach. Abdul was the only other man that had made me feel this way and as I thought about him, fighting a distant war in the bush somewhere, I felt wistful.

Carl gunned the engines of his Porsche and headed down Georgia Ave, then across Military Road into the northwest neighborhood. We drove through a winter wonderland, and I felt like a little girl staring eagerly at the lawn ornaments on either side of the street. Bright lights sparkled through curtain windows, and I spotted adorned Christmas trees towering up to ceilings within.

As Carl pointed out the most beautiful mansions, he spoke of the kind of home he wanted for his family one day. As Carl and I daydreamed together, thoughts of the housing projects, Aunty Khadi, and Abdul faded into the distance, and I imagined all the possibilities that lay ahead.

Chapter 7
Carl

The pyrotechnic display outside is so loud I can hardly hear my own voice. We are squeezed in tightly on the balcony of the penthouse suite at the Willard InterContinental, celebrating the coming of a new millennium. The venue offers a spectacular view of the surrounding landmarks and I drink it all in with gusto.

Angella is staying home tonight; Jennifer went to a party with Christine. Aunty Khadi somehow convinced Frank to drive her to watch night service at a nearby church because her mosque is too far from home and she is worried that if things go crazy at midnight, being an hour away from home is not a good idea.

It's the first time Carl and I are out together with friends, and he introduces me simply as Allison. I don't know what to make of the fact that he hasn't announced our relationship status. I eventually decide that it fits his conservative style.

"Are you excited?" Carl leans a little closer to ask the question. His eyes dance with mischief.

"Yes!" I yell back. I am trying to decide whether there is something profound I should say in a moment like this or just quietly take it all in. As we walked into the grand foyer earlier, I had felt bad for not splurging on a more expensive dress. I hoped no one would notice that my little black dress was off Macy's discount rack.

The other women attending the Inner Black Caucus affairs all seemed so sophisticated and polished. Their gowns looked expensive. Fancy jewelry glinted at their necklines and dangled from earlobes. I unconsciously touch my hair; quite sure it does not hold up to the women's perfect coiffures.

Ironically, I feel like I'm in one of the Daniel Steele novels that Jennifer loved to read and that I detested so much. A cliché tale of the rich and handsome prince taking in the poor but beautiful girl and showing her off to his friends. She feels small and inadequate, he reassures her that the opulence around them pales in comparison to their love, and so on and so forth. A scoff escaped my lips before I could catch it and I chuckled at my own humor.

"Care to share?" Carl inquires.

"I am not sure I fit in here," I stammer.

His expression is understanding, "But you will soon enough, Allison." He pulls me close and spins me around, so my back leans against his chest.

I feel silly for worrying about fitting in when I should just enjoy the night ahead. I barely ate anything during the day so I would fit into the clingy, silk dress, but I am ravenous now.

Carl had joked that there was always enough food to feed an army and I was impressed with the lavish menu. It promised five courses and an endless selection of desserts by a world-class pastry chef. I am not keen on champagne but when it was time for toasts, I agreed to try a glass. As Carl and I snuggle, I feel warm and happy and slightly dizzy. Looking out into the distance and waiting for the countdown to midnight, I think about how we have gotten here.

The past weeks were a whirlwind. I did most of the preparation for our move since Angella was busy studying. We now had our belongings mostly boxed up and ready to go. It took longer than usual to process our application because we had so little banking history. The landlord needed proof of at least three months of income and demanded a hefty deposit.

Although the delay made me restless, I didn't really mind staying with Aunty Khadi a little longer, and neither did she. She had been like a mother to us, and I would miss her terribly. I had fought back tears as I thought of Mama. On a night like this, she would have insisted we all be in church together. I thought of Papa. He wanted me to look after my younger siblings and I had done my best.

Now here I am, uncertain of what is to come. Here I am sipping champagne among some of the most influential people in the District, surrounded by elegance, and in the arms of a man with whom I am falling head over heels in love.

"Nine! Eight! Seven!—" Carl joins in the countdown as it grows louder. I join in as well, embracing the moment. If the world comes to an end, at least I will be with Carl.

He turns me around to face him and his mouth is moving. I struggle to make out his words, it is impossible to hear over the din of a clock's bell striking twelve, the blaring horns from cars below, and the fireworks lighting up the sky above the National Mall. I signal my inability to hear Carl by pointing to my ears and shaking with laughter and euphoria. He is grinning when he leans in close to my ear and whispers, "Allison Johnson, will you marry me?"

♋♈♋

Jake and Sarah's wedding was absolutely beautiful. The grass on the grounds of the Linganore Winery hidden far up in Mount Airy was lush and green. The sky was a pretty baby blue and the sun shone just brightly enough behind tendrils of fluffy white clouds, that it wasn't blinding.

Sarah was Carl's colleague at the bank and had become a friend to us both. Her bridesmaids were decked out in crimson, contrasting the rusty gold tones on the groom's side. Satin ribbons adorned the sides of white lawn chairs and magnificent floral arrangements stood tall on either side of the thick, white aisle runner that led to a wooden, lattice archway draped with garden roses, gladiolus, and hydrangeas.

I artfully dodged the champagne and chardonnay offered by the white-gloved waiters, and instead sipped daintily from a glass of lemonade. If Carl noticed, he did not comment. From across the room, his gaze instead was trained on Jamal Boykins, the only other black man on their team, who at that moment had my ear full of chatter and had done for much of the afternoon.

Jamal was a new arrival and not yet part of our circle of friends from Carl's firm. Jamal had never spoken to me at any of the bank's social events we attended together so I was surprised when he slipped into the empty seat beside me during the ceremony. Carl reached across me to offer his hand to Jamal, and I eased back to make room but was too late. Jamal's wrist brushed against my breast and Carl did not fail to notice. It was a slight almost imperceptible response, but I sensed it in the way he held Jamal's handshake just a moment too long, his brow slightly furrowed.

We learned from Jamal that his wife was home with a twisted ankle, which explained why he had gravitated to our side. During the ceremony, Jamal cracked jokes about Sarah's mother-in-law and a relative of the bridegroom who wore a morning coat, a top hat, and gold-tipped patent shoes. I smiled politely. I hadn't realized Jamal had such a sense of humor. All I could recall about him was what Carl mentioned about his less than superior education.

Jamal was a Howard University graduate and even though corporate preferred Ivy league stock for his position, he checked the other boxes including being a candidate of color. It was good for their image. From what Jamal was now saying, he felt the focus on him as a diversity hire detracted from his qualification and the fact that he was good at his job.

As I sipped my lemonade and listened, I found myself agreeing with Jamal's sentiment. I thought he had blended in well with his team and they probably saw things differently, but I didn't think he was expecting a response, so I nodded.

I wasn't surprised that Carl had not chosen to mentor Jamal. He was selective about the type of black folk with which he wanted to be associated. He was proud of his posh English accent which was still strong even after so many years living in the States. He continued buying his suits from London and showed disdain toward the fraternity culture which Jamal seemed proud of. Turning my attention back to my companion, I realized he was asking me a question.

"Allison, you look splendid in that outfit. It's African?" Jamal inquired curiously. "Do you mind if I take a picture? My wife would love the color."

I stepped forward, graciously obliging him. I knew the outfit I was wearing complimented my figure. The waxed cotton fabric was navy blue, with yellow and white silk embroidering at the bodice and sleeves, which hung off my shoulders and tastefully revealed my collar bones. I never wore necklaces but held my hair up so the silver earrings that dropped just past my jawline, picked up the accents of the embroidery.

Carl had walked over to join us just as Jamal struck up a conversation about Sierra Leonean culture. I did my best to describe the similarities and differences to other cultures in broad terms. Where the ceremony we had just witnessed had been brief, I tried to describe a typical Sierra Leone wedding.

"No way! So, three or four hundred guests would be normal?" Jamal was incredulous.

"Invited and-uninvited," I smiled; using air quotes on the last part, which I knew Carl couldn't stand. Ignoring Carl's snort, I explained that the crowds did tend to be large, and the ceremony often started ridiculously late, but in the end, the food, dancing, and carnival style celebration were well worth it. We both chuckled.

The reception was about to start, and as we made our way from the cocktail area over to the barn, I could sense the tension from Carl. Lately, his mood turned sour whenever we were out, and I was having fun. As the toasts continued, Carl downed one glass of wine after another. The other people at our table did not seem to notice, but I saw that Jamal was growing uncomfortable. Out of the corner of my eye, I caught him glancing nervously toward Carl and then back at me. I kept my attention straight ahead, trying to listen to the speeches and laugh at the jokes.

When the band struck up the music for the bride and groom's first dance, Carl leaned close to my ear.

"Time to go home, Cinderella!" he smirked.

The nicknames had begun soon after we were married. We had moved into a modest townhouse just off River Road and I enjoyed keeping it spotless. I spent hours scrubbing the shower stalls and the stove tops; tasks which were surprisingly relaxing to me. I often got lost in my thoughts, secretly reminiscing about Saturdays at King's Lodge. It was the one day on which Mama insisted we help with household chores so that Ms. Stella and Ms. Rosetta could focus on the extensive preparation that went into the Saturday lunch and Sunday dinner.

Mama had also emphasized that a clean and well-kept home was a source of pride for any Krio wife worth her salt. Guests could show up at any time and one must always be ready to host them. There was hardly ever a speck of dust to be seen at King's Lodge and even during the harmattan season, Mama had the expensive furniture draped with pretty crochet blankets to minimize the dust that settled on them when she left the windows open.

Carl had called me everything from porky to Cinderella, drama queen, Shaniqua, and dreamer. I had been shocked by "dreamer", seeing as we had spent so much time in the early days, dreaming together about the future. It took everything in me to keep myself from screaming at him to stop calling me names.

I was too scared to tell anyone, not even Angella, about Carl's bullying. I worried she would deride me for letting it happen or chastise me for not fighting back. Whenever I felt lonely or was smarting from his tongue lashings, I would turn on my music and lose myself in the soothing sounds of India Arie or Beverly Knight.

This was the first time he had called me a name in public and given the way he had been acting so far, I braced myself in case there was more to come. I slowly reached for my handbag and started to slide my chair back, but Carl thought I wasn't moving quickly enough, so he grabbed my arm and dragged me to my feet.

Jamal stood up in a flash, and hesitated, unsure how to respond. Carl ignored him and nearly knocked over my chair as he quickly ushered me away without saying goodnight to our hosts. I turned in time to see Jamal still standing at the table looking stunned. My eyes met his briefly and I gave a weak smile to let him know I would be okay, just before Carl yanked my wrist and we made our exit.

A wave of nausea rose in me, and I tried desperately to control it. By the time we reached the car and drove away, I was shivering. Carl was drunk, and as we sped down the winding roads away from the bright lights of the barn at the winery, I felt sick with terror. I hadn't told him I was pregnant.

♋

"Mrs. Wellesley-Coker, sorry to keep you waiting," the woman in a white coat beckoned to us from the doorway. Her auburn hair was a similar shade to her kneel-length pencil skirt and sensible shoes.

Lisa Wong was a graduate from George Washington University, and much sought after not least of all because of her reputation as an excellent obstetrician. She was Carl's top choice of all the doctors we vetted, and I felt lucky to have her. She had a kind manner that always put me at ease.

I was in the final months of my pregnancy, and lately, the little one's elbows and knees poked me nonstop. Carl had only missed one of our appointments. He listened keenly to every word the doctor said and made a note of all her instructions as we prepared for the big day.

We exchanged pleasantries, but I could feel Dr. Wong's unease as soon as we sat down opposite her. I did not expect her question.

"So Allison, you said this was your first pregnancy, correct?"

"Correct," I responded promptly. "Yes, of course." My response was a little less confident the second time.

Carl was already sitting up in his chair and I could feel the blood pounding in my ears. I wasn't sure what she was going to say, but her serious expression told me it was likely not good news.

"You have a significant amount of scarring in your vaginal and pelvic area that could make it impossible or at the very least, dangerous, to have a natural birth." She maintained eye contact with me as she spoke. Dr. Wong let her words sink in for a moment, then quickly followed with the reassurance that a cesarean section would be just as safe and the risk from complications was low.

"I didn't mention my findings earlier because I expected the tissue would loosen up as your pregnancy progressed. Sometimes this issue resolves itself but, in your case, unfortunately it hasn't."

"May I ask, were you circumcised as a young girl?" She sounded compassionate.

I shook my head vigorously, looking over at Carl as he had sat up in his chair. He looked alarmed and searched my face for answers. I stared dumbly back at Dr. Wong and waited for her to continue.

"We have to take the necessary precaution due to your age, and other factors. We don't want to add to the risk," she paused.

I nodded my understanding and avoided Carl's eyes which I could feel on me.

"So, in that case," she said, sounding more relaxed, "let's get you scheduled for your delivery!"

"I'll see you at the front desk," she said with a smile, as we rose to leave.

My hands trembled as I struggled to ease out of the paper gown and back into my clothes. Carl was quiet but I could sense he was boiling with rage. I had some explaining to do when we got home. To calm down, I practiced the breathing techniques I had learned from birthing videos. I could do nothing for the nub of pain in my chest that felt like the scar from an old wound. The doctor's words had just turned my world upside down.

I tried to run from my past, but it had caught up with me and would deny me the joy of bringing my child into the world naturally. I was left with no choice now. Carl needed to know the truth. I could feel a thin film of sweat forming on my upper lip.

Blinking back the tears that stung my eyes, I picked up my purse and followed Carl out into the waiting room.

"Allison, I can't believe you lied to me." There was pain mixed with confusion in Carl's voice.

Carl was silent for most of the drive. He changed gear in quick succession and the Porsche sped up. I could see signs for the Heritage Farm Neighborhood Park off Falls Road. We were almost home. We planned to buy a second car soon since the sports car wouldn't fit a car sea. I was looking forward to fewer trips at breakneck speed as Carl channeled his anger onto the road. His accusation had stung, but I was feeling nauseous and preferred to wait until we got home to talk.

We bought a new home one month prior, in preparation for the newest member of our family. A colleague at Carl's bank had handled the purchase and I had been pleasantly surprised when she showed me the size of loan for which we had been approved. The house at 8755 Crowne Point Way was grand by any measure. It had been custom-built and was being sold by the owner, a widower who was moving to Florida and was motivated to sell quickly.

"Maria, this is amazing!" I said as she walked me through all the details of my mortgage agreement.

She explained that she had been able to take advantage of federal incentives to encourage lending by minorities in our income bracket.

"Of course, the fact that Carl works for the bank was helpful," she had said with a wink. "His name can't appear in any of the documents though," she cautioned. "Just to avoid unnecessary scrutiny."

Our search for the perfect home had felt endless. With my pregnancy, it had gotten harder to make it to one showing after the other. When we first walked into the house we would eventually buy, it reminded me of walking through the doors of King's Lodge. It was as if Papa had led me here. The two-story building had a spacious foyer graced with a wainscot staircase, a large formal dining room, and five enormous bedrooms. It was surrounded by a meticulously landscaped yard.

As I gazed at the tray ceiling in the master bedroom, I couldn't help but wish it had a skylight so I could stare at the stars overhead. The room contained large walk-in closets, a soaking tub, separate vanities, and a shower booth with a marble bench.

Wandering into the dining room I felt nostalgic and pictured Mama bustling from room to room, pulling at her fine lace tablecloths and straightening the polished silverware. Mama was a gracious and warm host, and I looked forward to being the same.

Guests had always gushed over the centerpiece she displayed on the solid oak dining table in the center of the room. The previous owner had kept the stainless-steel appliances shiny and new. I smiled at the thought of Ms. Stella vying for her spot in the enormous space offered by the granite counters and massive island in the kitchen. There were lovely features at every turn, and I could tell the builders had paid attention to the tiniest details.

Many of the previous showings had been unimpressive. Although Carl discouraged me from looking at the houses through a professional lens, it was hard to resist the urge. I argued that it didn't seem fair that he would use his banking skills to get us the financing we needed, yet I wasn't allowed to use my architectural expertise to make sure the investment was sound.

When I made a case for the added aesthetic value of the floor-to-ceiling windows in the morning room and the sports bar where he could hang out and watch soccer, he finally acquiesced, and we put in an offer. Jennifer had let out a low whistle when I gave the address. She was just starting out with the Maddox Group and offered to find us the best value home insurance available. I was happy to sign on as one of her first accounts.

I loved coming home to Crowne Pointe Way but today a storm was brewing, and I feared things would go as badly if not worse than the night after Jake and Sarah's wedding reception.

I understood Carl's frustration. He had never been interested in exploring my body. He preferred to make love in the dark, his hands fumbling around and using the moist area between my legs to guide his penetration. I had learned to apply Vaseline, to soothe the searing pain I would feel afterward. Satiated, Carl would roll off me as quickly as he had climbed on.

Our bodies were never locked together long, and I was too shy to ask him to touch me in the ways that I yearned for. To feel aroused, I would think about Abdul and imagine his hands moving over my body. Since these were just thoughts, I convinced myself that it wasn't cheating. The longing was followed by an aching in my heart and finally poignancy.

When I became pregnant, Carl stopped reaching for me altogether, and at first, I was touched that he was being considerate. My hormones were in overdrive, but even after the doctor said sex was safe and encouraged it, caressing his thighs or brushing my breasts against him did not arouse him. Carl avoided any sexual advances so I left him alone, instead taking brisk walks around the park or putting up decals on the walls of the nursery to release my pent up energy.

ॐ♈ॐ

As Carl clicked the garage remote and the door swooshed open, I felt my tension ease. Now that we were safely home, I was ready to talk. I would have to start from the beginning. From the day we got into the canoe headed for Kychom. It felt like a lifetime had passed since then, but Carl deserved to hear the truth. Maybe this was a chance to heal old wounds for good.

Carl slammed the door, and I watched him retreat through the mud room and into the house. I felt a solid kick against the walls of my belly, and I had to stop and catch my breath.

"I know little one, the time is coming," I said softly, stroking my belly.

After I pulled myself out of the bucket seat on the passenger side, I set my feet on the ground and felt inside my pocket for the piece of paper. I had carried the note around with me lately. I would pull out the scribbled quote from Warsan Shire from time to time, and read it slowly, carefully, taking in the weight of each word. "No one puts their children in a boat unless the water is safer than land."

Years ago, when we were in danger, Mama put us on the boat to save our lives and she may have lost hers. The boat had carried us to land, and I had been running ever since. I owed it to Carl and to myself, to stop running. I wanted desperately to feel new and whole. The birth of our child would be my chance at that. I heaved my body out of the car and went into the house.

Carl had already poured himself a shot of single malt and was nursing a near-empty glass when I walked in.

"I didn't know Krio women got cut," he said, looking confused.

"No, I didn't get cut, Carl," I replied.

"Then what the hell happened to you?" he yelled.

150

I told Carl that I was raped by rebels outside the refugee camp in Guéckédou. He went quiet. I took his cue and started from the beginning. I described the awful memory of being overpowered as one after the other, bloodshot eyes leered at me. The heavy stench of sweat and djamba flooding my nostrils as men in filthy combat gear crushed and squeezed my nipples and penetrated me and ignoring my screams of pain.

I told him I could hear Angella screaming and hurling insults. The nightmare seemed to go on forever, then suddenly a knife flashed, and I felt a sticky stream running down my legs before everything went black.

Carl and I were both in tears as I spoke. I told him I had been in and out of consciousness for days, vaguely remembered the pain of urinating but little else. I recalled the doctors at the camp telling me I was lucky to still have my bowel and bladder function. Some of the women and girls they treated had been assaulted using AK-47s and other filthy implements and were less fortunate.

We talked late into the night. Carl agreed that it made sense for my old scars to have been mistaken by Dr. Wong as genital mutilation and he showed genuine concern. When I was done, I poured myself a shot of brandy, ignoring his questioning look as I took a sip. Mama had occasionally imbibed her favorite sherry when she was pregnant with Frank, and he seemed to have turned out fine. There was no way I could make it through the night with my nerves so badly shot.

Carl offered to set me up with an acquaintance who specialized in post-traumatic counseling, and I promised to consider it. It had never occurred to me to seek help before, but it was reckless of me to keep the emotions buried. I didn't need to continue pushing the assault down into the recesses of my mind or block out my gruesome past in the hopes of finally burying it.

♋︎♈︎♋︎

The Jetta was making strange sounds and wouldn't accelerate properly. It hadn't died on me yet, so I kept going.

The firm where I worked had a slew of small contracts which my boss Lani felt she wanted to shift over to me until she could trust me with the bigger jobs, with greater exposure. So, despite my late stage of pregnancy, my inbox filled up as quickly as I emptied it. Monique Robinson was the only other black woman in the office and though she looked over at me sympathetically as I struggled to adjust my stool, she said nothing.

Lately, I half-sat, half crouched over my drawings, swinging from my easel to my desk and back again. As the swelling in my feet and ankles worsened, I ditched my soft-soled moccasins for comfortable old slip-ons whenever I was at my desk. The slip-ons were a gift from Aunty Khadi. Our first winter with her, she had bubbled over with excitement one day when she returned home, arms full of boxes. Each one neatly gift wrapped in shiny aluminum gift paper.

"Open them, open them," she had squealed delightedly.

I could tell everyone was trying to hide their disappointment when they saw the house slippers. Aunty Khadi looked crestfallen, so I put my slippers on, making a show of them and parading up and down as if they were the best thing in the world. The memory made me smile, and the slippers were still going strong.

I turned a corner and the car whined. I wasn't ready to look for a new one just yet. Carl had suggested a mini van, but I was not interested.

"I don't want the soccer mom look," I protested.

Almost all the young families that lived in our cul-de-sac owned a mini van. They also happened to be mostly white and nearly all the women were stay-at-home moms. Carl didn't seem bothered by the fact that we were the only black family in the neighborhood and stood out like sore thumbs.

I had smiled nervously when a small welcoming party showed up at our door after we moved, oohing and aahing when they saw I was expecting. The last thing I wanted was a baby shower. I found the idea unfamiliar. In our culture, pregnancy was typically not discussed with strangers until a woman was showing, and even then, it was presumptuous to throw a party before the delivery.

Aunty Khadi warned me not to tell all and sundry that I was expecting. "Especially not her," she stressed, referring to Liz, Carl's mother. Aunty Khadi called her a wicked woman and was still upset that she hadn't shown up for our registry wedding at the Montgomery County Courthouse, choosing instead to invite us to dinner at the Bethesda Country Club along with a handful of her friends and Carl's godfather Matthew Steele, a sitting judge and close friend to Carl's late father.

Grateful that the car was behaving for the time, I maneuvered along winding roads, enjoying the vast landscape and trying to shake off whatever was causing my restless mood. I enjoyed my excursions. Driving through neighborhoods where the well-kept gardens reminded me of King's Lodge, I took guesses at who might live in the houses I passed along the way.

I wondered curiously where the owner might have discovered the passion for gardening or whether they hired a contractor. There was a growing number of Latino-owned landscaping businesses in the area. I lost track of time wondering to myself what it must be like to build my own business from scratch.

My daydreaming was interrupted when a sound like a thunder crack startled me. Since sharing my experience at Guéckédou with Carl, I felt restless and on edge. Angella, Jennifer, Frank and I had heard gunshots often enough and the sound was unmistakable. The occasional shots fired near the housing projects had been frightening, but in the years since we moved out, loud bangs were often ignored and our response to the sound of a backfiring car exhaust was usually a mere shrug. So, I chalked off the sound to just kids playing with firecrackers and kept going.

The sun was setting, and the clouds formed a breathtaking purple and orange swath ahead of me. The Jetta was starting to struggle again so I turned toward home, dreading another night of Carl's moodiness and silence.

My keys landed with a clatter as I dropped them onto the island in the kitchen. Carl rose from the bar stool where he had been sitting, at the end of the counter. His eyes were wide and frightful.

"Where have you been?" he snarled.

My mood had not improved, thanks to the car acting up. "I was just looking around the neighborhood." I shrugged casually. At least he was talking to me.

"Well, when you get your head out of the sky," he pointed angrily upward, "then maybe you will pay attention to what's around you. You may be accustomed to ghettos and violence, but you had better not put my child in harm's way," he warned.

I was stunned by the accusation. Ever since I found out that I was pregnant, I had been diligent and had done everything the doctor recommended.

Carl strode angrily over to the family room, and I instinctively followed. He grabbed the tv remote, turning it on and cranking the volume up to a deafening level. The news anchor's words were being instantly captioned in the scrolling banner at the bottom of the screen.

"Reports from Montgomery County police are now confirming that the shooting that took place this evening at the corner of Falls Road in Potomac, is linked to what the department is calling the D. C sniper attacks. Investigators determined that bullets from several of the first seven shootings were fired from the same weapon—a high-powered.c223-caliber rifle."

As I stared at the scenes on the screen, it dawned on me that I had been in that same vicinity around the time of the shooting.

"Allison, answer me! What were you thinking?" Carl's voice rose above the ringing in my ears, as I slowly realised he had been demanding a response. I debated whether to tell him and was turning toward him when a sharp sting on my cheek knocked me off balance. The slap rocked me backward and I sank down into the couch behind me.

The sounds around me seemed to fade into a distant tunnel as a haze of confusion clouded my mind momentarily. Looking as shocked as I felt, Carl rushed toward me. As he bent forward to pick me up off the couch, profusely apologizing, his eyes wet with tears, I noticed that the tips of his black lace-up shoes were wet. My water broke.

☾♈☾

I drove around the I495 inner loop for the third time, and the Baby Mozart was just ending when I realized that Natasha and Caleb had finally fallen asleep. My mind swirled with doubt and anxiety, but I had held back tears of frustration for as long as I could hear the giggling and babbling from the back seat.

I noticed that the red dots of brake lights ahead of me were beginning to dwindle and checked the clock on the dash. It was almost 11 pm. I checked on the kids through the rearview mirror before I popped in a Yolanda Adams cd, fading the speakers forward and inching up the volume just enough for me to catch the words of the songs. I was thankful that my car, an Acura MDX, had great sound controls so I could listen to music in my bubble and clear my head, without waking the kids.

I had not known Carl to have a wandering eye so the thought of an affair being the cause of his distant and cold behavior over the past eight months was far from my mind. He was close with his assistant Melissa, but he seemed to draw satisfaction rather than erotic interest from her reverence of him.

Searching his desk or car for clues was out of the question. If there was something going on with Melissa or anyone else, I bargained with myself that it would hurt less if I found out by accident rather than seeking the truth directly.

We weren't having serious money problems, even with Carl's taste for very expensive things. I had just gotten a raise after my firm made the winning bid on a contract to remodel the Beall-Dawson House in Rockville. The owner of the firm handpicked me to take lead on the project. He was surprised, then amused when I challenged him on the imbalance of my salary compared to a less experienced colleague who happened to be male.

He fully agreed with the argument and applauded my spunk. I think he realized it wasn't just about the money for me. I was excited about the work and although I had not planned to turn our meeting into a negotiation, it was only fair given the responsibility being placed in my hands.

I was part of the assessment team that visited the two-and-a-half-story federal house and estate before we tendered a bid. The building was constructed in 1815, with gothic framing in some areas and a crumbling Flemish brick façade. I had returned three or four times after my first visit just to look around, and I was eager to start work. I would need to bring in a plumbing contractor, but the restoration of everything else including the original brick dairy house, we would handle ourselves.

So, if Carl and I did not have money trouble and he wasn't having an affair, why did I feel an emotional draught? After all, we had been in this place for some time now. It wasn't new. Most days, he barely grunted a greeting when he walked in the door. He would head straight for his office, politely declining dinner. He stayed at his computer for hours, only emerging for a drink or to grab a handful of nuts from the kitchen.

After Natasha and Caleb were in bed and the house was still, I would lay in bed and listen for his footfalls on the carpeted stairs leading up to our bedroom. I chased sleep, watching the numbers on the digital clock by my bedside. He would shower for exactly five minutes. He came to bed naked, turned on his side, and promptly went to asleep.

Things had not been this way right after Natasha was born. We had grown close then. He came home earlier, was around more often; eager to hold her and feed her. A grandchild did little to lessen Liz's aloofness and Carl hadn't seemed phased by that. With Caleb, I had known when my time was near. I could feel his weight pressing on my bladder and my ankles were swollen and hurt, as they were when I carried his sister. My belly had been so big that my navel pointed out like a third nipple through my shift dress.

"Dis na boy pikin!" Aunty Khadi had exclaimed with a wisdom passed down through generations, determining that a baby carried high under the rib cage must be a boy. Her prediction had been correct.

"I suppose they think he had no business marrying a poor refugee girl," Aunty Khadi scoffed. She believed even more firmly than I would have expressed, that my Krio lineage and career choice of architecture should count for something. But Elizabeth Wellesley-Coker, who had emigrated to the United States in the early sixties, fully embraced her new American identity.

She wanted nothing more than for Carl to be part of the African American upper class and all her carefully executed decisions about his life led him toward that goal. A private school education, Cambridge University and then the London School of Economics, the Wall Street internship, and Morehouse MBA were all part of the plan.

Liz pushed her only son hard. His natural aptitude for numbers made his success seem simple. When he became the youngest vice president at his bank, he scored an interview with Forbes Magazine. Such were the heights Carl was expected to ascend and Liz would make certain he got there. She did not consider the way he spent money on luxury goods and expensive cars to be reckless. When he went to her for money to settle gambling debts, she responded with only a half-hearted rebuke, and always indulged him.

After Caleb was born, Liz in her own way seemed to be somewhat appeased. She now had the heir she hoped to groom in the same way she groomed Carl to continue the family legacy, apparently unbothered that he was born to the 'poor refugee girl' she ignored half the time.

I was torn by the desire to pack up and leave or confront Carl. The silence was killing me. Papa and Mama talked about everything. I remember hearing their voices on the verandah as they shared the details of their day. Other times, the hushed tones coming from behind the closed door of Papa's office or their bedroom, signaled their concern about the politics of the day and Mama's fear for Papa's safety. I had tried to have a heart-to-heart with Carl, had tried to talk to him about challenges at work, the discrimination I often had to ignore just to get through my day. He never seemed interested.

"You get too emotional, Allison," he said dryly when I told him about the rude manner in which our nanny had addressed me when I needed to make a deadline at work and asked her to stay a couple of hours later. My musical accent now seemed to irritate him.

"You sound ghetto," he had remarked once after he overheard Angella and I laughing and mimicking the way black Americans say 'girrrlll'. So, I adjusted my speech whenever I spoke with him. I kept a level tone and chose my words carefully. Angella's response to Carl had been to roll her eyes and change the subject.

Six years later, she didn't have to say she told me so, she could see how badly I was hurting. Angella was a rising star at her firm. She worked long hours and still made time for pro bono work with the legal defense fund. We saw each other as often as possible, and she slept over whenever Carl was out of town.

We reminisced for hours, salivating over the memory of Mama's jollof rice on Sundays or laughing about the time Ms. Stella teased me mercilessly when she realized I was sweet on Abdul. We recalled Mama's famous dinner parties and holiday picnics at the beach when Papa and uncle Emmanuel would swim out farther than any of us dared, their heads bobbing against the distant horizon.

Jennifer and I chatted on the phone sometimes. She was off chasing her dreams, and I was proud of her. She and Christine traveled a fair bit for work, so I treasured the times we could catch up. I did not want to burden her with my troubles, so I never talked about my marriage. Instead, I talked about Natasha and Caleb, and how quickly they were growing.

On nights like this, as the long drive lulled the children to sleep and I tried to clear my head, I listened to love songs, but they left me feeling empty and yearning for Abdul. Switching to gospel music helped. Carl wasn't religious and we never went to church besides on special occasions. I did not continue my mother's tradition of Saturday morning prayers. On Sunday mornings, Carl liked for us to take long walks along the C&O canal or George Washington Parkway, then brunch at a nice restaurant. It felt strange at first, but I got used to it.

I told my colleagues and Lani my boss just enough about my life outside the firm that I wasn't invisible. My weekend outings at least gave me something to talk about in the lunchroom on Monday mornings.

In the time since the war ended and peace was won, I had become an American citizen. Over the years I tried to blend in and 'belong' the way Carl did, but my heart was back home. I was able to find only one online newspaper that reported on the Truth and Reconciliation Commission. The terrible spelling and grammar irked me but I was grateful for news. The rest of the world seemed to have moved on from the devastation left in the wake of the war, but I could not.

Snapping back to present, I caught sight of the red and blue flashing lights in the rearview mirror. I slowed down and switched to the inside lane to let the squad car pass, but it pulled up behind me, so I switched lanes again and pulled over on the right shoulder. As I put the car in park, the police officer approached, and I heard Caleb whimper but saw with relief that he was still asleep.

"Ma'am, I need your license and registration please," the officer said after I had opened my window. I glanced at her and smiled weakly as I reached over to the passenger side. My heart almost stopped. I had been so distracted by my thoughts I left my purse at home.

I mumbled an explanation to the officer with my head still spinning and salt from the dried tears still on my cheeks. Jail was the last thing I needed to deal with in that moment. Whether it was because of my explanation or the sight of the infants in the back seat, I was let off with a fix-it ticket, which I decided that Carl need not know about.

☙ϒ❧

Potomac, Maryland

"It happened again last night, didn't it?" Carl's apprehensive tone was real. "I think you should start seeing Dr. Benson again." It wasn't a question.

"But I don't have time and besides, it costs so mu—" His hand was up against my lips before I could continue. The sessions cost three hundred dollars an hour, but they were supposed to help with my nightmares and insomnia.

"OK, I'll call him later today."

Carl already had the phone in his hand and was dialing. As I got dressed, I heard him repeat the appointment time. I was scheduled for five thirty which meant the nanny would have to get Natasha and Caleb ready for bed unless Carl came home early.

"Are you angry with me?" My furrowed brow must have prompted Carl's question.

"No. No, I was just thinking I might need to reschedule Pilates this week," I lied.

"Well, I think you look great my love." He kissed me on the cheek and left.

Mika, our nanny, had driven Natasha to kindergarten that morning and was taking Caleb to daycare for a few hours. I drifted around the kitchen, slowly gathering my folders and laptop. I had mixed feelings about seeing Dr. Benson. I was haunted by my memory, and I felt I might never be free of it; the smell and the sounds of that terrible night seemed burned into my consciousness forever.

Dr. Benson had prescribed a low dose antidepressant which also helped me sleep, but I hadn't taken the pills for some time because they clouded my mind and I struggled enough to stay present as it was. I needed my mind clear, for the children and for my job. That last brought me out of my reverie. Lani was considerate but she would not appreciate me showing up late for our annual budget review. With a deep sigh, I pick up my car keys and head to the door.

I thought I would take a walk during my lunch break. The leaves on the trees were turning red and yellow and the crisp air hinted at cooler days ahead. Pulling my favorite stole snuggly around my shoulders, I was glad I had grabbed it on the way out that morning.

A few years ago, I had discovered a cute little thrift shop in Chevy Chase and was thrilled with the high-end items on offer. I certainly did not need to buy second-hand clothes, but the pieces I picked up had more life and character than what I saw on the racks at Nordstrom or Bloomingdales. I spotted the Nina Ricci design from the window and curiously went inside. Since then, Mandy the store owner had come to know my taste and she messaged or rang to tell me about the arrival of new gems. The partners at my firm would never guess this secret and that suited me fine.

"So why do you think your nightmares are returning?" Dr. Benson asked.

The leather sofa in his office felt warmer than usual and the dull blinds were like a shroud. Threads of dark green and grey blended against the worn brown fabric funneling the lighting from the window into an unknown abyss underneath his chair. After I arrived, we had chatted about the kids and work.

He asked how I was coping with the stress of designing the new Lacks Research wing at Johns Hopkins but before long, we were on the subject of the reason for my appointment.

I thought for a moment before I spoke. "I think the news about the Human Rights Commission may have something to do with it."

I could feel him bristle. Dr. Benson had urged me to avoid stories that could retrigger my trauma. In fact, he had some strong opinions on the matter. I honestly had come to believe this was because those conversations made *him* uncomfortable. I didn't have the heart to tell Carl his Cambridge roommate wasn't the best psychiatrist in town.

Jerome was from Georgia. The two met during their second year when Carl had struck up a conversation with the other American standing in front of a post-modern installation at the Ruskin Gallery and they soon struck up a friendship. Jerome visited after graduation and didn't need much convincing from Carl to move up north from Oglethorpe and set up his office on River Road, a stone's throw from Carl's.

Like Carl, Jerome's impeccably tailored suits were never creased. Today he was in beige and brown. The hunter-green vest complimented his eyes which were currently inscrutable as he held my gaze.

"Does Carl know you are following the news again?" His disapproval was less veiled than at other times.

I complained to Angella that Jerome never experienced the violence of war. He could not possibly understand. She had urged me to see someone else, but I was worried about Carl's reaction. He told me I never gave anyone a chance and I had promised to do better, to fix what he described as my flaw.

"No, he doesn't," I retorted defiantly, not watching for Jerome's reaction.

I wanted to add, "not that it would make a difference," but I thought better of it. Jerome wasn't a marriage counselor, and I was beginning to realize that Carl and I sorely needed one. I'd always taken it for granted that the problems we were having were because of me. It was my history and my trauma that was to blame.

Meanwhile, Carl was skilled at maintaining the façade. Among our friends, we were a loving, happy, devoted couple. I thought if I told anyone how rocky things really were, they would not believe me.

Taking a deep breath, I repeated more evenly, "No Carl doesn't know."

"Well, Alison, revisiting your trauma and keeping that a secret is probably not helping you heal. The nightmares could be your way of expressing what is repressed."

No shit I thought.

I heard his words but that did not change how I felt. I needed to know what was going on back at home.

I scoured the stories for Abdul's name, yearning to find out how he was doing. Resettlement had petered out but every now and then news of a fresh group of arrivals would circulate in the community. Angella had her ears close to the ground and would call around to inquire. There was a spark in my heart. I hoped, no believed, that Abdul would come to America if he could, if for no other reason than to find me.

The distant sound of bells from St. Paul's reminded me we were only halfway through the session, so I sat up and faced Jerome squarely. He arched one eyebrow in a "So, what now?" look, and I flashed him a broad smile.

"So, I won't read the news anymore. Promise," I added, handing him my pinkie finger for a swear.

He cracked a smile, and I felt the tension ease. The silence that followed would probably last for the remainder of the session and Jerome and I both welcomed it. He was patient if nothing else; and bound by professionalism he would not disclose our conversations to his friend. So, he cashed his checks, and I had a dark quiet retreat for another half an hour, and I let my mind drift to my to do list for the next day.

ॐ♈ॐ

"Allison!"

I hear the car door slam shut and Carl's voice was loud enough that it carried from the garage through to the kitchen. He sounds angry and I know the reason even before he entered the house. Carl hated the smell of our traditional dishes, most of which are indeed pungent, but also very delicious. Early on in our marriage, Carl's mother had made it a point to educate me on Carl's tastes and sensitive digestive tract. For years, I had limited my cooking to the gastronomy of the far-flung cultures he sought happily to explore.

During both pregnancies when I had cravings. I tried a few local African restaurants that offered menu options which they touted as "just like home" but the food tasted nothing like Mama's or Ms. Stella's cooking so I gave up and instead would sneak down to Aunty Khadi's for cassava leaves, or crain crain sauce.

The food tasted like heaven and Aunty Khadi loved it when I cleared my plate and even chewed the chicken bones, or better still ate using my hand and licked my fingers afterward. She attempted cooking me jollof rice, which was always either too mushy or lacked full-bodied flavor. She would lament jovially that she still had not found the secret technique or ingredient that Krio women used to cook the dish perfectly.

I didn't mind. I was just thankful for her kindness. I had first tried my hand at cooking groundnut soup, which I thought was similar to Panang curry or some of the other Thai flavors Carl seemed to like. He had promptly snubbed the attempt, opting instead for takeout from Eggplant, his favorite restaurant at the time.

"What is that godawful stink?" Carl glares accusingly at me as he entered the kitchen. He makes a show of opening every window possible.

I had been longing for the taste of home, and desperately wanted to share that part of myself with the children. Since Carl was hardly around for lunch on weekends, I planned to cook a Saturday sauce, with rich red palm oil, ground egusi, beef, dried fish, bitter leaves, and spices, all bought that morning from an international food market in Silver Spring.

I hoped to have the meal prepared, and leftovers put away in the freezer by the time Carl returned but his plans must have changed, and he was home early. Seeing my reaction to the force of his words, Carl walked over to me and looked regretful.

"Look, Allison, it's not personal," he said.

He told me he had been moving toward becoming vegetarian for some time, and he reacted the way he did because the smell of the meat and oil was off-putting. He watched me closely as his words sank in. I was not totally surprised, but I felt silly for not asking him about it sooner, especially after I had noticed he only served himself the grains and vegetables from the food I prepared.

Later, Angella listened as I shared my frustration.

"I feel like we should be able to talk about everything without it becoming a tug of war or a confrontation, but as soon as I ask what I think is an innocent question, he looks at me like I offended him somehow," I said.

"As if I don't have the right to speak or share my opinion, even if it's for the good of our family."

I threw up my hands in defeat and Angella looked at me pointedly, offering no advice, which in retrospect was wise of her.

I was discreet when I brought up the subject with Aunty Khadi. I did not want to worry her, but I hope she could share some knowledge from her time being married. She had been in a long-term relationship for the last ten years and seemed content.

Aunty Khadi's beau had been a smart investor who scooped up a couple of the condo units early, moving into one of the units and turning over a neat profit by renting out the subsequent units and repeating the process over and again till he held a fairly large portfolio of units. Aunty Khadi had stubbornly refused his invitation for her to live with him permanently, instead insisting she would stay only until she found a place of her own.

At the time, I did offer for her to live with Carl and me, but she only clucked her tongue and changed the subject, eagerly showing off her latest Macy's employee coupons. Aunty Khadi never did move away from 14th Street, and years later, she and her beau still lived together and seemed quite happy. We never took the family trip to Las Vegas we had all talked about. There was always so much going on and we never did find the right time.

Aunty Khadi was at a loss when it came to Carl. She concluded that she must not "know much about shwenshwen Krios". I tried to explain there was a difference between Carl being conservative and aloof.

I did my best not to let the cracks in my relationship with Carl dominate conversations with my family, but I was finding it harder to hold the pain inside. I felt alone even when Carl and I were together, and if not for the children, I feared my spirit would wither away. What a dry place our marriage had become. Day in and day out, we woke up beside each other and got on with the day, exchanging only perfunctory words.

We had hired a babysitter when Natasha and Caleb started grade school and the routine at the end of each day was much the same. The sitter was a lovely francophone student. She was happy to prepare dinner for the kids, but most days I tried to be home early enough that I cooked their dinner.

Natasha and Caleb loved macaroni and cheese and could eat it all day if I let them, which I did not. I had to find creative ways to slip in carrots and broccoli into whatever they were having, meanwhile my own hips and thighs were filling out from eating rice; my comfort food, almost every day. I finally decided to make a change one day and looked up new recipes substituting rice with quinoa or couscous.

Carl came home late most nights and missed dinner so I made a plate for him and and kept it warm in the oven. After several mornings finding the plate untouched I stopped, and Carl didn't comment. One night after the children were in bed, I was in the family room watching Law and Order, excitedly waiting to share news of a pay raise from work with him.

"How much?" he asked, stretching up to touch the door jambe as he yawned lazily.

"Another five grand!" I grinned, proud of my six-figure salary.

"Is that all?" Carl scoffed, turning on his heel to go about his business.

I wanted to ask what he'd meant but changed my mind. I switched off the television and went upstairs feeling deflated and confused. I would probably never make as much money as Carl but that was not the point for me. We were not in competition. Still, Carl had a way of couching his words in derision, so, I was often left doubting myself.

His dismissal caused me to wonder whether my work as a black woman and an African immigrant would ever be valued as equal to my peers. He clearly didn't seem to think there was anything I had achieved worth celebrating.

I felt as though I was the one who had let Carl walk all over me. When we first got married, doing my best not to compare our life together with my parents', I was constantly finding ways to adjust to his quirks. I read relationship advice blogs and they all cautioned not to compare your relationship with others, but I only had Papa and Mama's relationship as my yardstick.

What I remembered of Papa and Mama's life together was nothing like mine. King's Lodge had been full of laughter. My parents joked and teased each other often. They sat on the verandah together, talking late into the night. They had valued each other's opinion and enjoyed each other's company.

No matter what mood Papa was in he had always treated Mama with respect, holding the door open for her and giving her his undivided attention when it was sought. He had made time for his children, taking us for ice cream at San Souci by the beach most Sundays, and he always went out of his way to answer our curious questions. Papa would pour Mama's sherry for her and tell her she was the most beautiful woman in the world.

I longed for the magic we shared that New Year's eve night on the balcony of the InterContinental Hotel when Carl asked me to marry him. He was no longer the talkative man I met at the coffee shop and there were days when I felt lost too. Outwardly, I looked like I had made it. I was a mother and a wife, a professional woman, married to a successful banker, and living in an expensive house in an affluent neighborhood. Inside I felt empty and broken.

Carl never hit me again after the day Natasha was born, but he still said things to me that were unnecessarily cruel. I learned to shake off the pain of the 'sticks and stones'.

"There really is no need to cook for me anymore," Carl said to me one day, as I stirred a pot of leafy greens with smoked fish and oxtail simmering on the stove.

I was emboldened when it came to cooking our cuisine and unapologetic of the smells. I had continued to cook the traditional dishes on weekends, though avoiding direct confrontation and making some effort to air out the kitchen once I was done. I scheduled my weekends so that I cooked the offending foods when Carl was not home, and after the children and I had eaten, I carefully froze any leftovers and tucked them away at the bottom of the deep freezer in the basement's cold room. I suspected Carl was aware of my defiance because although he had not commented, his request was not a surprise.

"From now on, I will fix my own meals, you just take care of the kids," he said.

"As long as you don't feed them junk food, I'm fine with whatever. Just don't ever cook that thing," he motioned to the pot on the stove, "in this house again. It stinks!"

I held my tongue and continued to stir, not wanting him to see through the blank expression I maintained until he had turned and left. I was enraged. If it wasn't so ridiculous it might even be funny.

I went back to my cooking, and for a moment considered omitting the ogiree from the recipe. The stuff was particularly pungent, but using just the right amount as Mama showed me, was what gave it the mouth-watering taste. I felt almost sorry for Carl. Maybe the reason he was so disgusted by things that brought me and others such pleasure, was because the culture was not handed down to him as a child.

My appetite was suddenly gone. I was angry enough with Carl to hurl the entire pot at his retreating back, but I had spent too many hours chopping the leaves, boiling the meat, and carefully washing the sand off the smoked fish, for my efforts to go to waste.

I eyed the soup, contemplating what to do next. In fairness, my actions these last months had been deliberate. I was hoping an exchange such as the one we just had would start a conversation. But it never worked.

I imagined our differences would compliment each other but that dream had since died. My taste in music, my love for family photographs which I displayed around the house, my colorful head scarves and elaborate traditional attire, the kabaslɔt and the kotoku like the ones my mother possessed, and the food that reminded me of my childhood, were all the things that made me Allison.

The sound of the gumbe drum or the balanji would always set my hips swaying and my feet tapping. It was in my blood. I felt honored to call the women who were older than me "aunty" even though we were not related. I felt proud to teach Natasha and Caleb how to *greet* everyone they met when we walked into a room. How could those things be wrong?

Our food is smelly and spicy and sealed with oil because that was the wisdom and the science of food preservation in a tropical climate before they had refrigerators. It was from those storehouses of wisdom that our people drew in times of hardship. I was beginning to see that Carl did not necessarily dislike these things, but rather he did not understand them and was indifferent to the value they held for me. I felt a sick sensation in the pit of my stomach as I realized that the survival of my marriage may require erasure of my past.

"Well, I'll be damned if I throw my soup away," I thought, sucking my teeth loud enough for Carl to hear from his office.

The kids were in the family room huddled over coloring books and comics and I hoped they had not heard their father's terse words.

The winter air bit the skin on my arms and neck, but I had left the house in a hurry and didn't want to go back inside for a jacket. I propped open the door leading out to the garage, balancing the heavy pot on my hip as I flicked the switch for the garage opener. As I carefully placed plastic sheets down inside the trunk of my car, I couldn't help but giggle at how ridiculous I must look right now.

Aunty Khadi chided women who stole entire pots of soup from kitchens at parties, tucking them away in the trunk of their cars, then hurrying back inside as if nothing was amiss. I could only imagine her expression when I showed up at her door with a pot of soup. The image made me laugh out loud as I pulled out of the garage. I laughed until tears streamed down my cheeks. Halfway on the journey to Aunty Khadi, my laughter quieted to deep sobs as I drove silently, my mind racing at the prospect that my marriage was over.

Chapter 8
Allison

Flight SN 812 to Freetown is packed and the cabin crew already looked strained as they respond to one call light after the next. The flight has not taken off yet. The excited chatter throughout the cabin has risen to a din, drowning out the sounds of fussing infants and the whirring white noise of the Boeing's engine.

"Marie du ya gi mi da plastic!"

The woman's apologetic smile does not prevent her from reaching an arm across my face. I press the back of my head firmly into my headrest as the said Calvin Klein shopping bag, appears from where it was tucked between Marie's feet. Bursting at the seams with brand new clothes and other goods still in their original wrapping, it swings dangerously close to my face before it is spirited away. The woman, Marie, settles back into her window seat to my right, and I watch as her friend wrestles the bag into an already jam-packed overhead bin a few rows ahead.

She succeeded at her task with a satisfied grin, and the bin's lock clicked firmly into place. Not for the first time, I contemplated upgrading to business class, but in truth, I was enjoying being among the throng. The familiar sound of my mother tongue filled me with a sense of peace amid the happy chaos.

Krio spoken in its diverse iterations and varied inflections gave away much about the speaker. There was a version spoken by other West Africans Nigerians, Cameroonians, and others who through their friendships, business dealings or family ties, had blended the language into their dialect to form a recognizable yet foreign hybrid.

There was the acquired 'diaspora' accent, which inversely revealed the length of time the speaker had been away by the amount of effort put into sounding foreign, so people back home would know you had newly arrived-a

Jos Cam or JC as they say. Local and diaspora accents fall into two main subsets; 'born' Krio speakers, and those who acquired the language in school, from the media, or visiting big cities. In the latter, tell-tale notes of the native dialect were common and often idiosyncratic.

The Christmas holiday home-goers were easy to spot even before they opened their mouth to speak. Glossy knee-high boots, embellished denim jackets, and bold-colored hair extensions were a reliable giveaway. Aunty Khadi had warned me not to take packages from anyone at the airport.

For a flight on its way to Freetown, a common enough sight in any American or European airport check-in area was of a traveler who overpacked and was unwilling to pay the excess baggage fee, struggling to rebalance his or her luggage, often forced to decide between practical items such as wrapped bundles of Kraft dinner or other American fare and gifts or special requests like pairs of gel bottom platform boots. They were not shy about asking fellow travelers who looked light to check in a bag on their behalf when the alternative would be to leave something behind.

The shared anticipation of returning home was palpable. The final group of passengers boarded and after several minutes of the usual messages and checks, and a taxi that seemed to go on forever, we were airborne. I caught glimpses of Dulles Airport as it gradually slated out of view, and the Potomac River disappeared into the horizon before the woman named Marie slammed the window shut, fixed a pair of the latest Dr. Dre Beats headphones over her ears before nestling her head in the nook between the window and her seat.

The man in the seat to my left had pulled out a laptop from a backpack tucked under the chair in front of him. I sighed deeply and leaned back, exchanging a polite smile with him before I closed my eyes.

I missed Natasha and Caleb but decided I had made the right decision not to bring them on my first trip back home. Carl had arranged for a nanny. She seemed nice enough, but I had an uneasy feeling she would lose the bedtime challenge.

Both kids had grown attached to their Nintendos and I had learned that a firm limit on gaming time always won over negotiation. Angella promised to call and check in often and I knew I could count on her. She and Carl weren't each other's favorite person. She still called him 'smart-ass' behind his back, but she loved her niece and nephew, and I knew she would be there for them in the next two weeks while I was away, especially as Christmas was around the corner.

In every one of the eight years since the war ended, I had broached the subject of returning with Carl, but each year he had refused, giving one reason or the other for why the trip wasn't worth the hassle of a day's flight plus the treacherous ferry ride to the capital and hours of waiting in between. He hadn't said so explicitly, but I sensed Carl thought I was being foolish to hold out hope that my mother was still alive, and perhaps sitting sick in a nursing home or hospital somewhere with no memory of her past.

The idea of going home left me feeling a strange mix of dread and excitement. I told myself I had good reasons for not making the journey earlier, but this was not true. I hadn't really needed Carl's blessing or his permission, but I had sought it anyway, knowing full well what his response would be. Maybe I was stalling but, in the end, it was a conversation about Angella that brought me to the decision.

My sessions with Dr. Benson continued over the years partly on Carl's insistence. He had made veiled references to the children and his concern they risked losing their mother due to my illness. I knew what he was insinuating, and I was damned either way. Staying in therapy was an admission I had a problem, stopping therapy without a clean bill of health would appear irresponsible on my part. Either option would not present well in front of a custody judge.

I still had nightmares and would wake in the middle of the night covered in sweat, disoriented, and clutching my throat for breath. I had continued to relive my memory of the night I was raped over and over during my sessions with Jerome. They say that to heal from post-traumatic stress disorder you should speak about the trigger event until you become bored with it.

I had gone from indifference as a way of hiding my depression in the beginning, to a cautious curiosity about my condition once I came to terms with my depression. I was still prone to panic especially when I awoke from a nightmare, but I had committed to practicing deep breathing and controlling my thoughts until I was calm.

I used to think I was unconscious in the days after I was assaulted, but in therapy I learned I could recall more than I first thought. Jerome told me I had dissociated after the incident and my brain tried to protect me by suppressing certain details. But lately as we'd talked, a layer would slowly peel away week to week, and I would remember. The faces of some of the women in the camp became sharply focused on my mind.

There was one woman in particular who had helped drag me back from the clearing where I was found. I remembered her name. And I remembered Angella. She had been with me when we were attacked in the bush. She somehow managed to escape and ran back to the camp for help.

It was on Jerome's couch that I revealed to him that Angella had killed a man that night. During my nightmares, the memories of my attacker's gaping throat slit open by her knife, was as vivid as when it happened. I knew she relived the scene when she had her spells in Aunty Khadi's apartment but never summed up the courage to admit it or tell the bewildered woman what we had been through.

It was something I never brought up with Angella either, I didn't know how to. I knew her thoughts on therapy. She wouldn't consider it. I had been struck by the fact that though we all had gone through so much and survived, we never talked about our trauma.

Dr. Benson had suggested I make the trip home with Angella as a way of starting the conversation. I was meeting Angella for coffee one afternoon in the spring. I sprung the question suddenly, as we grabbed a corner spot on the Starbucks patio, and Angella had eyed me skeptically, saying nothing at first as she took a dainty sip of her double mocha.

"That's a long way back, sis," she replied, avoiding my eyes and focusing instead on brushing an invisible piece of lint from the sleek line of her dark suit pants.

I knew she wasn't talking about just the distance and didn't know how to respond. We tossed the idea about briefly and she promised to think about it for another time, but she wasn't ready to go back with me this year. The more I contemplated the trip, the more I anticipated the possibility of seeing our Mama again. I had longed to hear the sound of her laughter and wondered what she would look like now.

I imagined it often enough, the lines at the corners of her mouth would be deeper, the neat bob of her hair might be silver at the temples. I imagined her welcoming me at the front door of King's Lodge, the aroma of her delicious jollof rice and stew wafting from the dining room. Soft music drifting through the house, carried along the gentle evening breeze from the windows opening out to the verandah. A glass of sherry perched on the whiskey stool by her favorite wicker chair overlooking the array of colors from the flowers in the garden. Mama.

☙❦❧

We landed close to midnight, but you couldn't tell the lateness of the hour from the energy in the air. The cabin burst into applause when the pilot touched down. The busy hum continued as the eager passengers exchanged how they planned to react once they got to their respective homes. I had shed my light coat and rolled it into my handbag. The blanket of air that hit us as we descended the steps of the plane and walked toward the terminal building was warmer and more humid than expected for harmattan season, but I welcomed the contrast to DC and set aside my concern that climate change may have made its way to the paradise I once called home.

Lungi airport had been modernized since the days of our family trips to England. I was surprised at the diversity in the nationality of people just at the airport and was seeing firsthand that in addition to bringing an economic boom, war had changed the shape of things for better or worse. I politely declined assistance from the eager swarm of porters.

I located my luggage without too much trouble and followed the exit signs casually following along and doing my best to blend in. Water taxi operators flashed signs boasting free WIFI and refreshment available for purchase in the comfort of an airconditioned vessel that made the trip across in half an hour. They ushered customers outside to waiting shuttles that would take them to the water terminal.

There was no one to tell of my arrival in town so my plan was to get on the ferry to Kissy terminal and then to Signal Hill. The ferry ride was longer than a water taxi, but I did not mind. I was beyond exhausted but despite my eagerness to arrive at King's Lodge I was determined to savor every bit of the journey. The idea of possibly being able to watch the sunrise from the ferry's deck filled me with a sense of nostalgia.

I picked a pleasant looking mustachioed man from among the taxi drivers lining the pavement outside and beckoning excitedly to travelers like me who had no transport pre-arranged. My driver introduced himself as Henry and was instantly judicious, carefully but firmly taking my suitcase from me and ushering me toward a white Toyota Hilux as he beat back others vying to usurp him.

"Make Madam pass! Give Madam Road please!" Henry sounded confident and official.

"Welcome, Madam!"

"Welcome, Aunty!"

I nodded politely and smiled at the young men who had called out resisting the urge to fish around my purse for single dollar bills to give out as tips. According to more experienced travelers, it did more harm than good to give people tips for doing nothing. It was the bane of the 'third world', the curse of the 'dregman culture' as one Sierra Leonean contributor had put it. Once inside the vehicle, Henry thoughtfully asked if I needed to purchase a local sim card or use his mobile phone to call someone. I thanked him and said no.

Once we had driven outside of the airport complex the countryside was mostly pitch black with the faint flickers of light scattered across the landscape. I distractedly answered Henry's polite questions about how long I had been away and how long I planned on staying, processing what I could see of my surroundings.

"Dis na dem Chinese, Ma," my de facto guide explained, pointing to a cluster of towering structures which were bathed in floodlights and apparently under twenty-four-hour construction from the crew and equipment I glimpsed through an open gate flanked by massive and lofty walls. I hadn't realized I would be able to observe so quickly and on such a scale, the impact of another notable extension of the *China Safari* I had recently been reading about.

As for the apparent shift from traditional development aid which post-colonial administrations had pilfered and treated like personal expense accounts, I was not an economist but intuitively could appreciate that the rise in micro-finance and other innovative mechanisms of funding signaled those economic fortunes in sub-Saharan Africa might finally turn a corner.

The potential that people could directly reap health, education and quality of life benefits from their stewardship over lush vegetation, waters replete with life-sustaining resources, and mineral deposits that enabled the technological revolution of our time, was a long time coming.

The war changed other things too. Some peacekeepers fell in love with the country or in some instances its people and returned to take back a bride or further burgeoning opportunities in business. A major commercial hub in the city was renamed Sani Abacha Street after a former Nigeria head of state and military general, and every tenth shop on the strip selling auto parts and electronics was run by a Nigerian.

There was a revival in entertainment as well. Music by a plethora of new local artists was making a splash in Sierra Leonean communities across the globe and others were starting to take notice; and many actors transitioned from the stage to the big screen while seeking refuge in Nigeria, the Gambia and Ghana. The field of journalism once monopolized by a single state-owned outfit had expanded dramatically. Increasingly, democratic and secular content as varied as soap operas or investigative reporting was now accessible to most people living in the smallest towns and even before I arrived in Freetown, the sight of a satellite dish on most rooftops was near ubiquitous.

The ferry was delayed almost two hours and I found myself accepting Henry's offer of a charter to my destination, instead of the single stop at Tagrin terminal. His rate seemed reasonable.

☙ Υ ❧

Signal Hill, Freetown

The gaping hole that should have been the roof of the King's Lodge welcomed the blazing sun in. Henry slowed the car to a crawl, inching gingerly up a dusty path. Knee-high weeds on either side replaced the flower beds Mama had delighted in, and it was moments after we passed through that I realized we had crossed the gap were the iron gate once stood.

When he could go no further, Henry parked the car. Although we barely got any sleep overnight, Henry had been chatting jovially on the drive through the city, continuing to deliver his surprisingly knowledgeable narration of recent history. His silence as we approached what was supposed to be my family home was suddenly deafening, an awful alert that the sight before me was real, as much as I wished it were a bad dream.

I stepped out of the car and walked slowly toward the main building. Its pane-less windows shaded with overgrown vegetation look ghoulish. The once thick Makore wood front door hangs rotting and charred from a few rusted hinges that hold it to what remains of the frame.

A lounge of lizards scatters in front of me as I make my way along the west wall of the property. I passed the spot where the boys' quarters once stood, now little more than an ashy platform. Carpet grass along the shady grove is replaced with dark green moss, and the paths that once led down to the garden are no longer there. I push through, thankful I am wearing sensible shoes.

I surveyed the damage from where I stood. The crumbling cement walls of the main house were mostly black with soot and branches of a mango tree stuck out from what was once the kitchen area. I thought I heard someone call me and was beginning to wonder if I was hallucinating until I saw Henry waving in the distance. He had climbed up on a low section of wall bordering the property and there was someone standing next to him.

Taking one last look around, my brain was whirring as I joined the pair who had moved to stand next to the car and were talking quietly. The man with Henry turned watery eyes and a big smile toward me, displaying a wide gap in his bottom row of tobacco-stained teeth.

"Miss Allison, welcome!" he said, nodding repeatedly and continuing to grin. It took me a few seconds, but recognition eventually dawned. *Mr. Johnny*!

Our former groundskeeper was bent over with age, but his grip was firm as we shook hands warmly. Over the next hour, I learned how surprised Mr. Johnny was when Mama and Ms. Stella returned to the house several weeks after we all left for the Northern border.

Their vehicle had been hijacked by rebels and the older women were lucky to be released alive. By some miracle, they reached Freetown with swollen feet and tattered clothes. My eyes filled with tears as the old man told the story in a combination of Krio and stilted English. He paused as I gestured to him so we could get into the vehicle. I feared my legs would no longer hold me.

Pa Johnny did not know the exact details but one night he had locked up and gone to his room only to be woken by the ash and smoke filling his nostril and choking him. The compound was ablaze. There was speculation a lit candle may have been the cause, while some thought it was a robbery gone wrong. The desperate attempts by Pa Johnny and the neighbors were too late and both women perished.

I saw Pa Johnny's lips moving but could not hear the words. A surreal out of body experience. As though I was watching my conversation with him from a distance. A part of me always knew Mama might not be alive, but hearing the words that confirmed it left a hole where my heart was meant to be. I clutched my chest with one hand and grabbed hair with the other.

"Allison," Pa Johnny brought me gently back to the present.

I recovered enough to thank Pa Johnny for doing his best to keep trespassers off the property over the years. He told me had secured the few items that survived the inferno-a handful of Papa's leather-bound volumes and one of Mama's portmanteaux, battered and burnt, some of its contents smoke damaged. He did his best to upkeep the place by cutting back the brush in the early days but with age his strength had waned.

He told me about Abdul. How he had been made Captain shortly after our departure. He had been mustering troops in the south unaware that his mother had not made it out of the country. My heart ached afresh when Pa Johnny told me that Abdul found out much later.

"I am so glad you were not here, my child," he says, unaware that the atrocities had stretched their ugly tentacles beyond the border into the camps in Guinea. I shudder.

Pa Johnny is in a talkative mood, and I listen to him recount his version of events after the coup. A countercoup had divided the military rank and file, peace talks collapsed, and Freetown was under a full-blown rebel attack. Pa Johnny like most was forced into hiding up in the hills while the house stood abandoned. Despite the danger, Abdul had returned as often as possible and given Pa Johnny money for food and medicine, encouraging him to keep an eye on the now dilapidated house.

I did not hide my disappointment when he said Abdul had not been back in a while and was probably on patrol. The UN and ECOWAS military personnel had identified Abdul as a strong leader and sent him on training programs in the region. He had even gone off to work with the British Army at times, Pa Johnny said with pride.

I was surprised when he mentioned Mama's brother, Uncle Robert. Our uncle had come to look around King's Lodge a few years back when he was in town to settle the Walcott-Taylor business. Henry chimed in then, recognizing the well-known name. I learned that the pharmacy was burned down during the invasion, and the few remaining family members had gone to England. Mama's childhood home was severely damaged, but Uncle Robert had arranged for the repairs, and the house was now being looked after by a caretaker.

Struggling to keep up with the barrage of information I agreed with Pa Johnny that I should go to Mama's family home and perhaps stay there rather than a hotel.

The car came to a stop. The afternoon sun had been high in the sky by the time we left Signal Hill, and I closed my eyes against its intensity. Jet lag was catching up with me and lulled by the movement of the vehicle, I had dozed off, waking just as we pulled up in front of my mother's childhood home.

I was grateful to have found Henry. He quickly explained to the gateman that I was "di Mami in pikin" and a short while later the caretaker Pa Sorie climbed with me up to the portico of the house as the older man rushed ahead with my suitcase, glad to ready a room for me.

I thanked Henry and paid him generously, accepting the cell phone number he proffered to me, scribbled on an old receipt. Refreshed after a bath, I flung on a loose-fitting t-shirt and opened the bedroom window, pulling the blinds to block the light from the blazing sun. I crawled into bed, falling asleep seconds after my head hit the pillow.

The next two weeks flew by and as much as I contemplated extending my stay by a few days, missing Christmas with Natasha and Caleb was not an option. I was immersed in my rediscovery of the city I once knew so well. I explored historical attractions with renewed curiosity and grabbed a drink at the new local hang-out spots. Despite Pa Johnny's objections, I made day trips to the provincial districts that had accessible roads.

Despite the unspeakable destruction, the city still bustled and I found myself constantly reminiscing. I was relieved to see that where many of the past problems with public services existed, access to consistent electricity supply, clean water, sanitation, health care, telecommunication were now privatized and for the most part seemed improved.

The population had quadrupled, and the real estate market was booming. The Walcott-Taylor house was now in the heart of a prime waterfront location which featured an impressively modern pier, with expensive boutiques and restaurants, and offices in gleaming glass towers that overlooked the bay.

Generations of entire families had emigrated elsewhere during and after the war, and although I recognized the landscape, hills, and beaches around me, I recognized no one and felt like a foreigner. I had heard the majority of the city residents were young professionals returning to take up high-profile positions in government or multinationals, or entrepreneurs buying up land for new manufacturing or agricultural ventures, but I didn't really know anyone who still lived here. I resorted to the internet to search for old acquaintances, scouring the pages for familiar faces or names, listed as living in Freetown that I might reconnect with.

Keeping in touch with the friends and old classmates now living in the States was something I was diligent about, but Angella thought it was silly and Carl was dismissive of it. It was probably the only thing she and Carl agreed on. Over the years, I traveled to Maine, New York, and Indiana to visit family; many of whom did not reciprocate but the gesture reminded me of what Mama did and I persevered. I understood Angela's sentiment, but she and I were different. Maintaining family and community ties meant a lot to me.

My childhood home had been a hub, a nest that brought together some of the most brilliant minds and influential personalities. During Mama's soirees or Papa's parties, they laughed and talked late into the night over Star beers and fine whiskey, hatching a vision for a beautiful and strong country with beautiful and strong people who stood united for justice, prosperity, and peace. I had dreamed big dreams then and the world was a magical place I could reach out and touch. Despite the pain of Papa's death, and losing Mama, I desperately wanted to capture some of that magic and pass it on to my children.

The morning after I arrived as I wandered around the rooms of the house, Pa Sorie pulled out a very worn flip phone from his pocket, dialed a number and handed it to me.

"Allison, welcome home!"

I was delighted to hear Uncle Robert on the other end of the line. I hadn't realized before just how much like Mama he sounded. Uncle Robert told me how he and his wife had left Pepel by boat to Conakry, then on to England. He tried many times to locate us but only hit dead ends. The internet at that time was not the goldmine it would become.

Unable to hold back the emotion, we both wept as we talked about Mama. It had torn him apart not to be able to return for his sister. He sent money to cover the costs, but it was Abdul alone who bore the responsibility to bury his mother and mine during that terrible time. I anxiously asked Uncle Robert if he knew where Abdul was, but he said they lost touch early on.

When the war finally ended, it had been a struggle for Uncle Robert to get his hands on the deed to King's Lodge since there was no will. Probate was a difficult fight to win long distance, but he had persevered with the help of Uncle Imma. It was finally only on his last visit that he convinced the courts to appoint him executor of his late sister's estate and was able to start plans to restore King's Lodge and access Mama's financial accounts.

We hung up with a plan for my siblings and I to connect with him once I returned to the States. The conference call to my sisters and brother was much more difficult. With so many years without word from her, our worst fears that she had died were unspoken. Now with the confirmation, the relief of closure was palpable in the long silence that followed.

I visited Mama's graveside that very day. She was buried beside Papa and not far away was Ms. Stella's plot next to her mother. I returned over the following days bringing fresh flowers to each site. Three days in a row I sat in the quiet, deserted cemetery on low whitewashed pavestone that bordered Papa and Mama's lot and poured out my heart to them.

I told Mama about my marriage with Carl, and my fear that the pain would reduce me to nothing. I wanted to leave him, but I didn't know if I would have the strength I needed for the inevitable fight. I talked to Papa about my hopes for his grandchildren's future and my desire to bring them home. I revealed my deepest thoughts and recounted darkest memories. I held nothing back. There was no need for carefully choosing my words. There was no need for a brave face. I spilled out my feelings unchecked and for the first time in a very long time, I felt truly free.

When I called Jennifer and Frank again, gushing over the things I had seen and learned, hoping to get their buy-in, they were ambivalent about King's Lodge. I placed the call prior to my return so we would start the conversation before we actually met with Uncle Robert to discuss the fate of the home. Neither of them was particularly interested in keeping it.

"Whatever you decide is fine with me, Allison," Jennifer had responded distractedly. She was on speakerphone, battling New York City traffic, and running late for a client visit.

Angella had been surprisingly measured when I excitedly gave her all the latest developments. She thought it was a good thing that I was thinking about renovating the house and keeping it in our family.

"Do you mind contacting the UMC diocese for me while you are in town? I have the address" Angella said.

"Yes, I'm sure I can find it," I replied.

Angella mentioned that a few months earlier she was contacted about a package in her name. I knew that Angella had been born and raised at the mission house in Bo before Mama and Papa took her in, so I was curious.

Honoring tradition, I made sure to pick up bottles of hard liquor to take with me on the last visit to the cemetery, I wanted to show Papa that years living overseas had not erased all my memories. I uncapped the sherry and poured out libation next to Mama's grave followed by Papa's favorite whiskey.

Over the years, as Evangelical Christianity spread in West Africa, the ritual had grown out of favor among many Krios and I myself was not sure how to reconcile it with my faith journey, so I did not dwell on those questions. It had felt strangely empowering to pour out the offerings. I had been holding on to everything in my life like a drowning man clutching at straws and I was finally understanding what it meant to let go. The darkness had slipped away. I thanked them for taking the load of my heart and left the cemetery.

☙γ❧

The attendants tried unsuccessfully to board the plane on time. I was fine with the delay because it meant the layover in Belgium would be shorter than the five hours mentioned on the itinerary. I had downloaded pictures of the ruins at Bunce Island to my laptop for the flight and would spend some time studying them if I wasn't able to fall asleep.

Carl would have insisted I use the American Express card to gain entry to the Business Class lounge at Brussels Airport, but I didn't want to miss out on interacting with people in the transit terminal. I took in as many of the conversations as I could without seeming too inquisitive. An hour into our wait, although my head was buried in Barak Obama's *Dreams from My Father* and I had on headphones, a number of my fellow travelers said hello or tried to strike up a conversation to pass the time, so much so I eventually gave up on trying to read.

Carl had read the memoir several times and urged me to see for myself what all the buzz was about, but I had been wrapped up in the final stage of the Beall Dawson House restoration at the time and hadn't picked it up before. I hadn't really paid attention to the Democratic nominee and Senator from Illinois until a few weeks before the 2008 elections. By election night, despite the frosty relation between Carl and I, we had both watched in awe as the tall man with big ears and swagger, strolled out to the stage in victory.

Natasha was glued to the television screen, awoken by our whooping and hollering as we high-fived and danced around the family room. Caleb, whom I had laid on the couch beside me, stirred briefly but went right back to sleep after I picked him up.

Barack Obama's passionate activism and quiet strength reminded me of Frances Claudia Wright. Like Wright, he was too black to be accepted into his white ancestry but too white to be fully embraced by all black folk. I could relate to this duality by way of my Krio identity. There was a kinship with black people in America, but something about the way we carried ourselves, dressed, and spoke, triggered the inevitable question "I hear an accent, where are you from?". After sixteen years, I had long realized I would never be one of them, and the question often annoyed me.

"Mek di plane nɔ lef mi!" a lady beside me exclaimed as she stood up to join the queue in front of the boarding gate. I was confused when I realized almost everyone else was pushing their way forward to line up. As far as I knew the plane had not even arrived so it was highly unlikely, she or anyone else would miss the flight.

The plane would be boarded in the usual order and unless the airline had made an error and overbooked, we would all eventually get to our assigned seats. Perhaps a deep distrust of some systems and order was the reason for such irrational behavior. Nevertheless, I had come to appreciate the quirks of my countrymen. Feeling self-conscious now that I was the sole passenger still seated in the waiting area, I stood up. I guess they weren't the only ones anxious to get home.

"Yes, oh!" I chimed in with a knowing smile, filing in behind her to join the queue. Our collective desire was thwarted when twenty minutes later the announcement came saying the flight had been canceled due to bad weather in Washington DC. A rumble of displeasure ran through the group and erupted into near chaos as representatives from the airline came out and explained that we would receive transport and accommodation vouchers for a nearby hotel for the night until our flight was confirmed the next day. Great, I thought. I was definitely going to use the American Express card now.

I met Paul on the escalators as I was heading down to the taxi stands. He had reached forward and grabbed my shoulder as a backpacker rushed by, almost knocking me over. We chatted casually at the bottom of the stairs after I thanked him for saving me from a fall.

He was an engineer from North Carolina and in town for a conference. He was burly and had a small potbelly. His clothes were well made, and his facial hair impeccably groomed. His smile was warm and friendly and when he flashed it at me my heart stirred in a way it hadn't in years. He had a quick wit and an ease with words that had me laughing as we exchanged travel horror stories. When he asked if we could meet later for a glass of wine, I agreed and gave him my phone number and hotel name.

"No later than 9 o'clock—" I had said, giving him a flirtatious wink that surprised even myself.

I was in my oversize nightshirt huddled over the laptop and working on some design ideas for King's Lodge when my phone signaled an SMS.

"Red or white?"

I stared at the message on the screen for seconds trying to figure out what it meant. The number was unknown. The phone buzzed again "—Wine" a smiley face accompanied the word. I cursed under my breath, thinking quickly how best to gently reject this stranger. What had I been thinking? Also, for all I knew, he could be a serial killer. I definitely had not expected him to follow through.

The phone rang.

"Pizza hut can I take your order?" I sounded corny as hell and cringed at the lame joke. The laughter on the other end of the line was deep and rich and I could feel my insides melt as playfulness took over. His reaction was disarming, and I was surprised at how strongly attracted to him I felt. The heat building below my belly was thrilling and irresistible.

"Beautiful and a sense of humor to boot," Paul was clearly amused. He hesitated for a second and I waited, wondering briefly if this was going to progress beyond our flirting on the phone. I did a quick mental checklist. Who was he really? Was he married? Did he have children? I wasn't really looking for answers. As I debated whether to take any action, my spontaneity got the better of me. When he cleared his throat and asked in his best Barrie White imitation if I wanted to meet him at 9 o'clock, without hesitation, I said yes.

Chapter 9
Faith, Hope, Love

"Dirty scoundrel," I muttered under my breath, drawing a sharp glance from Angella. I shifted my weight in the chair, trying to find a comfortable spot to ease the ache in my shoulder from sleeping on her lumpy futon.

Angella held on to old furniture like a bad habit, and the bed was ancient. Natasha and Caleb were wild sleepers, so I left the twin beds in the spare bedroom of Angella's chic little condo to them, preferring to deal with achy shoulders rather than wake up with feet in my face. We were in court to file some final papers, but the grand jury's decision had been rendered in our favor. I would not be indicted.

When we had signed the papers for the new mortgage loan, Carl assured me that my mediocre credit score was exactly the type of qualification his bank was looking for to implement their new financial instruments.

"You fit the bill, Allison. This is perfect," he had told me.

Carl still knew how to switch on the charm and be cajoling when it came to money. I questioned how I could be qualified for the loan that had been secured in my name, but as always, he had a good explanation. I quickly grew tired of arguing over why my name had to be on his real estate 'investments', while I was totally in the dark about his finances. The jargon he used to rationalize this was just as confusing as the reasons for his golf vacations, expensive trips, and luxury goods, and left my head spinning.

I figured that ultimately it would not hurt as long as Carl kept up with the payments and turned it over as quickly as he said he would. The way he described things, the money would make a tidy nest egg for both of us and secure the children's future. He explained that needed to separate himself only due to the sensitivity of his position with the bank.

Before the last deal that precipitated federal charges being laid against Carl, I had been nervous and yet elated about signing my name on the dotted line. An eight-million-dollar mansion in Potomac was extravagant beyond my imagination. Angella cautioned me against going forward with the plan because the entire thing would raise red flags despite my six-figure income. I heeded her advice, but Carl had fudged the paperwork and pushed it through all the same.

The case against Carl went to trial and my whole world was overturned. It only made sense that I should give up our house, and by the time I had untangled the financial mess Carl landed me in, I was lucky to still be able to afford a mortgage for the quaint colonial I had found nestled just behind Sligo Creek Parkway. It had a neat little garden and I planned to plant as many flowers and shrubs as I could, just for Mama.

During the worst of the crisis, Jennifer and Frank called to check in now and then, and Aunty Khadi was also very supportive, but it was Angella who was most constant; a rock to me and the children. She freed up her schedule to make sure she was available when I started divorce proceedings.

When Carl went to jail, she helped me sort through the remaining documents in his office that had not been seized and came by every day until the house was all packed up. I sold what I could of the expensive furniture and donated the rest. Natasha and Caleb thought downsizing to temporarily move in with their Aunty Angella was an adventure. I didn't have the heart to explain to them the details of why they could not see their father, and why we had to leave our home.

There had been other encounters after Paul. I didn't feel guilty for having casual sex with strangers, but I knew my habit would become unsustainable. I started to see Dr. Benson again around the time of the trial. He was surprisingly insightful, and I agreed with him that my actions were out of pent-up frustration from more than a decade in an emotionally abusive marriage, the financial troubles I had been thrown into, and other typical mid-life stressors.

I would do better to tackle the root cause of my issues rather than continue on a path of self-sabotage. I hadn't loved Carl for several years and the divorce was a relief, but the mental and emotional pressure from the scandal and gossip sometimes felt unbearable.

Liz blamed me for enabling Carl, for being a bad influence. She barely had a polite word for me since his arrest and only called to talk to the kids. Early on she had made some noises about her 'rights' to be able to care for her grandchildren but I put a decisive end to that foolish talk. After that she avoided my calls, letting them go to voicemail and sending me an apologetic text message in response.

It was two years since my trip to Freetown, and everything since then had happened so quickly. I felt a childlike thrill when my friend requests were accepted, or someone liked my mundane posts. I felt connected sending condolences to someone in mourning. The interactions brought me into community circles. Attending a pull na doh was more than just an act of politeness or an opportunity to eat your fill of jollof rice and beans. Social interactions were integral to how we had survived as a people.

Krios as a minority had historically been squeezed into an ever-narrowing geographic space and then simultaneously dispersed either due to the war and diminishing economic opportunities or more naturally through intermarriage and other social changes. It was the connection to people, shared stories, food and music that formed the core of consolation and even therapy, for many of us, especially when hopes of attaining the American dream were frustrated.

I was shocked to learn online that my childhood crush Sam had died suddenly from a heart attack while he was playing soccer with his high school alumni league. The silent blight did not discriminate, taking the young and otherwise healthy as easily as anyone else.

My body image issues up to that point had been superficial. I took brisk walks as much as possible but still found it easier to gain the pounds than lose them. I secretly liked that my breasts were fuller, but this was at the expense of my belly poking out, and having to deal with scathing looks from Carl when he walked into the bathroom as I was about to step into the shower.

Reflecting on Sam's passing I decided to make some changes. I started to run a couple of times a week and signed up for a Salsa class. I got a new haircut, agreeing to bronze highlights, suggested by my hairdresser. Angella had grinned in approval when she saw the new look, calling it 'young and exciting'.

The court accepted my petition for a name change. I had stared at the notice for a long time as a wave of sadness rushed over me. The small victory felt empty. A wry smile crossed my lips as I imagined Papa's booming voice saying, "Daughter, you have tenacity!" I imagined his eyes sparkling and an affirming nod that needed no further words. I placed the notice on the kitchen table and thought about how I would explain it to Natasha and Caleb.

Carl's appeal was successful. He was released from jail to serve the rest of his three-year sentence under house arrest. The Washington Post had lost interest in the case and there were no longer reporters lurking about or accosting me randomly on the street or outside my office. I buried myself in work when I wasn't driving Natasha and Caleb to soccer or piano practice.

I had spearheaded the Helping Homes project and it was just wrapping up with resounding success. My new boss Adrian was very flexible and let me make my own hours, and working from home three days a week for almost a year. I thought I noticed a few junior partners dart curious looks in my direction but no one at work talked to me about my ex-husband's legal troubles besides Adrian, and he was always understanding. Distancing myself from the office was probably good for everyone until the cloud lifted.

While my finances were tied up in the mess at home, the renovation of King's Lodge had been able to proceed with the money from Mama and Papa's estate. It wasn't much. Frank, Jennifer, and Angella willingly offered some additional support.

The money had been just enough to hire a reliable contractor and see the work through to completion, with Uncle Robert supervising as best he could. Henry had become a trusted aid and an invaluable set of quick feet on the ground in Freetown. With King's Lodge completed, I joined a Fourah Bay College alumni group of architects and engineers and dedicated any spare time I had to the bucket list of projects.

One afternoon, I was at my desk sketching designs for a new children's home and streamed BBC Africa on my iPod. I was curious to know how things were fairing since the recent national elections. I perked up as Ofeibea Quist-Arcton started reporting a segment on Sierra Leone. She introduced the piece as a ten year retrospective on the end of the civil war. She was interviewing a returned military officer who had initially joined the Revolutionary United Front out of his frustration with the status quo. Abdul's voice was unmistakable.

She let him narrate his story of how he and others who had been student activists were specifically sought out and recruited. He described his sense of disillusionment after witnessing atrocities committed by the RUF against civilians at the Liberian border and decision to switch sides and realign with the Sierra Leone Army. Though he was not part of the group that stormed the

State House in 1992, he told Ofeibea that he was in support of the coup. I got goosebumps as I recalled that day.

The feature lasted close to an hour, and Ofeibea peppered Abdul with questions about his loyalty to the Sierra Leone military, his experience fighting side by side with the ECOMOG troops, United Nations Mission to Sierra Leone, and the role of the British Forces in securing victory over the rebels. She asked about his time living in Ghana and the reason for his return. When she pressed him about his personal views on current events and whether he had any designs on entering the political sphere as a number of his equals had done, he maintained a steady, cool tone.

"We were not taught to idolize power and material wealth," he replied firmly, echoing one of Papa's favorite admonitions.

"By we, do you mean your family Major Kamara, or your company?" Ofeibea was unrelenting.

"My family," he said, "Definitely my family."

I had called to say I was on my way over right after the radio program ended and I was screaming even before I got out of the car.

"Angella, I found him!"

♋

I had to pinch myself several times to prove I was not dreaming.

"And then Papa banned both of us from driving and hid his car keys!" I screeched with laughter rolling over in my bed and trying not to fall off the edge. Abdul and I had been chatting for hours.

"That old man was something else you know," Abdul mused.

"I had looked forward to the day I would stride up to the front door and declare my intention to put stop for you, but I missed the chance."

He studied my face intently, as his warm baritone trailed off into the world of possibilities for how different our lives might have turned out.

I gazed at him for a long time, taking in his features through the screen on my tablet. His image would be seared in my mind until we could meet in the flesh. A few years after we had first arrived in America, I remembered how I panicked when I couldn't remember his face. Without pictures, the image faded, and once I married Carl, the image was clouded further. Now it was only a matter of time, a few months at the most and we would be together again.

☜♈☞

Angella was getting impatient because I was taking too long to put on my makeup.

"Lilli, it's a seminar, not a fashion show."

The careful strokes as I applied eyeliner seemed to exasperate her further. I puckered my lips to make sure they were evenly covered as I put on more lipstick. Unlike Angella's, my lips were a dark hue that contrasted with my skin in a way that stood out, so I covered them with a plum color, which I thought accentuated them better and looked more natural.

My eyebrows had grown wayward since I cut down my visits to the nail salon, and cringed at the extra $13 charge for a wax. I was conscious of every penny spent these days and had tried my hand at shaping my brows myself. They turned out much thinner than I intended so I tried to fill them out as best I could.

Angella had requested that I attend the event with her, and I was happy to oblige. The seminar was being held at the Silver Spring Civic Building. It was aimed at helping illegal immigrants and undocumented workers navigate the new immigration-related ballot measures. Angella loved her work and was passionate about educating people about their rights under the law.

"We got lucky!" she often reminded me. Many others could not say they had made it as far as we had. Families were torn apart. Others had to live the rest of their lives maimed. We had our share of scars but in the grand scheme of things, we came through alright. Lately, she seemed to have an insatiable drive to get involved and give back, maybe even return home to continue Papa's quest. As she scooped us her car keys, the signal that she was heading out the door, I took one last look at my handiwork, smiled to make sure there was no lipstick on my teeth, and ran out to meet her.

The auditorium was packed and though I saw a few familiar faces from our time with Aunty Khadi but there were many faces I did not recognize. After a number of embarrassing episodes of Carl walking off to the car because someone sitting beside us at a funeral smelled of freshly cooked stew, or forcing us to leave a wedding reception early because they was traditional drumming and masked devils dancing as men carrying fake hunting guns splashed water on onlookers, I had gradually limited my attendance to only social events not these wider community affairs. The number of immigrants had grown since we arrived in the States, but I had not realized just how much.

We scoured the space. Spotting two empty seats near the front, we made our way over and sat down. The stage was set up with a lectern and a table for the panelists. Angella raised her eyebrows disapprovingly at the all-male panel, squinting to make out the names beneath the pictures. The participants were a mix of men and women mostly African or black with just a sprinkling of Caucasians and a few East Indians.

The organizers bustled up and down the aisles, trying to get things going which I hoped would be soon, considering I only arranged for the babysitter for three hours. Angella was livid when I told her I was not willing to accept the alimony payment Montgomery County Court had ordered Carl to pay.

It was bad enough that he had been jailed for his crime, the revelation of his affair with his business associate Maria Russo, a hot-headed woman with a fondness for red bottom shoes, was the last straw. Angella had painstakingly explained the details of their scheme to me and how the Dodd-Frank Wall Street Reform and Consumer Protection Act was supposed to prevent such practices from going unchecked in the future.

"My head was in the sand," I confessed to Angella.

"No, your heart was in the right place," she had assured me.

Our wait finally came to an end as the audience started to applaud, signaling the entrance of the chairperson as he walked on to the stage followed by the panelists.

☙♈❧

"Dr. Berkowitz, you don't need to sugarcoat anything," Angella's voice is high-pitched. She eyes the doctor with apprehension.

"I know I have few options left, so stop it with your stupid hypotheticals and give me an answer or some damn morphine please!" she yells.

If Angella hated anything it was hedging, which her oncologist though unintentionally, appears to be doing today. I touch Angella's hand lightly to try and soothe her, and turn apologetically toward the short, balding middle-aged man. The thick frame of his glasses makes him look like one of the crazy scientists on the children's cartoon networks.

His appearance does not do his knowledge justice. He is brilliant in his specialty and I feel blessed that Angella is under the care of his team. She is a fighter, and we were all relieved when her bone marrow was cleared after the first phase of treatment. But then her numbers suddenly deteriorated, and she is now looking at a third round of chemotherapy.

I was still getting used to the fact that Angella and I shared the same blood type. It wasn't so long after she revealed her diagnosis of Acute Myeloid Leukemia, that she showed me the letters that had been left for her by Mary Rogers, the nursing sister, and Angella's caregiver from the time of her birth until she was brought to Freetown to live with us. I was filled with indignation, anger, shame, and other emotions that I couldn't even identify. She had known for the last four years that Papa had had an affair with her mother and she was as much his child as Frank, Jennifer, and me, yet she kept silent about it.

More than ever my heart was filled with compassion toward this woman who had grown from being my best friend to becoming my sister. It only seemed natural that we indeed shared the same blood. She loved me fiercely and boasted about being my guardian angel, but I realized the jest was all too real. She had kept the secret to protect all of us from thinking less of our father, and only opened up about it because her life had depended on it.

We talked for hours about the things which confounded us as children. The reason for Mama's lashing which always seemed over-done when it came to Angella, the similarities in our features, especially our eyes. Those things all made more sense now.

After the bone marrow donation when I was laid up in bed, I wondered what to do. Sister Mary Rogers and Father Fred were probably long dead so they wouldn't be able to give us any answers. I knew Papa loved Mama deeply and was confused by the idea that he could have shown such weakness. But as the spiritual leader Pastor Joe reminded me when I presented my conflicting judgment to him, we are all human. Born of sinful flesh, our nature by default was sinful. While Pastor Joe spoke my mind ran to my own sexual indiscretions and I felt a deep sense of conviction. I could not be my father's judge.

Thanks to the miracle working powers of Dr. B, as we fondly referred to him, Angella was accepted into a new drug trial which was showing promising results. In a matter of months, things took a sudden turn for the better and before too long Angella began to show signs of improvement.

She didn't complain about the hair loss from her treatments and even after her hair grew back she kept it low cut. She had lost a drastic amount of weight, but she was slowly regaining her strength. She joked about being skinny enough to fit into her jeans from the days when we lived in the housing projects. I suspected she was serious about still owning those pants. Angella held on to the strangest of things.

Less than a year out of the woods, Angella was back working with renewed frenzy around the clock with the young attorneys she mentored back home. We both launched into our projects with an unspoken urgency, burning the candle at both ends. A small team I worked with had secured funding for the Bunce Island restoration plans and I worked feverishly to meet deadlines.

Angella had beamed gratefully when I swore not to tell Dr. B that in between therapy she planned on a trip to a country with almost non-existent health care. He would not be impressed but I knew how much it meant to her. Her work had earned her an advisory role with the Anti-Corruption Commission and she was anxious to finally meet her colleagues in person.

Abdul was at the airport to meet us when we arrived. Our reunion lasted a long time as we embraced, then stood apart taking in the sight of each other in a lingering gaze, and embracing over and over again. After months of talking by video, we could feel and touch and kiss each other. We were finally home. Angella squealed in delight at the sight of everything, from the simple bougainvillea that lined the boulevard leading away from the airport, to the sight of street hawkers selling roasted peanuts and peeled oranges.

Abdul insisted that these days, the road was safer than the ferry or water taxi. The route around Port Loko and into the east end of the city would take almost four hours but I did not object. His time in the military was evident in his decision-making; it was always strategic.

As we chased the orange blaze of sunset I looked over at Angella. She glanced at me with a smile and went back to staring wistfully out the open window, the breeze whipped gently at her face which looked serene in the dying light of day. The road would be dark soon, and the mountain scenery would vanish into silhouette, but I was just happy to breathe in the air and be in that place at that time with the ones I loved so dearly.

☙ ♈ ☙

Abdul hands me the stack of sealed envelopes. Every one of them is stamped 'undeliverable'. Intrigued, I carefully remove the letters and begin to read.

June 10th, 1993

My dearest Allison,

How I miss you!

The situation here is unimaginable. They are using all kinds of intimidation tactics. They rape, they cut open the stomachs of pregnant women, cut off people's hands and feet. Many women have been kidnapped and taken to be their brides. I am so happy none of you are here to see this Lili. We have monsters among us.

The days are very long and I see fear all around me, but I have hope. My platoon has been very fortunate to receive supplies from the ECOMOG forces. You should have seen how we all rushed at them. Toothpaste after so many days. And corned beef. I can't wait to have it with some warm fulah bread. The potato leaf sauce they cook at the makeshift canteen is full of spice and watered down but at least it's better than nothing.

We are headed to the eastern region again tomorrow. Our plan is to take back the diamond mining areas. Every time we go out there, I pray that I find one of the stones that I hear you can find just below the soil of the muddy river running through Kono district. If I ever find one, I hope it is big! If all these Lebanese traders can play with our diamonds, ship them abroad and make money, then I want to do the same. I want to give you a big diamond and watch your eyes sparkle when it shines. And your smile too. I want to see your bright smile.

I have to be careful when we go there. I saw a boy once and he was wielding two AK-47s almost as big as he was. They kidnap children as young as ten to fight on their side. They give them drugs and make them crazy. I wish I had a way to tell him that this was not good for him or any of his family. I am sure he will die soon. They are not trained in combat. Just how to put fear in people.

I don't have any news from Ms. June or Aunty Stella. I found no trace through the refugee office. I heard that a big convoy was hijacked by the rebels.

They scattered and some made it over the border, but the Guinean government sent them back. Many were put on a boat back to Freetown while the younger ones took their chance and headed for the Guéckédou camp where you were. I wish I had been there. I promise to find them soon.

April 18th, 1994

My dearest Allison,

I have news of Ms. June and Aunty Stella, but I want to wait until I can see you and hold you to talk about it. Stay strong. As for me I will keep fighting hard. To save my people, to save our beloved country.

I dream of the day we will meet again my Lili.

Always,
Abdul

December 22nd, 1995

My dearest Allison,

Happy birthday to you! I sang heartily as I bathed this morning and the officers teased me.

They all know that I have a woman all the way in America somewhere. The woman I love and miss very much. I hope you are having a nice day. Are you in a place that has snow or is cold? Do they celebrate Christmas? I dreamt of Ms. June's jollof rice and roasted pork. No chance of that today but I will manage. When we meet, you have to cook me a whole pot that I can eat on my own (smile).

I think the rebels are taking time to rest during this Christmas time as well because the scouts we have watching their camps have not seen much activity for almost a week. They are probably also low on ammunition. They are poorly trained and disorganized at times which gives us the chance to go in and overpower them. Executive Outcomes, a private military company from South Africa are fantastic. You should see the tactics they use. Now that there is some calm, I hear the president may come back to the country and they will hold elections.

My plan is to go to King's Lodge as soon as possible. Pa Johnny has been keeping watch, but I heard Sullay left to go to his village and protect his family. Many small villages are attacked, their sheep and chickens stolen, and their rice taken back to the rebel camp. There is a lot of hunger, Allison. Hunger is making people desperate. Some young men are rising up and forming militias to help in the fight. They mainly use machetes which I don't think stand much chance against the guns, but they also believe that the amulets they wear from the poro bush will protect them. God help them.

As for me, I will keep fighting hard. To save my people, to save our beloved country.

I long for the day we will meet again, my Lili.

Till then,
Your only,
Abdul

☙ ♈ ❧

I tell Abdul I am contemplating making a permanent move back. I wish to finish work on the Bunce Island project, a relic from the slave trade era that captured my imagination ever since I first set foot there.

"Papa would want me to do this." I know it was unfair to pull that card, but I want to be sure I have his support. I tell him how inspired I was by my visit to the Gullah people in South Carolina and Georgia and that I want to bring that inspiration home.

Abdul is still contemplating my words when I venture to say I was also toying with the idea of running for office.

"What?" Abdul exclaims.

I've never heard Abdul raise his voice like this before.

"Lili, I think living abroad has changed you too much. You have become like them," he complains. "You are very aggressive now, eh?" he sulks.

"I want my Lili back," he groans, rolling over in the bed we share at the Radisson hotel right on the beachfront.

"I am your Lili," I assure him, snuggling up close. He takes me in his arms, and we lie in silence. With everything that has happened, I am not the same Allison he knew and had loved. Pastor Joe would say it is to be expected. Old things pass away, and new things come. Abdul would have to learn to love the new Allison or find someone else to love.

For a while, life back in Maryland felt like it was in a holding pattern. I had the enormous challenge of figuring out what was best for Natasha and Caleb while thinking about my own plans. Natasha's depression worsened as time went on, and she would not take the medication she was prescribed. Caleb's grades were abysmal. Carl's sentence was coming to an end soon, and the children had talked about wanting to live with him part of the time. There were things to be taken care of until then, but Angela and I both decided unequivocally that we were bound to return home.

I'd started attending church more regularly after Angella's diagnosis and my dedication to walking the Christian path was reborn and grew stronger each day. Angella was not a believer but this did not offend me. Rather it encouraged me to continue praying for her eyes to be opened and to accept salvation. Pastor Joe had urged me to give it time and let the Holy Spirit do the work. Natasha and Caleb had no desire to participate, accusing me of being hypocritical.

"So if you are such a good Christian now, then why haven't you forgiven Dad?" Natasha had asked one day.

"You've not once been to see him either!" she screamed at me.

She was right. I hadn't contacted or gone to see Carl. I was still working through my feelings of hate and anger toward him, so I didn't argue.

Angella had agreed to attend a prayer meeting at Sanctuary of Praise with me one night. She'd been feeling restless and needed a distraction. She didn't mind my newfound love for God and all my rantings about faith, but she had warned me she couldn't promise not to laugh if any of the members including me got possessed by the 'spirit'.

That night at the service, Sister Beatrice, who always caught the holy ghost dramatically, was running up and down the aisle when she shoved her large bottom in our direction and bumped into Angella.

I heard the sick sound of a crack as Angella lost her balance, falling over and hitting her head on the pew in front of her. An angry bruise appeared, and the area was swelling quickly. The singing and praying stopped as others joined me to try and raise her up. Blood started dripping from her nose and it took everything in me not to scream while someone dialed 911. She was rushed to the hospital and admitted to the inpatient floor at the Sidney Kimmel Cancer Center. Dr. B wasn't on call, but I reached him on his cell phone.

The next morning as we waited for Dr. B to do his rounds, I noticed Angella biting her lip. She seemed agitated and fidgety. I asked what was bothering her and she told me she was worried her current health situation would keep her away from our projects too long. Now the Anti-Corruption Commission had gained the confidence of the international legal and human rights communities, the timing was right to push for reform. She had relapsed and this was a setback.

Before cancer, I joked with Angella that I couldn't believe I needed a spot in the schedule to see my own sister. If she wasn't in court, she was on the phone, in meetings, at rallies, shelters, anywhere someone needed her help. Her firm was happy for her to take the pro bono work while others brought in paying clients. She thrived on her wins.

Every time she succeeded in reversing a deportation order for hard-working honest people trying to make a new life in America, every time she saved someone from losing their savings or home because of a wrongful dismissal or some other injustice, she added a sticker to her victory board; a ten by ten cork board hanging behind her desk bearing miniature images of clenched fists, stickers, and pins, representing each case she had won.

She was convinced that often, just showing up to fight was half the victory. The battle at home was much the same she said. Reversing the lack of accountability by government officials, and the continued misuse of the country's vast resources did not only require expertise in the law. It required someone willing to stand up for what was right.

Now, sitting beside her on the hospital bed, I struggled to comprehend what she was saying to me, but as she continued to speak about the wasted years that could have been avoided if men like Papa were not silenced, I found myself becoming indignant and agreeing with her. Angella asked me to look inside her purse. I found her VPN card for the Library of Congress as she directed. She urged me to take it and use it to search up reports by the World Bank, IMF and the State Department. She thought it would be eye-opening for me.

"The influencers can be trusted, sis," Angella said. Her voice was weak but insistent.

"They know what must be done. And since I cannot go–you must! You have to carry the mantle, Allison."

She smiled wanly, " Papa wouldn't want it any other way."

☎♈☎

"Pleasure to meet you Mrs. Wellesley-Coker or can I call you Allison?" the bald gentleman at the head of the conference table says, beckoning me to take the only empty seat across from him.

"Actually, I go by Johnson now," my response elicits nods and satisfied smiles around the table. My father's name still carries weight.

The men and women gathered all wore suits and had a sleek-looking dossier set out in front of each place. I was self-conscious about how I looked in my V-neck sweater and slacks, but I advanced as confidently as I could and took my seat. I had stopped wearing heavy makeup for some time and stopped using chemicals to treat my hair. I realized that my natural look was fresh and reminiscent of Mama and I saw fragments of her when I looked at myself in the mirror. It made me happy.

Looking around the table I recognized former Ambassador Blake; Susan Cummings, the first female representative to the United Nations; Steven Harding, a renowned Harvard scholar and Alusine Sesay, the deputy director of the World Bank's Africa Bureau. I didn't have to read the word CONFIDENTIAL embossed on the dossier to understand the nature of its contents.

"My name is Elijah Pratt. Before we start, I must tell you that everything we say in this room is completely confidential. We will need to hand us your cellphone and any other recording device that you have in your possession. I will also ask you to open the dossier in front of you. The first documents states that what we discuss in this room can never be repeated or described to anyone. Ever. In other words, you take it to your grave."

My heart races. *What on earth had Angella gotten into?* I think. Angella told me she believed this mission would be retribution for Papa. But I struggled to understand how I could help. I knew the current government had started out well. The President's promise to run the nation like a business was a concern to some.

By the end of his second term, he appeared to be dragging his feet and hinted at changing the constitution to allow life-time presidency, in the name of maintaining stability. Despite evidence of some improvements during his administration, the consensus was that he and his stalwarts, many with family connections to di Pa's regime, pocketed far more than they could spend in their collective lifetimes, leaving disgruntled youth and civil servants no better off than in the twenty years prior when the nation and its economy had collapsed.

I recalled Abdul's views that some within the military rank and file were pleased with the President's strong support that built the forces up to a formidable might, while others questioned his agenda. All eyes were now on the National Electoral Commission to ensure the election and transition were free, fair, transparent, and peaceful.

Feeling as ready as I ever could be for whatever task is ahead, I flip open the folder to read the words on the page in front of me. I look around the room the I pick up the pen and sign in the blank space reserved for my name.

"Thank you, Allison." Mr. Pratt stands up and I wonder if I should as well. Before I can decide, he continues.

"We won't beat about the bush. We consider ourselves gatekeepers, if you will, and we believe that this, country is ready for a woman to hold the highest office. If you agree and accept our proposition, we have the power to make that a reality." He shifts his weight and grimaces. "Angella was poised to assist with our mission but it would seem fate and serendipity has turned the tables." He looks at me pointedly and asks directly " Would you be willing to lead?"

As shocked as I am by the realization that I have just been offered the opportunity to be the flag-bearer in a presidential election, I am glad I have not stood. My knees feel like sponges. Fine beads of sweat are breaking across my brow and I grip the arms of the leather chair I am sitting in, to stop my hands from shaking.

Freetown

"How come *we* don't get to fly first class?" Caleb whined as I packed my suitcase. He had been in a bad mood for the past week and complained about everything. It was hard to ignore him because he had a way of following me around the house, so close on my heels that if I turned around suddenly, we both would end up in a heap on the floor.

I had politely declined the Influencers' offer to fly business class. I might be the flag bearer but was still determined to have some autonomy in certain decisions. About the only characteristic I sought to emulate in the style of the late Robin Benton, was mingling with constituents. He famously drove unaccompanied up and down the beachfront on weekends looking for good deals on fresh barracuda.

Natasha had retreated to her room earlier, slamming the door to show her disgust for what she called her brother's "bratty B-S". I knew Caleb was trying to get my attention because he missed me when I was gone. It was hard to manage the life of a single mother and the strain had increased when Angella got sick and more so when the presidential campaign began in earnest.

"Don't worry, dear," I said, coaxing him. "When you are old enough to work and you earn your *own* money, then you can fly first class as often as you please!"

I tried not to sound too righteous when encouraging them to be frugal. Natasha tended to think I was taking a swipe at Carl, got touchy on many occasions and she rushed to his defense.

"Dad isn't a crook," she had spat the words angrily at me. "It was all that woman, Maria's fault."

When she got into that mood, I did not argue with her. I knew they were still reeling from the reality of our new life, even though they had shrugged off the embarrassing questions from their friends after we left the grandeur of 8755 Crowne Point Way.

"Our neighbors were too far away anyhow," Natasha had said, sounding unusually practical.

"Yeah," Caleb chimed in agreement. "And I was tired of that old man at the 7-Eleven accusing me of stealing his candy just because I am black!"

As I continued packing, I thought about Frank. No one had heard from him in months and I was worried sick. He had disappeared before, only to show up and assure us he was fine—he just needed to get away for a while. He had never been gone this long. With Jennifer moving further away, we talked less often and there was little chance we would meet up before my inauguration. She wasn't keen on visiting Sierra Leone. Now that I was leaving, I had no idea how easy it would be to stay in touch.

My bid for office did not really hit home for any of my family until a year into the campaign when Abdul insisted Natasha and Caleb accompany me home to get to know their roots. I did my best to prepare them for the experience but the mad rush of supporters and reporters that met us at the airport had left them in a daze.

To make it worse, they both had the worst imaginable bouts of diarrhea and missed what should have been enjoyable parts of the trip like going to the beautiful beaches, or meeting local artisans at Big Market. They were able to join me for a visit the Outamba Kilimi National Park on our return and picked out one food item after the other from a roadside vendor on the way from Kabala until we practically bought all her wares.

The Influencers were responsible for my security detail and assigned guards in black pants and camouflage vests by my side from the moment we arrived at the airport and every step forward. Natasha and Caleb cringed nervously at the sight of the AK-47s they lugged casually over their shoulders. I was nervous as well but did my best hide it.

⚏♈︎⚏

As hard as I had tried to bridge the gap between Jennifer and Angella our entire lives, she never seemed to have gotten over her resentment for having to share our home with an outsider. It seemed useless to tell her about the bone marrow match or the secret letters now. I still marvel at how uncanny it was that Papa's one out of wedlock child, ended up in our home. To her credit, Jennifer did come to Angella's funeral and had been the one to arrange for a care for Natasha and Caleb when the news of my candidacy and election victory made headlines.

As I shoved the final pair of flats into a corner of my suitcase, I noticed the time on my bedside clock. It was time to pray. Like most days lately, I was up doing one thing or another, well past midnight. Pastor Joe had suggested using the opportunity to have midnight prayers which he claimed were more powerful than during the day.

"Evil agents and spirits start their mischief when they think we are all asleep. Paul and Silas were praying at midnight when there was a great earthquake and the prison doors flung open!" he had said, his hands gesturing wide on either side of him.

He explained that it was at midnight that the Lord smote all the first-born of the land of Egypt. Jesus himself prayed to God all night as recorded in the book of Luke. I had to admit that he was right, and I always felt better afterward.

A group of Christian women who worked at State House called themselves the Praying Ladies set time aside whenever I was in town to pray with me. It was comforting to know they had my back. I got wind that the Hunting Society and the Freemasons were not impressed by my display of faith and declaration of being a born-again Christian. They couldn't fathom that I would honestly lead without permitting members of my administration to compromise integrity and accept bribes or inflate contracts with excess charges to line their pockets.

The Influencers had worked tirelessly to garner the support of investors and experts from all walks of life. I *was* the face of a revolution in the nation's politics and never ceased to be humbled by the awesome responsibility of it all. With Angella not far from my mind I closed my bedroom door, prostrated myself on the floor as Pastor Joe had shown me, and started to pray.

☙❦❧

Abdul retired from active duty soon after we reunited and was running training exercises at the International Military Training and Advisory Team Sierra Leone compound in preparation for peacekeeping missions in the region. It was a position the Influencers had initially expressed some ambivalence about given his romantic relationship with me.

"I'm a big girl, Mr. Pratt," I had said, assuring my mentor I could handle myself.

Abdul was shocked that I did not want to get married right away if nothing more than to avoid the rumors about his car being spotted emerging from the Presidential residence at a late hour. I had not decided if I wanted to be married at all and knew I should tell Abdul that the frolicking in bed had to stop until I made my decision. The state of the nation had become my first love and Abdul being a patriotic military man, should understand.

The extent of erosion to the economy was evidenced from the poor quality of primary education to the persistent maternal death rates and the hawkers, hustlers, and disabled beggars lining the street leading to the State House every Friday. I saw the way Abdul's jaw clenched at the sight of so many victims brutally mutilated in the war, who never received the promised recompense.

As he traced the scar from my cesarean sections, I suspected he wanted to ask me how I felt about having more children.

"I am an old woman now," I joked, hoping to get him to open up about his expectations of having our own family. We both knew the discussion of age related risk was secondary to the real reason more babies would not be in my future. The question of other women never came up. Abdul was handsome and commanded authority. I hadn't caught any overt signs of him pursuing other interests for which there was ample opportunity, though I knew there must have been others before.

In his typical manner, he smiled and only smirked mischievously, which I knew meant he wasn't going to let me draw him into the conversation until he was ready. He was adjusting to my 'American' ways. My being bold and vocal had made him uncomfortable in the beginning, but he'd soon begun to accept that some things would never be the same as he had imagined all those years we were apart.

With every sector clamoring for attention, my calendar was filled up a full year ahead. The World Bank country representative had not yet arrived, and I was already hearing rumors of side meetings with lobbyists. The Sierra Leone diaspora had grown into a large and unwieldy force with great influence that would best serve the nation if we could find common ground. If only Angella were here, I thought.

As we rushed along the beach road past the Golf Club I wondered why Ibrahim had chosen to go this way. Thankfully, it was seven o'clock on a Friday morning and the road was mostly free of auto traffic so the diversion would not cause a disruption. I made a mental note to privately ask Joe, my state chief of protocol whether there had been changes to my weekend routes.

There was a scattering of runners and cyclists along the beach road. They powered forward with intent and I admired their strength and discipline. I felt tempted to jump out of the Jeep and join them. My legs could use the toning, I mused. I had not yet made time in my schedule for an exercise routine and I made another mental note to correct this.

We approached the Congo-cross round-about and slowed. A throng of young men rushed toward the convoy shouting and waving white hand towels.

"Mami na power!" they chanted. Despite Alex's look of horror, I put down my window and shook my fist in the air, smiling and waving to the crowd. The familiar words had been a rallying cry during my campaign and still brought a smile to my lips whether it came from the market women at Sani Abacha Street or the guards on the hill as we entered the State House.

Youyi building was coming up on the right and I was pleased to see that the contractor had kept his word and completed the new paint work in time for the Africa Climate Change Convention. My entrance would be a surprise, but I felt inclined to make Honorable Jim Conteh feel special. He was one of the few that took heat for backing a female presidential candidate and did not waver.

The games politicians play are dirty and can be even dirtier when the stakes are so high. Jim had no idea how much his actions meant to me, so I decided to return the favor with a very public acknowledgment. My chief of protocol was not happy.

After all the handshakes and speeches were over, and I had left behind the camera flashes and hopped back into the vehicle, I wondered what people would think if only they knew how powerless this woman of power felt. As Ibrahim sped away I shifted anxiously in my seat and gasped with trepidation as street hawkers pulled their fare out of the way to avoid being run over. Whatever was the matter with the man. I resisted the urge to correct him right there and then and instead added to my growing list of things to have a talk with Alex about.

Later with the staff dismissed for the night and Abdul away for the weekend I had the house all to myself. As I wandered the hallways of the villa, I tried to push the busy thoughts of the past few days out of mind, starting my prayers with a request for God's forgiveness for any wrongdoing. I could feel a calming presence around me, and I smiled, content that I had emptied myself enough to make room for the experience. Abdul was still wary of my prayer time, unsettled by what he described as a glow on my face when I emerged from my prayer closet.

The house was tucked away on a hill off Spur Road and had been the official residence of the late Aroun Sesay, former Minister of Lands. He had been an affable man with a hearty laugh, fondly remembered by friends and colleagues at the Ministry. Sadly, his unhealthy lifestyle had cost him. Like many men in his position, a breakfast of loaves of bread stuffed with fried fish-balls and onion gravy, chased with a generous portion of rice and meat-laden sauce for lunch, topped off with assorted grilled meats and more rice for dinner, was a fitting reward for their burden of responsibility.

Abdul had not known the man well and was not put off from scooping up the place when it became available. We split our time between the Presidential Lodge and our private residence. The house had been well kept and its discrete location offered privacy when the convoy picked me up to drive into State House on Monday mornings. After the renovation of King's Lodge was complete, I could not bear to live there and instead rented it out to a South African businessman. The proceeds went directly into an education foundation for underprivileged children which we started in Mama and Papa's honour.

I had collected Mama's old portmanteau from the Walcott-Taylor house where Uncle Robert had kept it safe. I didn't need to explain to Abdul why I wanted to keep the few trinkets and clothes that belonged to Mama, or why I wanted to recreate the room from King's Lodge in a bedroom across the hall from mine. Abdul helped me pick out the bed, I added a rocking chair and a bookcase where I displayed the books from Papa's library. I carefully selected the lace used to sew a replica of Mama's favorite curtains.

The shrine, Abdul warned me, was bound to attract ghosts. I argued that it was better than going to the graveyard and talking to a headstone, so he let it be.

The setting sun cast long shadows across the patio overlooking the swimming pool. As I stroll around the edge of the clear still water, I read Psalm 139 from the bible I am carrying, uttering each verse slowly to allow a full understanding of the inspired words of King David as advised by Pastor Joe. I am in search of clarity and guidance.

I have to contend with a feeling of powerlessness that comes from being separated from my daughter and son for much of the year, as they continue their studies living with their father in America. On the other hand, I have yet to fully wrap my head around the power suddenly resting on my shoulders as Head of State.

Everything still feels surreal. The longing in my heart for Papa is a hollow ache inside. It throbs worse on some days than others. He modeled a balance of humility and authority that I can only hope to emulate. I am grateful to have reunited with Aunty Lolo, although she lives in England now and was unable to travel to my inauguration due to poor health. She calls me regularly and even offered to write and record a song in honor of the first female president. Aunty Khadi is also there for me. We text and talk on the phone as often as possible, and she tells me I am always included in her Isha'a.

Their support helps to calm my frustration at the vicious backlash to my election. The vast majority of the political establishment is male and as the reality of a female head of state sinks in, the verbal attacks have escalated. The tabloid newspapers blasted full-page photos of Abdul and I having a meal at the Golf Club with a heading "Her Excellency's lover was a rebel" and "Mami na pawa-ɛn mami na bed". The former statement was a lie of course. The Influencers had thoroughly investigated Abdul's past and found no evidence he ever officially joined the RUF.

As for being a woman, I am proud to join the ranks of female leadership around the world-across every sector in society. I am convinced those in my country who still resist the tide of change will eventually have no choice but to accept it. SLBC had recently aired a series on Women in Power that featured the stories of women at the highest levels of industry, business, and politics. I was proud to see that many like me were alumnae of the Annie Walsh School.

The biggest challenge facing my administration is capital. The country's coffers leak faster than they can be filled. We lose fortunes in import and export revenue, paying off grossly exorbitant hard currency debt to the International Monetary Fund. Saddest of all, we lose untold amounts from untapped human resources.

Still, there is some good news. The Influencers spearheaded a joint commission whose mandate was to recover illegally extracted diamonds being tracked around the world, and reports of progress had so far been positive. The nation desperately needs an infusion of revenue but Sheku Mansaray, the Minister of Finance wants more time to draft the financial reform policies and he refuses to be rushed.

"Madam Allison, we need to get it right this time," he explained to me in his quiet, reassuring tone.

His solid credentials and methodical approach are exactly the reason I supported his appointment to cabinet, but I worry his quest for long-term perfection will come at the sacrifice of being good enough in the immediate term. At least he is trustworthy and so far has not been named in any of the scandals real or imaginary, being ginned up by my opponents. Even my Vice-President, Desmond Peters who was carefully vetted by the Influencers and came up squeaky clean, is being accused of accepting bribes.

The outside lights automatically turn on. It is getting dark and I return to the house forcing my troubled thoughts back to my prayers. I flip open my *Bible* again and read the words on the page in front of me.

O lord, thou hast searched me, and known me. Thou knowest my downsitting and mine uprising, thou understandest my thought afar off. Thou compassest my path and my lying down, and art acquainted with all my ways. Whither shall I go from thy spirit? or whither shall I flee from thy presence? If I ascend up into heaven, thou art there, if I make my bed in hell, behold, thou art there. Search me, O God, and know my heart, try me, and know my thoughts. And see if there be any wicked way in me, and lead me in the way everlasting.

It is close to three in the morning when I finally shut my eyes. I am drained from praying for so long, my hairline is matted with sweat from my forehead, but I feel at peace. As I crawl into bed, I consider pouring myself a shot of the Remy Cognac which was a congratulatory gift from African Development Bank Manager Adama Ouattara, a young Ivorian with a wardrobe of flashy custom-made suits. The bottle was outlandishly large and came wrapped in a huge red bow and a note that read 'Congratulations, Madame Presidente!'

The brandy would definitely help me fall asleep better, but I have been struggling with Pastor Joe's admonition to keep the body pure. I try not to be skeptical and question why some things I enjoy including the occasional alcoholic drink, though not explicitly prohibited in the scriptures, are discouraged because of the pleasure they provide. What is the point of life if not to be enjoyed?

I start to drift off to sleep when the smell of lavender strikes my nostrils and a cool chill wraps around my shoulders. My eyes fly open and I try to cry out, moving my lips soundlessly. I have felt this terrifying sensation once before and asked Pastor Joe about the possibility of Mama's or Angella's spirit visiting me. I have smelled this same scent before in the moments between sleeping and waking. It is light and lingering as if they are searching for a way to pierce the veil that separates us, reaching out to warn me of something.

"No, I don't believe in such things," he had said emphatically. "You shouldn't either."

He grew up in Ghana, but like many, he gave up the animist beliefs of our common West African ancestors and embraced an uncompromising interpretation of the Christian faith. All things considered, I was grateful that close to the end he had been able to convince Angella to accept Jesus Christ as her Savior. In readiness for the simple communion service, we held in her hospice room, I had painted her nails a bright red to cover the telltale signs of chemotherapy.

"I feel like a hooker seducing a priest," she joked as she held the chalice to her lips. Pastor Joe's hands supported her weak grip and trembling fingers. As soon as she passed, funeral service was held at Hansen's funeral home on Rhode Island Ave in DC. It was a quiet affair followed by cremation as Angella had requested. Pastor Joe had officiated.

When I hear the faintest rustle of fabric against a wall, the house is no longer completely silent and my instinct knows I am not alone. I lie still, paralyzed by dread. I wonder if this is a waking dream. I hope it is. The illuminated rectangles on the bedside registers 4 o'clock. A figure appears before me quite suddenly. As the intruder moves into full view, his eyes like mine have adjusted to the dark and our gazes lock. I notice how startled he appears when our eyes meet.

His feet must be clad in soft-soled shoes because I did not hear his approach. He looks only slightly taller than my five-foot frame, but he is muscular; his bulging forearms and biceps strain the loose fabric of his black t-shirt. His black trousers are snug, showing the sinewy outline of his thighs. Midnight dark skin peek from under his face mask, but it is impossible to make out any other features.

As I rise from my bed, his eyes wander over my scanty attire and he hesitates. Most people assume the president actually resembles the daunting portrait carefully crafted by The Influencers. Seeing me in the flesh and observing my slight frame surprises the intruder. My hair is disheveled, but I do not brush away the stubborn strands falling forward on my face. Squaring his shoulders, he approaches.

I feel the silencer's cold tip against my skin as he presses a handgun to my right temple. As frightening as the situation is, I am calm. The words from Isiah 54 verse 17 are clear before my eyes, bathed in the shimmer of a bright light. *No weapon that is formed against thee shall prosper, and every tongue that shall rise against thee in judgment, thou shalt condemn. This is the* heritage of the servants of the Lord, and their righteousness is of me, saith the Lord. The invincible and defiant smile on my lips might have surprised my executioner, even as he clenched the weapon firmly and squeezed the trigger.